FACE
THE
MUSIC

A novel by Joe Anderson

DISCLAIMER

This is a work of fiction. Any reference to any real person or organization living or dead is wholly fictional and entirely of the author's imagination. All trademarks used in this work are the property of their respective owners and used in a wholly fictional fashion. All purported news clippings are wholly fictional. Any other similarity to any person or entity, living or dead, is entirely coincidental and not intended by the author. All foreign languages are used in parody.

WEST BUTTE BOOKS
615 SUNSET AVE., STE. B
VENICE, CA 90291

ISBN 13 # 9780989025119

Cover designed by Julie Arden Rosen
Interior Design and Layout by Stefanie Motte

DEDICATION

For Mom, whose unconditional love and support knows no bounds and who knows this isn't an autobiography. I think.

TABLE OF CONTENTS

Grammy® Nominations/Song of the Year Category
I Turned Around – Zack Fluett (Wendy Harper)
Another Whole New World (Gilligan's Theme) – Alan Menken, Tim Rice, Sherwood Schwartz (Natalie Cole & Michael Bolton)
The Streets of Orlando – Bruce Springsteen (Bruce Springsteen)
Insanity Salad – Lena Rifka (Lena Rifka)
I Love You Because I'm Lonely – Diane Warren, Richard Marx, Max Martin, and Andreas Carlsson (TJ Corey)

Daily Variety, December 18, 2008

PART ONE

BILLBOARD® TOP 10 WEEK OF OCTOBER 10, 1996
1. (1) CULTURAL WASTELAND – This Is Gonna Get Expensive – *Defiant Groove*
2. (2) ALANIS MORISSETTE – Jagged Little Pill – *Maverick*
3. (5) GARTH BROOKS – Fresh Horses – *Capitol Nashville*
4. (4) MARIAH CAREY – Daydream – *Columbia*
5. (8) FUGEES – The Score – *Ruffhouse*
6. (10) WAITING TO EXHALE – Soundtrack – *Arista*
7. (6) TUPAC – All Eyez on Me – *Death Row/Interscope*
8. (9) SHANIA TWAIN – The Woman in Me – *Mercury Nashville*
9. (21) THE MCCANN CLAN – New Pair of Shoes – *Rising Tides*
10. (3) CELINE DION – Falling into You – *550 Music*

CHAPTER 1

HERE COMES THE FEAR again. Just when I was get-ting over it. Shit. I knew I shouldn't have done this. This was a bad move. I should not be standing here. I should exercise my well-honed flight instincts right now. I should get the hell out of here and back to Woody Creek where I belong. This just isn't me anymore.

It seemed like such a good idea at the time. "Go on out there," I said to myself. "Get out of the snow. Hang out poolside at the Beverly Hills Hotel. Go to the damn show. It's a once-in-a-lifetime opportunity (well, not really, but kind of). What can it hurt you to try to ease up on the running away and hiding from life?" That was all well and good in the abstract, but now that I'm here, did I really have to pick Music's Biggest Night to try a psychic makeover?

I reach into the pocket of my brand new tuxedo and pull out a pack of Marlboros. It occurs to me that this is the first time I've worn a tux since my first wedding, fifteen years ago. It's unseasonably warm for L.A. in February, and I'm starting to sweat. I regret the de-

cision to accessorize the tux with my best black Stetson. Right now the only thing I do feel good about is wearing the Old Man's custom-made black dress boots, also fifteen years old, but it's going to be something of a chore to get them off later, alone. I'll be glad I've got them on once I get inside the Staples Center, though. Thinking about it, I shiver abruptly, despite the heat. I light a cigarette and take stock of my situation.

Like the well-dressed crowd around me, I'm standing on a red carpet, waiting for them to open the goddamned doors and get this over with already. It's not the real red carpet, the one with idiotic dirty-laundry flacks asking you what you're wearing. It's just here to make all of us feel better about not being on the real red carpet, like we're somehow being treated the same as the folks who are performing on the show. I'm actually fine with not having to run the gauntlet of the real red carpet, but I don't like being made to stand around in the heat, either.

I drop the cigarette on the carpet. It lands on the logo for the National Association of Recording Arts & Sciences. I watch the cherry begin to melt into the fiber of the gramophone and smile grimly but with childish delight at the tiny act of protest. I'm reminded of feeding my big sister's Barbie to the dog when she got to go to Jaws *with the folks while I was deemed too young. I sigh resignedly and crush out the butt.*

The last time I attended the Grammy Awards, over a decade ago, I did walk that real red carpet, as far as I remember. That night, as I'm sure I pointed out to some walking advertisement for plastic surgery medical malpractice insurance, I was wearing thousand-dollar one-of-a-kind Roberto Cavalli jeans, a bumblebee pattern Versace jacket, and a watch that cost as much as a Korean car. That was appropriate enough, as I was playing rock star that night on TV as a Grammy nominee for Record of the Year. Technically, it was my band, Cultural Wasteland, that was nominated, and even more technically, it was not my band, as I would soon find out. It turned out to be Lark Dray's band, and I was just the keyboard player in it.

That night, like many over the past twenty years, remains hazy. I presume there was a limo ride with cocaine, Crown Royal with cocaine, a backstage blowjob with cocaine, then several beta-blockers. This is a fair presumption because that was my routine every night before a gig back then. After the gig there would be champagne with cocaine, then someone might pull out some Ecstasy, then there would be another limo ride to a hotel suite or a house in the hills, frequently followed by frenzied but generally incomplete attempts at sexual congress, and occasionally followed by auto theft, incarceration, and bailment.

But I digress. The last time I did this, I was not sweating in the bright sunlight outside the Staples Center, first, because the Grammys were held at Madison Square Garden that year, and otherwise because, as a performer, I was spared such indignities. Tonight I am just a spectator. This whole experience is most likely another in my long series of lessons about karma and just what kind of a lady she is.

Looking back on that long-ago evening in New York, I do recall giving a decent performance of our huge Grammy-nominated hit, "This Is Gonna Get Expensive." I also specifically recall being surprised when that nice group of little black girls who had been giggling in their seats in front of us screamed and then went up on stage to thank God and collect the Grammy for Record of the Year. I also recall watching Lark Dray mount that *same stage, grin his famous wicked grin, and thank God and everyone in the world except his band for the Song of the Year Grammy he had just received for writing "This Is Gonna Get Expensive," which he did not.*

I don't recall much else of the evening, with the exception of breaking Lark Dray's nose with a punch that, unfortunately, also shattered the fifth metacarpal of my right hand. That resulted in my being replaced by Ben Felder on keys for the thirty-show Cultural Wasteland European tour that began ten days after the Grammy Awards. By the time that tour was over and my hand had healed, I had been replaced by Ben Felder in Cultural Wasteland, period.

Try as I might, I can't resent Ben. Never could. I have resented a whole lot of people and institutions and companies and deities and parents and wives and girlfriends and doctors and dead batteries at the absolute worst time, but I never resented Ben. He was just a damn good musician in the right place at the right time. I never resented any bartenders either. But that's a different point altogether. I do, however, resent the hell out of Lark Dray.

I feel that old, hot resentment rising again as the heat rises from the pavement beneath the red carpet in the parking lot of the Staples Center. I breathe deeply, do my mantra, and focus on the moment, trying to drive decade-old demons from my mind. I find it hard enough to drive the hours-old demons from my mind without fucking around with ancient history, but none of it's easy, out here with all these schnooks in the parking lot of the Staples Center.

Wait a minute there, Zack. Easy, cowboy. I look around and really take in my compatriots for the first time. I breathe. Just over there with the leonine white hair is Jerome Golding. He's won more Oscars for Best Film Score than I've seen movies. I particularly liked the one he did for that modern Western a couple of years ago, I forget the name, and that boxing movie, Ballyhoo. Bad movie title, but the score was good.

I also see Anita Sparks talking to some young rapper. She won Album of the Year a couple of years ago. I think she's nominated for Best R&B Single this year. Apparently she isn't performing either, so I shouldn't feel too insulted to be out here with her. Peter Kelsing is just over there; he's nominated for Engineering virtually every year. I would love to work with him someday. Maybe I'll bump into him inside.

Better now. These people are not schnooks. They are talented, dedicated, industrious people here to celebrate their industry with one another. Although it is an industry I generally detest, if I am to make it through this evening, I had best hold off on the hypocrisy for a while, accept the fact that I have chosen to attend, and agree that I am not a schnook either. I am also a talented and hardworking person worthy of being here, but no more worthy than anyone else.

I breathe and try to focus. The Fear begins to fade. There's nothing to be afraid of. It's only your past. Everyone has one. I am not going to run away from this. This is a big night, after all. I repeat to myself the almost unbelievable truth—I am Zack Fluett, and I wrote "I Turned Around," a Song of the Year nominee. The doors to the Staples Center suddenly open, and we all gratefully move toward the air conditioning.

CHAPTER 2

LAST CHANCE SALOON
321 Clement Street
Thursday 9:00 pm
AUGUST WEST
23 Fillmore
$5 cover/Ladies Free/$2 Jäger shots

S.F. Examiner September 28, 1989

IT WAS LATE SEPTEMBER, and I really should have
been back at school. No, I was not with Maggie
May; I was with Lark Dray, and instead of attending
my junior year at a prestigious Northern California
university, I was rocking the Last Chance Saloon in
San Francisco, along with the Ramos brothers (Peter on lead guitar, Chris on bass), and Hugh "Huge"
Howell on drums. We had only been playing together for about two months at the time, but the
chemistry was apparent from the first couple of days,
and I was having a lot of fun. So, in my first great
act of open defiance of the rules that had governed
my existence up to that point, I decided to "stop out"

from my classes and give rock & roll the old college try.

I was the only college boy in the band, and it was the confluence of several seemingly unrelated events that resulted in my winding up on that small, hot stage that fall. Upon arrival at school, I had looked like an eager beaver Young Republican. I was valedictorian of a very small, rural high school from a sparsely populated state. I had great SAT scores (especially verbal, always better with words than math, as my unbalanced checkbook attests) and outstanding extracurricular activities. In other words, I was a wet dream for a college admissions officer looking to show a little geographic diversity in a class full of exceptional prep school types.

But the resume was just a ruse. All the hard work that went into creating that carefully sculpted front, to the point of feeling like an imposter much of the time, had been employed solely for the purpose of getting out of that small town. It was the only way I felt I could become the person I was meant to be. It was the only way I could think of to become more than just the Old Man's son.

My political science major satisfied the Old Man that I remained on the right track and kept the tuition, room, board, and Budweiser checks coming, but it was the drama and music minor that brought me a new kind of sanity. Once away at school, I did everything in my power to stay away, sometimes subconsciously, unconsciously, or in a blackout, as the case may be. That particular, magic summer, I managed to convince the folks to let me stay in San Francisco because I had finagled myself a job working in the library of a big law firm. I had made this happen because, unbeknownst to them, I needed to stay in the Bay Area that summer due to the little matter of my appearance being required at a trial for driving under the influence and leaving the scene. Sadly, I was the defendant.

Fortunately, my smart young public defender convinced a jury of people whom I felt most certainly were not my peers that I had not, in fact, gotten utterly shitfaced, borrowed a car, run over a rack of bicycles outside a sorority house, and then taken a little snooze under the dining room table of said sorority, which I was later confused to discover was not the one to which my girlfriend belonged. The public defender accurately pointed out that there were no witnesses, and that although I was certainly recovered by the police in an utterly inebriated state, nobody had seen me behind the wheel of the car. Further, by the next morning, the rack of damaged bikes had disappeared completely and could not be placed in evidence. (A similar rack of bikes would be discovered several years later during a major drought when the administration saw fit to drain the campus lake.) Reasonable doubt prevailed.

That minor inconvenience aside, I was free to spend a pleasant summer not working on the family ranch. My then girlfriend Shelly's parents had a lovely place in Woodside with a pool and a tennis court, and we spent weeknights in the city, smoking dope and drinking and screwing, and weekends in Woodside, smoking dope and drinking and screwing and swimming. Never did like tennis much.

Shelly had modeled in New York during her teens, keeping up with her studies through tutors and correspondence courses. She realized that she wasn't going to make the leap from just plain model to supermodel, so she decided to go back to school to study drama. I met her when we were both cast in the fall musical. I offered my services as rehearsal pianist for her big number, and I accepted her offer of repayment late one night atop the white concert grand in Memorial Auditorium. After that, we rehearsed a lot, which turned out well for me in more ways than one.

Shelly's folks threw a party on the Fourth of July, and Lark Dray, all six feet five inches of him, showed up with his Bon Jovi hair, movie star looks, and acoustic guitar. Battle lines were promptly drawn when Lark started playing his guitar, sitting cross-legged in the living room, and Shelly joined the rest of the girls in going all gooey over him.

If Shelly's little sister Sherry hadn't begged for piano lessons when she was thirteen (giving them up at fourteen), everything would have turned out differently. But there it was in the living room: a Kawai baby grand. I had to fight fire with fire before Shelly just dragged Lark back to her room right then and there. I had no doubt she would do this because her years in New York had inculcated in her a certain moral ambiguity of which I had been the beneficiary for over six months. I was painfully aware I could lose her in about six minutes. I sat down at the piano and listened to Lark's song for a few seconds, a simple E major blues, and at the turn of the verse, I joined in.

Lark turned, surprised and annoyed. He lost his place and stopped. I smiled kindly at him and slowly replayed the previous measure as if he were a rank amateur. His eyes flashed as he gripped his guitar and jumped right back in. It was on. We played through the verse and a chorus, then, gracefully and without missing a beat, he rose to his feet and stood next to me through the next verse, allowing me to carry the chords and rhythm while he picked out a more complex guitar line.

Not to be outdone, at the next chorus, I harmonized in thirds in a clear high voice, not too loud, that complimented his whiskey baritone. We both started to smile. Instead of singing the next verse, he took a solo, a good one, then nodded at me that I should take one as well, which I did. Now focused entirely on one another, we played three more instrumental verses, trading off solos, and then he sang a final verse, and we harmonized on the final chorus twice and finished.

We grinned at one another. The girls started clapping and cheering and we both turned, surprised to find them there. We took extravagant bows and shook hands. I started for the bar, but Lark strummed another chord.

"What about this?" he said, beginning a new refrain, more complex than the last, haunting and mournful. I sat back down.

"B minor?" I asked. He nodded. I quickly figured it out, and then began inventing a countermelody in the right hand. Lark's eyes lit up, and he broke into the smile that would later become the foundation of a merchandising juggernaut. We played on.

I'm not sure when the girls got up and left, but when the fireworks started there was no one in the living room but us. We hurried out to take a look, checking out the display, pointing to the sky, and oohing and aahing along with everyone. After a time,

I looked around for Shelly, but she was nowhere to be seen. It was not her style to stand around and watch while the guy she was screwing and the guy she wanted to screw fell in love with each other.

Lark and I had a couple of things in common. We grew up in small towns in the middle of nowhere, and we felt like we didn't really fit in where we were. Lark had it worse than I did, however. His parents were Jehovah's Witnesses, the kind who knock on your door with *Watchtower* pamphlets. They didn't celebrate Christmas or Thanksgiving or even birthdays, and he wasn't allowed to stand with his classmates and recite the Pledge of Allegiance. He also grew in huge spurts that made him ungainly and awkward.

Lark was private and sensitive and seemed to think that he was missing something everyone else had. When he evinced an interest in art and music, his parents complained that he was ignoring his own spiritual growth and forbid him from participating in organized school activities. He apparently did not get along with the church elders and was constantly being punished for questioning their word and for pursuing his interests in anything other than a course of conduct intended to ensure his path to heaven when Armageddon came, which was apparently right around the corner.

Lark figured that he just wasn't going to make it to heaven if he had to play by the Witnesses' rules, so he decided to try a new set of rules. He left home at sixteen and headed for California, winding up in San Francisco, as so many outsiders do. He found work sweeping up hair clippings in a Castro salon and bought his first guitar, couch surfing for a year until he graduated to shampooing clients' hair, at which time he moved into a group house in Noe Valley.

He was working toward getting his cosmetology license when he answered an ad in the Bay Guardian for a lead singer and met Huge and the Ramos Brothers. They saw his obvious potential as a front man and brought him in, forming themselves into a band they named Danger Zone. They played at a little pub called Boone's in the Marina once a week for a crowd of drunken yuppies eager to hear covers of the hits of the day.

Lark wanted Danger Zone to be more than just a cover band, and bringing me in was part of his plan to take things to the next level. The other guys were not particularly interested in adding keyboards to their sound, however. To them keyboards meant synthesizers and overwrought, overproduced, egomaniacal outpourings. This was not an entirely unjustified viewpoint at that time in music history. Howard Jones's popularity was at an all-time high. Nonetheless, Lark prevailed on them to give me a chance, and we rented a stifling rehearsal space south of Market with an old upright piano for three hours on a Saturday afternoon. Little did we know at the time that we would not relinquish that space for over two years.

The chemistry was immediate, no different than it had been with Lark on the Fourth of July. Because I had to pound the keys in order to hear and be heard, I played big blocky chords for the most part or occasional broken chords in eighth-note runs, putting me securely in the rhythm section with Chris and Huge. They liked this fine, as it freed them up to explore opportunities they had previously avoided in order to keep the beat simple and strong. Likewise, this more complex foundation freed up Lark from playing so much rhythm guitar and allowed him to weave his guitar with that of Peter, the band's other guitarist. Synthesizers, no. Dueling lead guitars? Hell yes!

We leased the sweatbox on a lockout basis so we didn't have to keep setting up and breaking down and so we could practice whenever we felt like, even in the middle of the night. I cashed my tuition check and bought a used Fender Rhodes 72 electric piano and a new Kurzweil synthesizer because I liked its organ sound. I plugged them into a used Peavy keyboard amp, and we pushed the old upright into the corner of the rehearsal space for use when Lark and I wrote. When the whole band was there, I could now compete in terms of volume, allowing me to pound less and play more, and we cranked it up constantly. We played so loud for so long in that echoing oven that now, in middle age, I can't hear well enough to keep up a conversation in a crowded restaurant.

We practiced every weekday for at least three hours, usually twice that, and often all day on weekends. We changed our name to August West, a fairly obscure reference to a Grateful Dead song. I learned to cover "Ramblin' Man," "Sugar Magnolia," "Sweet Home Alabama," and the entire Spin Doctors oeuvre that had won Danger Zone the Boone's gig in the first place. At the same time, Lark and I started writing original songs together that we slowly but surely incorporated into the act. We played Boone's once a week to ever-increasing crowds, until it got to be a fire hazard, and that's when we got invited to play the Last Chance Saloon.

The Last Chance Saloon was almost a proper venue. It was out in the Avenues on Clement Street. There was a bar and pool hall on the ground floor. The club was upstairs. We hauled our equipment up the narrow wooden stairs ourselves; the place was its own kind of fire hazard even before you drew a crowd. There was a small stage that had a support pillar in the middle that Lark and Peter had to dodge around. There was a small PA system with a soundboard and an engineer. Theoretically there were monitors, but I don't remember ever hearing anything come out of them. There was a storage room in the back that we used as a dressing room when we changed from our "roadie" t-shirts into our "gig" t-shirts.

There was no riser for Huge's drums, but he was Huge, so it didn't really matter. Chris set his bass amp stage left, and I set up my rig far stage right facing toward the band, leaving the center clear for Peter and Lark. Our little following from Boone's did what they were supposed to do, followed us, and the Saloon did a little advertising, so we had a pretty good crowd our first night.

We played hard and loud and drank beer, as always, and the crowd was with us, dancing and singing along to the covers (and sometimes to the original stuff too). More people came in from off the street. The electricity in the room got higher, and the beat was pumping, and I was playing my ass off, when suddenly I was utterly euphoric, and I felt as though my rig and I were levitating above the stage, looking down at the cheering crowd and those beautiful cats that were banging away with me. I knew at that moment that I was going to be a professional musician for the rest of my life. I made a mental note to grow my hair and get a tattoo. And I knew at some point I was going to have to tell the Old Man about "stopping out."

CHAPTER 3

I HAVE MADE IT through the metal detector, contraband undetected, and am standing in line to get a Squirt from one of the Staples Center concessions stands. The air-conditioning helps, but I still feel paranoid and claustrophobic. There are just so many people. It used to be that the Grammy Awards were an industry function, but for some time they have simply been an excuse to throw an arena-size "all-star" concert (generally quite mediocre if not downright bad) and tape it "live" for television (unless you live in the West). If it ever really was about awarding excellence, it was a pretense that had long since passed. It is now about selling tickets at more than a hundred dollars a pop to the taping of a Sunday night TV show during February sweeps intended to keep people in front of their tubes the week after the Super Bowl. Most of the people surrounding me are not even in the music business.

Part of the problem with the Grammys arose from the bona fide good intentions of its Trustees many years ago to acknowledge as many forms of music as possible. Un-

fortunately, there turned out to be many, many, many forms of music, and artists are always creating new ones, while generally not abandoning the old. There are now somewhere around one hundred different categories of Grammy Awards. You simply cannot fit them all into a single show, even a bloated three-and-a-half-hour special that almost never finishes on time.

Almost all of the Grammys, those for Best Polka Album, for example, are given away at the fairly execrable pre-show, during which there is no music or entertainment. A few smarmy industry vets herd the process along as quickly and, frankly, rudely as possible. Most of the nominees surrounding me attended the pre-show, were ushered out of the Staples Center so the stage could be reset for the real show, and then came back in with me. Many of these people already know they have lost and are probably still seething inside at the talentless hacks that did take home the miniature gold-plated gramophones.

I am a little ashamed of my negative feelings toward the whole process. After all, most of these people are just here to have fun. Those who are here as nominees at least seem to be acting happy to be here, despite the sure knowledge of four-fifths of them that they have already lost and there is no alcohol allowed or sold at the Staples Center during the Grammys.

A good five hours separates them from the Governors Ball, at which time they can finally get drunk or, in the case of the gospel artists, at least get something free to eat. Why should I feel low when I had lunch at the Polo Lounge while everyone else was at the pre-show, my award (one of the four "major" awards—Best New Artist, Song, Record, and Album) is yet to come, I haven't lost yet, and I have a smuggled flask of Fortaleza in the Old Man's custom-made boots?

I shiver again at the thought and complete the Squirt purchase. Although it has been over two years since my last drink, I readily recall that Squirt is a perfectly acceptable mixer for tequila if you can't just do a straight-up margarita. I do not want to admit to myself that the tequila will make me feel better, but I know that it will, just as soon as I can get to the bathroom and pour it into the Squirt and then into me. This is the plan. Prepare for and face the Fear.

"Are we getting married again?"

The plan will have to wait. I turn around, and there stands the former Miss Claudia Rankin of Sag Harbor, Long Island. The first Mrs. Zachary Fluett.

"I'm available."

"Same tux?"

"New one. I got it at the Men's Warehouse two days ago. The tailoring took only twenty-four hours. I like the way I look."

"It looks the same," she insists with a smile.

"The classics never go out of style. This one just has twice as much fabric," I respond, patting my well-tailored paunch.

She looks fabulous. She always looks fabulous, and she always did.

"You look fabulous," I say, proud of being genuine and in the moment, if at least fifteen years tardy.

"Thank you," she says. "I like the hat."

"It's too hot, and I feel like a phony."

"Well, you come by it honestly enough, and it's appropriate for this evening. Congratulations, by the way."

"Do you know something I don't?"

"Don't you know that it's an honor just to be nominated?"

"Bullshit."

"See? The hat suits you perfectly. Are those your father's boots?"

"They are."

"Off the wagon?" she asks, not unkindly.

"Not yet, but I will be soon. Just for tonight. I gave myself permission. Special occasion."

"That's your call, Zack, but if you're going to do it, I do suggest that you not drink alone."

Is that an invitation I hear?

CHAPTER 4

Rankin/Fluett – Claudia Morgan Rankin and Zachary Robert Fluett were married Saturday at Sagaponack Presbyterian Church in Southampton. The Rev. Neil M. Jordahl performed the ceremony. The bride is a graduate of Wellesley College and a publicist at Calloway & Carrington; the groom is a member of the music group Cultural Wasteland. They live in Los Angeles.

New York Times – Sunday, July 27, 1994

THE OLD MAN HAD the boots made for the wedding. It was a rather extravagant affair in the Hamptons, and both he and Mom wanted to make a good appearance. They did not want to look like a couple of hayseeds from Montana, even though that was pretty much what they were. It was what I really was as well, but I was in denial. In any event, they were very nice boots, soft and supple black leather with a rounded toe, low heel, and no decorative stitching such that, at first glance, they could pass for regular dress shoes. Except that most dress shoes don't have a built-in sleeve that holds a ten-ounce pewter whiskey flask.

The Old Man could have simply worn dress shoes. Mom just wore a pretty dress and pumps, and she looked great, but I think he wanted to make a little statement and be his own man amongst the investment bankers, fund managers, and trust funders that made up the bride's family and friends. I also think he truly felt he needed to carry his own supply of bourbon. The Old Man did not care for champagne, and I believe he feared that might be all there was. Having spent most of the previous year in a Seattle hospital, the Old Man also feared "the AIDS." He probably figured that with the San Franciscans and junkies he imagined I was hanging around, it was best to have a bottle over which he had complete dominion and control.

Claudia found this perfectly charming. She found Mom and the Old Man perfectly charming in general, and she loved them. When they came to find that she was an utterly genuine person, notwithstanding her parents' home address, they fell for her too. Marrying Claudia was the first thing I had done right since I left Montana, as far as the folks were concerned.

Claudia's people didn't come over on the *Mayflower*, but they were probably on the second boat, whatever that was. Her great-grandfather was a banker in the House of Morgan who went down on the *Titanic*. Although I don't think they technically had to work, her father was also a banker in Philadelphia and her mother was a real estate broker representing people seeking homes that George Washington had slept in.

I never got very close to her parents or to her sisters. She was the youngest of three, and I was never able to figure out if her folks were distant because they didn't approve of my lifestyle (or me, for that matter), or if it was just because that was their nature. Although she was the youngest by several years, she wasn't treated like the baby. Her parents did not dote on her, and she grew up quite independent. At the wedding, she focused far more on making sure that my people were happy than worrying about the social obligations that were part of the day.

Claudia had spent a great deal of time riding horses in Palm Beach, lying on the beach in Sag Harbor, and playing field hockey at Choate, all pastimes utterly foreign to me. She attended Wellesley College, as had her mother, and continued her equestrian pursuits there while studying journalism. She was the editor of *The Wellesley News* for two years and had dabbled with the idea of becoming a serious journalist, but after a spring break trip to California, she decided she wanted to try the West Coast. It turned out that she had been a closeted reader of tabloids and gossip magazines for years, and that interest, combined with her solid resume and natural desire to be helpful to others, wound up changing her career path such that it intersected with mine.

Claudia was the first publicist assigned to Cultural Wasteland when Defiant Groove Records, an L.A.-based indie with major label distribution, signed us. She was just out of college and at her first job at Calloway & Carrington, the big PR firm. Representing a new band with a new record coming out was very exciting for her, even though by C&C standards, we were of virtually no significance whatsoever.

At her first meeting with the band, she was very eager, very nervous, and very, very cute. She wanted to get historical backgrounds on each of us so she could begin crafting a story. Of course, we thought we were as funny as The Beatles. Our answers went like this:

"I am the shadow that comes and goes in the night," said Lark.

"We are members of the royal family of Argentina," suggested Peter and Chris.

"I'm a superhero," was Huge's response.

Always looking for an angle, I figured I could say something seemingly wacky too, but later when she learned it to be true, she would be impressed and have sex with me.

"I'm a dirt farmer from Montana."

"This is great stuff!" Claudia enthused. "I'll get right to work on putting a press package together. Also, I'm going to set up a photo shoot for next week. I'll get you some books to review so you can decide which stylist you want to work with. Then we'll go shopping!"

In typical Claudia style, she took each of us at our word, willing to believe that it was all the truth. As I came to learn, for the most part, it all was.

CHAPTER 5

4:25 p.m. PST

I EMERGE FROM THE bathroom stall, where I had just pulled the flask of Fortaleza out of the sleeve in the Old Man's boot and poured some into the Squirt. The smell was intoxicating, but I resisted the temptation to take a straight shot before replacing the flask. Best to step into this thing gently.

I take off my hat to see if I look better without it, checking myself out in the mirror. I really don't do well in the heat anymore. I'm a little puffy and red, and I've got a sticky band of sweat through my hair. Looks like the hat stays put. I wash my hands and splash some water on my face, then dry off and head back onto the concourse of the Staples Center.

I walk through the crowd, taking in all the photos of Lakers and Clippers and Kings, along with pictures of big shows that have played here. I recognize one from the boy band The Coreys, and I am reminded that the Staples Center has not always been a hateful place to me. That was a pretty fun night, in fact. I have lower expectations for tonight, but things are about to get a whole lot better, I hope.

Claudia has secured a table near the concessions and awaits me, talking on her cell phone. It is so nice to see her. She motions to me to sit down and holds up her index finger and thumb an inch apart to indicate that the call is almost over. I place the plastic cup on the table between us and take the top off, then pull two straws from my pocket, take off the paper wrappers, and put them in the drink, one facing her and one facing me. She snaps her phone closed and looks at me expectantly. I raise my eyebrows and take a deep breath, then grin at her.

"Here goes?" I say.

She nods slightly and we both lower our heads and take a sip from the straws. I envision us as a parallel universe version of a 1950s Norman Rockwell painting of teens sharing a malt. The concoction is sweet, with a zing. I am a bit apprehensive at first, but the old familiar feeling down the throat and the flush outward when it hits the stomach reminds me that drinking is something I will probably always be very good and very, very bad at. Tonight I want this feeling to soothe my jangly nerves, first simply because of being nominated but now also at seeing my ex-wife—the ex-wife who knows good and well that I probably shouldn't be drinking.

"Who do you have nominated tonight?" I ask. After several years at C&C (and after leaving me), Claudia formed her own boutique publicity firm and had done quite well with it.

"No one," she responds. "I don't represent entertainers anymore."

"Good thinking. What are you doing here then?"

"Aren't you glad to see me?"

"I'm very glad to see you."

"I could just be here to root you on."

Dare I hope? "You bought a ticket to this craziness

just to root me on?"

She smiles and shrugs. "Well, actually, no. I'm representing Greentricity, the solar power company that installed the panels on the Staples Center roof. They're providing 'clean, renewable, zero-emissions electricity for Music's Biggest Night.'"

"That so?"

"That's the tagline. It's my story, and I'm sticking to it."

"Well, it's better than some I've heard you tell."

"Yes, but you were the subject of those stories. Bad input, bad output."

"Touché. Where are you sitting?"

"I'll be moving around. Greentricity is one of the lead sponsors of the show, so I'll be trying to get everyone to talk about how excited they are that the telecast is actually helping to eliminate global warming and how all you at home should go out and do your part too."

"I put solar up in Woody Creek. I actually believe all that crap, you know."

"So do I. Otherwise I wouldn't be doing it. Leave your date in Colorado this time?"

I give her a look.

"No, she should be getting home to her mother just about now, telling tales of drunkenness and cruelty."

"No, Zack, that would have been me. No date, eh?"

I shake my head no, smiling.

"Good. Give me your extra ticket so I can find you inside. I'll drop by and keep you company and drink your drink so you don't."

I give her another look, but it doesn't feel like she's being too judgmental. She's just doing her best to help. I give her the extra ticket. She zips off, leaving behind the familiar scent of Chanel No. 5, lavender soap, and the

Atlantic Ocean. She also leaves behind the almost full tequila and Squirt. I take another drink, a longer pull using both straws, pleased to be drinking from the one she just used.

I'm starting to feel good. Maybe it's the tequila, but maybe that's not all.

CHAPTER 6

STEVE'S GUITARS
123 Second Street
Saturday 9:00 pm
ZACK FLUETT (Cultural Wasteland)
Tickets $20

Aspen Times October 21, 2003

ALL THE RECOVERING ALCOHOLICS I have met refer to "hitting rock bottom." This was never the case for me. My drinking is more like an anchor that simply cannot find a purchase on the ocean floor, allowing the ship above to continue to be battered hither and yon in the storm. Dragging anchor, I believe it's called.

I have quit drinking many times, but I always return to it. As I have geezed my way into middle age, I have managed to quit and stay quit from the Percocets, the Demerols, the Vicodins, the Ecstasy, the mushrooms, the LSD, the cocaine, and even the marijuana, but I always come back to the booze. And I never leave the cigarettes. They are by far the toughest addiction I have ever faced.

The most recent time I quit drinking was an anchor drag that had more to do with someone else's misfortune than with mine. After I got kicked out of Cultural Wasteland, I then got fired from my paid gig as keyboard player for the boy band The Coreys, and after that Melanie, the original GDT (Gold Digging Tramp), took most of my money and all of my self-respect. Well, then I took an old buddy up on a kindly offer and moved into a beat-up trailer in Woody Creek, about five miles outside of Aspen, Colorado. L.A. was finished with me, and I couldn't go back home, because there was no home to go to. The Old Man was long since dead, and Mom had wisely sold the ranch and moved into town. Where else to flee?

I had pawned my keyboards to buy the last of the cocaine that had worn me so thin in L.A., so, when I moved on, I found myself without an artistic outlet for the first time in memory. Once in Woody Creek, I laid off the blow for a while and, for something to do, I picked up an old Martin six-string copy at a pawnshop and started to teach myself to play guitar.

I learned to play "Uncle John's Band" and "Take It Easy" and "Lawyers, Guns, and Money," and then I figured, what the hell, and I learned to play "This Is Gonna Get Expensive" and "Monte Carlo Blues" and "Baby All the Plants Are Dead" and all of the rest of the Cultural Wasteland songs I hadn't played in a hell of a long time. It was interesting, relearning those songs on a new instrument, solo, being responsible for all the music coming out and singing the melody using an instrument that, by dint of several years' disuse and the ingestion of truly heroic amounts of booze and cigarettes, had become the voice of a man with a history.

I started off with a solo gig at Steve's Guitars in Carbondale. It's a nice place to play because it's not a bar. It's a guitar shop that Steve has set up with chairs and a stage, and he brings in offbeat public radio-type artists, and offbeat public radio-type listeners show up and listen respectfully. This is a nice environment in which to try something new, rather than trying to sing over the sound of some drunk hitting on a girl at the bar.

In any event, I called up Steve and asked him if I could try a little something, and he knew who I was, but he said sure anyway. He put up little posters around Carbondale, and twelve people showed up (just like a jury, I thought). I played and sang for about forty-five minutes, including a couple of new things I was working on, a smattering of Cultural Wasteland hits, and a cover of "Brokedown Palace."

The audience was very polite, and Steve invited me back, giving me eighty bucks that I promptly spent next door at the Black Dog, a dive bar full of bikers and Vietnam vets and George Bush fans. The need to get completely hammered in that environment resulted in my spending the night in the Carbondale jail on another DUI, resulting in the loss of driving privileges in Colorado. Thereafter, about monthly, I would take the bus from Woody Creek down to Carbondale to play my show at Steve's (with an increasingly large following, I might add), and then spend most of the proceeds on a cab back to Woody Creek, where I would either just get drunk at home or drink with Davy at the Woody Creek Tavern, just a ten minute or so stumble from my trailer.

After about six months of that, I got a semi-regular gig at the Belly Up in Aspen, opening about once a week or so for whatever act was coming through town without an opening act in tow. The Belly Up was a nice place to play, and because they could afford it (this being Aspen and all), they brought in some pretty good artists. Often I would be asked to hang around and sit in a little, and on more than one occasion somebody would want to cover a Cultural Wasteland tune, and I'd actually get to play piano on stage again.

These were not bad years. There were a series of girlfriends of a variety of shapes, sizes, and ages that came and went, some in a month, some in a week, and some in a night. There was enough song publishing money finally coming through again that, after servicing the GDT-induced mountain of debt, I could afford my rent and booze without having to submit to a day job. Ultimately, the gigs at the Belly Up caught the attention of a small-time promoter who sent me out on mini-tours of college venues and clubs, after I got my driver's license back. I was back in the music business.

The routine was simple for me: wake up in a cheap hotel in the afternoon, brush my teeth, throw up, rebrush my teeth, have the first beer and tomato juice of the day, restring my guitar, then head to the venue to eat the free cheese and veggie tray before the show. After the show, drink myself into bed, preferably with a local who had seen the show. Get up, drive to the next town, and do it again. It was from just such a tour of New Mexico and Arizona that I had returned to learn that Davy was dead.

Davy was my drinking buddy at the Woody Creek Tavern. He took pity on me when I was penniless and staked me drinks in exchange for listening to his story. He was a local boy. He grew up in nearby Aspen, where his parents had owned a liquor store for decades. Davy went off to L.A. to try the movie business in his twenties, and he had pretty solid success for a time as an assistant director, mostly on series television. He made a nice living and married a nice enough woman, and they had a nice baby who drowned in the pool one Saturday when Davy was passed out in front of the USC game.

He didn't contest the divorce and simply gave her the house and the bank accounts and drove away. On the trip back to Colorado, he stopped in Vegas for the night and woke up in jail three days later. He hocked his car to pay his fine, caught a Greyhound, and arrived in Aspen to the news that his folks had been killed when a truck rolled over in front of them on Highway 82. Davy sold the liquor store, moved into his parents' modest place in Woody Creek, and began the process of drinking himself to death.

That I was a party to this is something that will always haunt me. It was apparent to everyone that this is what was happening, but we kept on drinking with him and sometimes doing blow with him (whoever his connection was in Aspen had the very worst blow I ever snorted, but we did it), even though we knew he wasn't well. Every couple of months he would wind up in the emergency room, and they'd keep him there to detox and filter his blood, but when he'd get out, we'd all just party again. I was the worst offender, though. I was nursing my own regrets, and I honestly enjoyed listening and talking to Davy and getting loaded with him. I just did it, knowing it most likely wouldn't end well.

I had begun to have some hope for us, however.

Once I started getting out on the road and playing again, I got worried about what was happening back in Woody Creek to Davy without me at least to make sure he walked home safely. As a result, I convinced him, over several days and several hundred drinks, to try to get a job with a production that had come to town to shoot a new TV series called *Snow Job*. Thinking that a change might do him good, he went for it.

On the basis of his excellent resume, he was hired as second assistant director. They shot six episodes, and Davy stayed sober, showing up on time for the five a.m. calls and otherwise doing a solid and competent job. He got along with the actors, the directors, and the executive producer, and when the show was cancelled the morning after the third episode aired, the executive producer invited Davy to come back to L.A. and take a similar post on another series that was shooting there.

Davy didn't want to go. I argued with him for days. I told him that he was looking so much better after nine weeks of being back on the job. I told him that he was a kind and funny person who was loved by many people, myself included. I told him there was no reason he could not start again, go back to what he loved, forgive himself, and still have a full and complete life. I told him that drinking himself to death on a barstool next to me was no way to live, and I promised him that I would take my own advice as well. I promised that if he went back to work in L.A. for the run of this series, then I would get sober and make a solo record.

We drank and talked about big things and we had big hopes, and Davy finally agreed to go. He flew out to L.A. a few days after I left for my mini-tour of the Southwest. On the day I returned, word made it back to Woody Creek that Davy had been found dead in a motel room in Hollywood. They have much better coke in Hollywood than they do in Woody Creek.

Unbeknownst to me, Davy had made out a new will before he left, leaving me as his sole beneficiary. I don't know why he did this, except perhaps that I had been the last person on earth to tell him I loved him. We had a wake at the Tavern, a full-on blowout from which I awoke two days later. Then I thanked the staff, but informed them that they needn't save my stool in the future. I moved out of the trailer and into Davy's parents' little house, now my little house, and I spent the last of the liquor store money putting in a home studio. I started recording.

CHAPTER 7

I FEEL GUILTY ABOUT the tequila in my belly, but not so guilty as to stop drinking it. I think of Davy and how he would have been happy that he was going to see me on TV, my picture showing for a brief moment as they introduce the nominees, and he would have gotten a kick out of knowing that I have a flask of tequila in my cowboy boot.

"You've just stepped off the wagon for the evening," I say to myself. "Tomorrow you'll get back on, but this time you'll be able to have a beer when you watch a game, or have a glass of wine with dinner, or even drop in for a nightcap at the Tavern." I take another sip and look around a little bit.

One of the things that's wild about the Grammys and distinguishes it from the other major awards shows is the variety of clothing on display. The major reason for this is a desire for credibility. At the Oscars or Emmys or Golden Globes, the guys wear a suit or tux ranging from simple to splashy and the women wear elegant evening gowns by designers desperate to have their creations shown off on the red carpet. At the Grammys, your attire must match your music genre.

For some, this isn't that big of a deal. Pop stars like Beyoncé will always have clothes that pretty much look the same whether they're on the red carpet at the Oscars or Grammys, because she pretty much just wears high-end fashion all the time. She doesn't have to give anyone a hint as to whom she is except those who aren't watching anyway. For most everybody else, however, it's important to help people figure out who you are (or who you want them to think you are) because there are something like five hundred nominees trying to distinguish themselves from all the other folks trying to enjoy or endure "Music's Biggest Night." Plus, there are lots of seat fillers, more than one might guess.

In any event, I am surrounded by a dazzling array of fashion weirdness. Because most of the nominees for the big awards are performing and are thus backstage or soon will be, most of the folks surrounding me are from the awards that won't get announced live on TV. So now it's time to play, "Guess Who's Who!" OK. It's pretty clear that the fellow over there is in the Best Polka category. Why else would you wear a red vest and a hat with a large feather in it? That was pretty easy. Let's see what else we've got.

The country music stars, the men at least, all wear cowboy hats of some description. I am sort of lumped in with them this evening because Wendy Harper's version of "I Turned Around" started off on the country charts before it crossed over, but I am wearing basic black, whereas most of them are in brighter colors with placketed jackets and, occasionally, rhinestone appliqués that remind me of Porter Wagoner or, in the best cases, Gram Parsons.

The hip hop artists are all about the bling, with those on the gangsta rapper side of the fence staying true to form in baggy jeans, Nikes, baseball caps, and adding the full mouth grill in diamonds and gold. The R&B guys tend to wear their own clothing lines, sporting highly visible quality white suits with fedoras and no grill. I thought about having my own clothing line once, but it turned out that the flannel space was already pretty well occupied.

The rock gods wear motorcycle boots, jewelry by Chrome Hearts, bandanas, and pretty much anything by Roberto Cavalli, as long as you can still see at least thirty-six square inches of tattoo. This is the category I fell into the last time I attended the Grammys. The alt-rock guys look pretty much the same, except their t-shirts and jeans cost about a tenth as much as the rock gods. They are purchased along the same stretch of Melrose, just in different stores. I still have a few articles of clothing that would fit in with these guys if only they would fit on me.

I see someone that I presume is a nominee in the Best New Age category, because she is dressed like a fairy. Then again, she could be an Icelandic nominee in one of the dance categories. Or maybe she's a real fairy. Speaking of the dance category, towering over the scene is RuPaul, stunning in a long purple dress, hair and makeup perfect, and, frankly, with the best pair of legs in the house.

I am disappointed to realize that, because they have spun off the Latin Grammys into its own show, you no longer have nearly the number of great sombreros and studded suits of the Tejano and mariachi bands, which were really fun, if difficult to be seated behind. The jazz guys, as always, look cooler than everyone else, but not as cool as Miles Davis, even though that's what they're hoping to achieve. The gospel contenders are wearing pretty much the same basic outfits as the jazz guys; they just picked theirs up at Tent & Awning. It's odd how Herbie Hancock's aubergine Nehru jacket looks like a tapestry in an 8XL on the tenor from the Harlem Men's Choir.

The reggae guys look, sound, and smell reggae. I may be one of the few to sneak booze into the Staples Center, but the fellas from Jamaica seem to have kept up their end of the bargain too. I can smell it.

One of the primary looks of the Grammys, however, is hooker. This is simply another aspect of the music business. Whether high-end call girl or escort service hooker, a host of the jobs in the still male-dominated music industry tend to be populated by men who cannot or will not take a real date (like a girlfriend), a nomination date (like your mother), or no date (like me) to an awards show like the Grammys. These jobs include agents, managers, music industry attorneys, label executives (including Christian), misogynistic musicians (except gospel), all radio personnel, and closeted gays. In fairness, some of the men in these categories did not arrive with hookers; they arrived with their wives, who possibly used to be hookers, really look like hookers, or are simply successful Gold Digging Tramps.

The lights flash, warning us that the show is about to begin. I sip down the last of the first tequila and Squirt. Man, is that stuff tasty. I feel pretty good now. I'll maybe have to get another one during the first commercial break. I start through the peacock-clad folks still milling around the concourse and catch a glimpse of an unmistakable face towering above the crowd. Shit. I feel worse. I am about to cross paths with Lark Dray and, if I don't miss my guess, that is the GDT, the original Gold Diggin' Tramp herself, on his arm. Here comes the Fear again.

I am tempted just to turn and run, but now it's too late. He sees me. He smiles that wolfish smile of his and steers his small entourage toward me. He sticks out a hand, which I ignore. He hesitates, and then goes right on ahead.

"Hello, Zachary."

"Lark. Melanie."

The GDT says nothing and looks at the ceiling.

"Hey, congratulations on the nomination, man. Good luck tonight. We're all pulling for you."

"We are? Who, exactly, are we?"

"Well, me, Melanie, the band."

"I can't speak for you, but, as she no longer has any financial stake in my success, I find it hard to believe that Melanie is rooting for me."

While looking at the ceiling, Melanie nods her agreement. I appreciate the honesty.

"And I don't think I know anybody in your band, these days."

Lark's smile fades. Melanie ends the silent treatment. "You are such an asshole, Zack. He's just trying to be nice."

"I'm afraid nice went out the window when my best friend kicked me out of my own band and started fucking my wife."

"Dude, you might just want to take a little responsibility for yourself from time to time," *Lark responds.* "Anyway, we're out of here. I have to get changed for the show."

"Enjoy it from out front," *Melanie hisses.*

I believe I will get that Squirt and find a quiet spot for a cigarette near the reggae guys right now.

CHAPTER 8

GREAT AMERICAN MUSIC HALL
859 O'Farrell Street
Friday 10:00 pm
AUGUST WEST
Train
$10 Cover/$3 Bud

SF Weekly January 18, 1991

THE NIGHT OF OUR farewell show at the Great American Music Hall (we had outgrown the Last Chance Saloon by a long shot) was also the night we changed our name to Cultural Wasteland. I always liked the name August West, but it did give off connotations of being a Grateful Dead cover band, especially in San Francisco. We were now playing strictly original songs, and our sound had gotten tight and pretty slick, good enough for us to attract the attention of Defiant Groove Records, a well-respected L.A.-based label that agreed to sign us. The label suggested that we come up with a more original name, and Peter commented that having someone from the cultural wasteland of L.A. tell you to try to do something more original seemed ridiculous. Lark loved that comment and suggested that we just fight fire with fire, so we went ahead and took on the roll of being the purveyors of art from a cultural wasteland.

We made the big announcement of our name change at the gig, along with the news that we were going to L.A. to cut a record. The crowd cheered enthusiastically in support of us, which was nice, but I had half-expected sobs and depression and "you can't leaves." But no, everyone knew there would be a next "big new thing" along in a minute, and now we were in the category of, "Cultural Wasteland? Oh, I saw them back when they were still August West. Before they sold out."

The sellout was not for much money, although it seemed like it at the time, but there certainly was a lot of excitement. I realized almost immediately that we were made for the L.A. scene, because Lark was made for L.A. He was tall and lean and had those piercing blue eyes that gleamed out from under a shock of jet-black hair as he howled our songs. And he was funny too, back then. Once we got down to L.A., we really started to feel like this whole crazy dream of pursuing a life in music might actually come true. We might not ever have to have day jobs again.

We played the Whisky and the Key Club and the Viper Room and all the usual L.A. haunts. The girls showed up, so the guys showed up. The label had us spend about three months just playing as much as possible and getting our name out there, and then they pulled us back and put us in the studio.

We had signed what amounts to a standard new-band indie deal, which at the time seemed pretty great to us but, as we would learn, was actually absolutely horrifying in the long run, especially for yours truly. We signed up for seven records with Defiant Groove, which meant in reality one record if we stank and seven if we were great, but the decision was at the label's option, so they basically had us tied up for years at a price negotiated when we had no leverage because no one had ever heard of us. We got a half million-dollar advance against artist royalties from sales of the first record, which seemed awesome, but in practice that didn't go very far.

First, twenty percent went to the management company the label had hooked us up with, and another five percent went to the law firm that the management company advised us to retain, then another three percent went to the business managers that the law firm put in charge of keeping track of the money, undoubtedly to make sure that the lawyers and managers actually got paid.

Next, the producer that the label had chosen came in and sat down with us and set a budget for the record to be paid from the advance, which of course included his fees, those of an engineer and assistant engineer, studio rental time, gear rental, tape costs, and miscellaneous expenses (which wound up including pot, booze, and cocaine, and got pretty expensive). Once this budget was presented to the business managers, they got back to us with what we would have to live on during the sixty or so days scheduled to record. Nothing.

So our managers and lawyers went back to the label to see what could be done. I knew they had to be good for something, but I didn't realize what it was going to cost us in the long run. The label agreed that it would be best for the recording if we got out of the cheap hotel they had been putting us up in and if we were able to feed ourselves, and our managers thought it best to rent us a rambling old house in Topanga so we could work on songs when we weren't in the studio (and most likely so they could keep an eye on us). As a result, everyone agreed we should enter into a music publishing deal with yet another $100,000 "advance."

Music publishing isn't just for selling sheet music of songs we wrote, like I assumed at the time. It also includes royalties paid for radio play and for the manufacture of records. What I didn't realize was that by taking this deal, we were letting the label pay us reduced rates and, worse yet, actually take ownership of our copyrights in perpetuity, amongst other indignities too annoying and legalistic to mention. We didn't understand for years that "advance" would eventually mean, "you're going to pay for this, sucker!"

In any event, after our business managers paid themselves, our lawyers, and our other managers their fees and withheld enough for taxes, we now had about $10,000 each to live on while we recorded the album and waited for the royalties to start coming in. What we totally ignored was that our record wouldn't come out for months and that royalty statements would only be delivered twice a year after that, which meant that it would wind up being a long time before we were even theoretically owed any money. Tragically, it turned out that theoretically was the operative word, because even once we started making sales, the label first got back the "advances" it had made from our royalties.

The word "royalties" turns out to be similar to "advance." The royalty rate we got for our first album was fourteen percent "all in," which was pretty decent for an indie act, or so our managers, attorneys, and business managers told us. That fourteen percent was calculated on the Suggested Retail List Price of a record, which back then was about fifteen bucks, so our finger-counting math suggested that was around two dollars a record. Not so fast, it turned out. That "all in" royalty included four points for our producer, which was OK, but then was subject to a lot of bullshit deductions for packaging, "free goods," budget sales, foreign sales, and pretty much anything else the label could think of to screw us.

The bottom line is that our artist royalty turned out to be less than a dollar a record, sometimes quite a lot less. We eventually figured out to our horror that even at a dollar a record, it would take at least a gold certified record (500,000 units sold) to recoup just the $500,000 advance, and that didn't include additional label expenses for publicity, promotions, videos, and all that other good stuff, all of which were also considered advances. Gold records do not grow on trees, and even if we might be so lucky as to get one (and we were), we would still be in the hole with the label.

Because we did get that gold record, however, the label exercised its option for another record and issued us another advance to go back in the studio, and that advance was then "cross-collateralized" (I know, who comes up with these terms?) against royalties otherwise payable on the first record as well as the second and any others. This process could go on indefinitely.

It took me years to understand it, but once I did I began to appreciate the upside of staying in school and becoming a lawyer, accountant, or businessman. You can rip off dumb (or at least wasted and distracted) musicians. Although I was a member of a big-time rock band that sold millions of records, while I was a member of that band (and for many years thereafter), I never actually received an artist royalty check. I am not alone in this regard.

The upshot of all of this is that the label took a big risk up front that we would wash out (and many bands do). But once we started to have success, they took their profits from the sale of each record while recouping their at-risk money from royalties otherwise payable to us, and, at the end of the day, they owned the master recordings and the copyright in the albums and songs. Even had the records sold millions and millions of copies, the profits received by the label would have far exceeded the royalties that would ultimately need to be divvied up among the five members of the band.

This was by no means considered a bad record deal. We just didn't understand all its intricacies at the time, and I would not be around long enough to enjoy the fruits of that other reality of the music business known as "renegotiation." That little bitch karma got back at the music industry later on, however, when both illegal and legal downloading would take a huge chunk out of a business that was built around the concept of selling plastic discs rather than music.

None of which mattered to us on that beautiful June morning when we moved into the house on Entrada in Topanga, however. From the perspective of a twentysomething college dropout, life was about as good as it could get. I had $10,000 in my checking account, the label had made a deal with Korg to deliver a brand new top-of-the-line keyboard that I could keep, and we had five bedrooms with four and a half baths and a swimming pool out back. Also, that cute publicist Claudia had said, "Maybe I will," in response to my suggestion that she bring a bikini when she dropped by later to show us the example books from various stylists for our first photo shoot.

Huge was in the kitchen tending to a blender of margaritas; Chris was in his room downstairs screwing the actress from the Herbal Essences commercial; Peter was breaking in the brand new Stratocaster that Fender had given him; and Lark and I were lying in the Southern California sunshine, fresh out of the pool.

"This sucketh not," commented Lark.

"Low on the suckage meter," I agreed.

"A veritable suck-free zone," he went on.

"It does lack a certain suckability," I said, starting to giggle.

"The sucking has ceased and desisted!" he shouted.

"Suck this," said Huge, grabbing his crotch while at the same time setting down a tray of margs, blended with salt on the rim and sporting colorful straws, all quite proper. This struck Lark and me as one of the funniest things ever said, and we proceeded to make ourselves nearly sick with laughter. Huge pretended to ignore us, smiling quietly behind his sunglasses and sucking noisily on his straw.

Suddenly Lark leapt to his feet and ran up to the house. He returned moments later with his acoustic, and sat back down, strumming a couple of chords with a bright, syncopated blues rhythm. Then he started singing.

"I've got a Margarita headache and there's leaves in the pool. Cry for me. Cry for me."

I chimed in, "My Victoria's Secret girlfriend

brought her bi friend to play too. Cry for me. Cry for me."

"My Lamborghini's in the shop, the loaner's just a Benz."

"If I didn't pay for them, I think I'd have no friends!"

Then, Lark pounded out a distinctive triplet pattern and Huge joined in instinctively with both of us as we shouted out the staccato punch line.

"This sucks! This sucks! This sucks! This sucks!"

Well, damned if we hadn't just written our first number-one single.

CHAPTER 9

ENTERING THE ARENA AFTER my smoke and another quick tequila and Squirt, I take my seat and get a gander at the program, which is roughly the size of an NFL playbook. Despite the large number of Grammy award categories, only about a dozen of them will be given out live tonight, but there will be lots of other non-award related stuff to pass the time between commercial breaks.

I am pleased to see that they have returned to a hosted format. That funny lesbian comedian I always enjoy will be seeing us through the evening. She's actually pretty cool, so maybe this won't be all bad. Although, from the looks of this program, it certainly will be somewhat weird, if not downright cheesy.

In addition to the actual awards, there will be the fifth salute to the Beatles in six years for no apparent reason, this one involving a roller-blading team and Disney's Country Bears. There are going to be lifetime achievement awards presented to Alan Parsons and Joe Satriani, who have twenty-six Grammy nominations and no wins between them. There will also be a special presentation to Bela Fleck thanking him for participating in the Grammy process but barring him from further competition to prevent him from winning in every single category. This seems reasonable to me. Let him go pick on the Latin Grammys for a while.

In the major categories, multiple nominees take up many of the spots. The Boss is tied for most nominations for the year with a newcomer indie chick, Lena Rifka. They have six each, and both of them are nominated in my category of Song of the Year. This does not bode well for me. They are also nominated for Album of the Year and Record of the Year, and she is nominated for Best New Artist. Lark Dray will compete against them for Record of the Year, which is for a single, and my girl Wendy Harper will compete against them for Album of the Year, which, as it sounds, is for an entire album.

There are a couple of other nominees in my category whose names I recognize, but whose songs I don't. Diane Warren gets nominated for Best Song a lot, and she is nominated again this year, but in collaboration with three other songwriters, which is pretty unusual for her. I don't know the song, but the artist is TJ Corey on his solo debut away from his boy band The Coreys, and I certainly do know him.

The other nominated song is from a Pixar movie based on Gilligan's Island. I'm pretty sure that if it wins I'll have to go ahead and kill myself, and I don't even care that much about winning. Losing to Gilligan, however, is unacceptable.

The real trouble is Springsteen. He's won something like eighteen Grammys, and the Academy loves him. I positively worship the guy, though I must admit that am not too familiar with his most recent album, The Streets of Orlando, *the title track of which was written for a Spike Lee PBS special about the plight of theme-park workers. He has in the past won for AIDS patients, Vietnam vets, and modern Okies, so this could be stiff competition. On the other hand, this Lena Rifka could turn out to be a twenty-first-century Sheryl Crow, who routinely beat up on the Grammys back when I was in Cultural Wasteland.*

I am especially hopeful for Wendy Harper in the Album of the Year category. She faces the same stiff competition as I do for Best Song; however, she's getting to that stage of her career where it's her turn to get a Grammy, even if it's awarded in part for her body of work. She's been nominated something like five times for Best Female Country Performance as well as in other country categories, but she's never won. Dreams of Tomorrow, *the album that "I Turned Around" is on, was her first big crossover success, and this is the first time she's been nominated in one of the "Big Four" categories.*

As far as I'm concerned, she's nominated in two, as my nomination for Song of the Year wouldn't exist without her, but it would be especially great if she could win for herself for the Best Album of the Year. That's a nice one to get. If you care about those kinds of things. Which, of course, I don't. I'm just here for the air conditioning.

CHAPTER 10

THE FIRST SUMMER AS Cultural Wasteland was
magic. Leon Richard, the producer assigned by the
label, turned out to be an excellent choice. He was
a low-key guy and an excellent musician who knew
infinitely more about music and recording than we
did, but he also recognized that we had a certain
sound and chemistry that worked. Thankfully he
didn't try to turn us into something we were not, but
simply helped capture what we were.

Leon liked to work at night, so a typical day constituted getting up at the crack of noon and lounging around the pool all day working on songs. Then we'd all pile into the orange 1970 VW camper bus that I'd bought to haul around our equipment during the August West days, go to Lila's for Mexican food, and then into the Valley to the studio around six.

We'd work for anywhere from six to ten hours, depending. Lark and I summed up that experience and more in the song "Graveyard Shift," the first single off our second album, *The State I'm In*. It wasn't exactly like I expected it to be, though I didn't really know what to expect. Leon ran a pretty tight ship. He believed that you got to work at a set time, put in your eight hours, fewer if you were either great or just sucking, more if you were either great or just sucking, and that you put sounds on tape. There was not much sitting around. Leon had an idea of what he wanted to accomplish in a session, and he gave clear directions. Although he could be as eloquent as he wanted in discussing the intricacies of melody, harmony, rhythm, and songwriting, his producing style was generally to say one of three things: Yes, No, or Do It Again.

Leon had attended most of our L.A. shows and had heard all our songs. He picked fifteen to record, from which twelve would ultimately make the album. The suits from the label added "Cry for Me" (the "This Sucks" song) during the process. It was a very dangerous play, adding that track, because it was essentially a novelty record, but it was just so damn catchy and funny that the label felt it had no choice. We were lucky that Leon made sure there was enough solid stuff behind that song to keep us

from becoming a one-hit wonder when they got behind "Cry for Me" as the first single.

The basic drill was that the whole band would get
together and lay down the track live, two or three
or more times until we got a nice tight version of it.
Then Leon would work with us individually, starting
with Huge and Chris to perfect the rhythm tracks.
My turn next. Often I would have several tracks
to myself because I might use multiple keyboards,
from grand piano to electric piano to organ to various synth sounds. We kept it pretty straightforward
rock, but I learned a lot from Leon about what can
be done with layers and with very subtle background
washes that don't take away from the heart of a five-
piece live rock band. Then Leon would work with
Lark and Peter on the guitar parts, then start the
process all over with vocals.

Everyone but Chris sang live on stage, and we
were pretty proud of some of the harmonies we had
developed. In the studio, however, Lark quickly became the sole vocal focus. He simply had the best
voice, and he could do so much with it. With Leon
helping, he learned to do even more. Harmony lines
that I had always sung live (and would continue to
do so on the road), were doubled and tripled by Lark
alone in the booth. There was a good reason for this:
it sounded better. This could have been the source
of considerable friction if it had not been for the way
Leon handled it. He had me sing my parts; then he
had Lark sing my parts. Then we A-Bed the two
mixes, and the whole band, myself included, agreed
immediately on which was better. I admit that my
pride was a little hurt, but there was nothing unfair
about it.

Interestingly, many of Peter and Huge's vocals stayed, because they were more flavorings and counterpoints than harmonies. I had always been the second-best singer in the band, even singing lead on a few songs, and so had done all the tight harmony work. It was all that work (including singing lead on anything) that was turned over to Lark in the studio. Despite spending many hours in the vocal booth, the only place my voice can be heard on our first album is on the shouted chorus of "Cry for Me," and there I am joined not only by the whole band, but also by Leon, both engineers, and the studio security guard, whose rumbly über-bass actually makes the record, if you ask me.

Leon was also strict about hangers-out. There were none. Not that we had much in the way of an entourage at the time. We didn't really have many friends in L.A. outside of one another, but there were girls, of course, and a few drug dealers and the like. All were forbidden from entering the studio. The only people allowed in, and then only from time to time, were Ross Stuart, our A&R man from the label, and Claudia, until Leon learned I was sleeping with her and then she too was banned.

There was always cold beer and booze and coke around, but never too much. We were all expected to keep our shit straight. Leon liked to smoke pot while he worked, so he couldn't be too fascist about it, but none of us abused the privilege. Although Cultural Wasteland would make other good albums, there would never be another recording experience like the one we had when our egos were in check and Leon was in the center chair.

After we finished recording all the tracks for a

given song to Leon's satisfaction, he'd give us a day off and take to the studio alone with the engineers to make a first pass at the mix. I think he did this because he knew we'd be bored just sitting around listening to the same thing over and over again with minute little adjustments and so, for something to do, we would try to be helpful. In order to avoid having to deal with such helpfulness, Leon would send us to the beach for a day.

We'd go down to the Pier at Santa Monica and eat burgers at Big Dean's, then stroll around, maybe take a ride or two on the dinky little roller coaster and try out the bumper cars. Then we'd have air hockey tournaments in the arcade or we'd go into Venice and get tattoos. I already had a likeness of my old cutting horse, Sundee, on my right shoulder from back in the August West days. That summer I got myself inked with a wild dragon that pretty much sleeved my left forearm, and I added a Charlie Russell bison skull on my right pectoral. Huge got a Maori design on his leg, and Lark put a lark on his shoulder that we all agreed looked gay. The Ramos brothers declined to get tattoos, admitting that their mother would kill them. I made fun of them for years about this, until I actually met her.

That summer the five of us spent virtually all of our time together. Even when Claudia and I started seeing more of each other, we didn't much go out on dates by ourselves. She would just hang out with us, as did all the rest of the other girls who rotated through the house.

When he was ready, Leon would bring us back into the studio to listen to the mix. We'd work with him on finalizing it, and he would often seem to make small adjustments based on our comments. Years later he told me that there were two knobs and two sliders on the mixing board that did absolutely nothing. Frequently he would twiddle with one in response to an idea one of us might have and, invariably, we would all agree that the change made all the difference. The engineers and he would then smile and nod—how they kept from cracking up is beyond me—and we'd move on.

In this fashion Leon built each song like a house from the foundation up, and then put the record together like an eclectic but harmonious little neighborhood. The album cover artwork mirrored this approach, with a funky, rundown little house showing through the jewel box and then folding out to display a whole neighborhood with several different abodes seen in the twilight, five very different dogs roaming its streets. The label was very pleased, as were we.

After the record was finished, the label sprung for a trip to Baja, justifying it not only as a reward for having knocked out a good album on time and on budget (that was Leon's doing), but also to shoot a video for "Cry for Me." We used the tropical resort beaches, bars, and even golf courses to show the sad and difficult life of a privileged rock star, with Lark as the main focus, of course.

At first the rest of us were a little pissed off that we were pretty much relegated to the background, aping playing our instruments at poolside or in a greenside bunker while lip synching "This Sucks!" Once we learned that making a video really does suck, however, we were happy that the director made short work of us, spending most of his time getting

Lark to mope his way through the shoot, champagne glass in hand and a variety of bleach blondes by his side. We laughed amongst ourselves, drinking at the swim-up bar at the Hotel Cabo San Lucas, amused that Lark was outside in the hundred-degree heat in full rock-star getup, leather pants and all, doing the sixty-seventh take of a five-second sequence in what was a heroically stupid video. Looking back on it, although it was funny at the time, this really was the beginning of the breakdown of the band as a band and not just as a backing group for Lark Dray.

Adding to the nascent sense of separation was my growing relationship with Claudia. She was technically working and spent a fair amount of time scouting locations for photo shoots, the deserts of Mexico being an interesting place to shoot a band named Cultural Wasteland. Having had enough pool time in Topanga, I took to accompanying her, and the more time we spent together alone, the more I fell for her. She had an extraordinary sense of humor, was smart as hell, and I never got bored around her. She was also quite willing and even eager to pull off to the side of the road or run off into the sand dunes for a quickie whenever the spirit grabbed us. Which it often did. I think we both realized on that trip that this was not just fun and games. We were, in fact, falling in love, something neither of us had done before.

The summer ended, as summers do. We stayed in the house in Topanga for another month, playing the circuit in L.A. as we had before we went into the studio, and then the label sent us out on the road. We opened for Bobby Craft, an artist on Defiant Groove who had been around for years, in and out of major label deals and rehab. Bobby had a couple of hits in the seventies but had never made it to the top of the mountain. Part of this was because his music was simply too sophisticated, literate, and darkly humorous for most people to appreciate except in small doses, and part of it was because he had been a legendary drunk with a vicious amphetamine problem and a penchant for handguns. Lark loved him immediately, and I would learn to over time.

Bobby traveled in an RV with his handler and sound engineer, Winston. Bobby had been sober for several years, but it remained pretty much one day at a time. Getting clean had revealed a solid bipolar disorder along with compulsive behavior, so Winston drove the RV, ran the sound, and made sure that everything went just the way it was supposed to in order to keep Bobby on an even keel.

We followed behind in a converted Greyhound packed full of equipment and dark, evil smells. We'd drive all night, get into town and check into the cheapest hotel we could find, try to get some shuteye, and then go down to the venue and set up our shit. No roadies for us. We'd play an opening set, and then we'd become the backup band for Bobby.

Bobby was not just compulsive; he was a perfectionist. He was constantly screaming at Chris and Huge to refine the beat down to a level where it was almost mechanical in its perfection but still had the swing of a live sound. He gave Peter all kinds of directions about how he wanted notes bent. And he expected me to work out, write, and teach the rest of the band the arrangements. As I result, I was the one who caught most of Bobby's shit when things didn't go exactly as he wanted, which was almost exactly always. It was hell on wheels, but our time in the studio with Leon and three months on the road with Bobby did, in fact, turn each of us into an honest-to-God musician, and not just a member of a band.

CHAPTER 11

5:35 p.m. PST

I'M SWEATING STRAIGHT THROUGH my tuxedo jacket. The air conditioning is not keeping up with the hot lights of the crowded Staples Center Arena. I have my hat on my knee and am grateful once again that I elected to cut my hair. Long hair would be brutal on a night like this, and besides, I was starting to go gray and was looking like an old hippie instead of a grizzled veteran of the rock wars. Unfortunately, I fear that I now look like a Republican fundraiser instead—some guy named Joe Bob who owns several Cadillac dealerships in Austin and Oklahoma City.

The Crips and the Bloods seem to be mounting a production of West Side Story *on stage, or perhaps it's* Guys and Dolls *with a dogfight in place of the crap game. The producers appear to have successfully imported the Northern Lights and one supernova into the confines of the Staples Center. The speakers are pumping out the sounds of what seems to be someone attempting intercourse with an unwilling bull moose, which is never a good idea. It's hard to tell exactly, because my seat seems four hundred rows back, partially obscured by the soundboard to my left and a camera boom to my right. I am, fortunately, on an aisle. A kindly enough production assistant said she would take me to a seat closer to the front when the Song of the Year category comes up, but that will be hours from now.*

The Grammys have grown appreciably since I was last in attendance. Even though I don't particularly think my seat is appropriate for a Song of the Year nominee, I also recognize that I really am a nobody compared with the people up front that the TV camera pans across on the bumpers in and out of commercials. As bad as it is, I must admit that I have a better seat than about nineteen thousand other people. The amount of energy being used to power the show and the taping of the show is astounding. Good thing Claudia's solar team had a nice hot sunny day up there on the roof of the Staples Center.

A hand alights on my shoulder. "Scoot over," Claudia murmurs in my ear. Her breath is cool on my neck. I oblige.

"Don't you just love this band?" Claudia grins.

"Kickin' it old school, aight." I suddenly feel much better.

"Is the tequila gone?"

"I'm trying to make it last the whole show, but it's going to be a close call."

"I want a shot. Let's take a walk."

I gratefully haul my ass out of the folding chair and we hightail it out of the arena, keeping away from the cameras and hopping over the twists of heavy cable. We run up the tunnel, our way blocked by a yellow jacket.

"No in and outs during the performances," says the burly fellow.

Claudia flashes her All Access pass. "Best Song Nominee. I have to get him backstage pronto." I fumble for my medallion that does indeed signify that I am a "Nominee."

The guard nods officiously and pulls back the drape. We slip through quickly, then out the crash doors and back into the relative cool and quiet of the concourse.

"You are a lifesaver. I was starting to go mental in there. Where did they get that moose?"

Claudia eyes me, smiles. "I'm not sure I follow you as well as I used to, Zack, but I think you're talking about the lead singer from a gospel group from northern Maine."

"Ah. All right then. That explains it." I notice that the concessions have closed.

"Jesus Christ, the concessions have already closed," I point out.

"Yep. Once the show starts, the producers want everyone to stay put as much as possible, I guess. That's why I asked for a shot. No mixers left."

I put my foot up on a garbage can, pull up my pant leg, and retrieve the flask. I hand it over to Claudia. She takes a quick pull, then another little nip, and hands it back to me. I test the weight; there will not be enough to stave off the white knuckles. There's nothing to be done now, so I take a pull too and offer it back.

"No thanks, I just wanted to see how you were doing, really. I have to get back in a minute. The moose is going to make a statement to the press about global warming and the importance of solar power."

"He's your client? Well, I understand that northern Maine is one of the places hardest hit by global warming."

"Just so."

The tequila plays through me warmly. I feel safe again.

"Well, I'm doing fine now, thanks to you. Remind me why we got divorced again?"

"Because I caught you red handed in a pile of smelly French groupies."

"We all know the story, but what was the real reason?"

Claudia's smile fades. "Honestly?"

A sudden wave of fear comes over me. Do I really want to know this? I forgot what diminished judgment does to my communication skills. What happened to the sense of well-being? Can I get back to light banter?

"Honestly," *comes out of my mouth. It sounds not at all like light banter but like a desire to hear the truth while standing outside one of the great, annual black holes of entertainment industry hypocrisy.*

Claudia stares at her feet for a moment, and then looks me straight in the eye. We've gotten close, but we haven't actually gone here before.

"Because you were only sorry that you got caught. You weren't sorry that you cheated; you weren't sorry that you hurt me."

My brain screams out a combination of "I didn't really cheat on you" and "that doesn't really matter!" at the same time.

"You were just sorry because you knew it was going to mean that I was going to be upset, and that was going to be a pain in the ass for you."

I mentally check my emotional landscape. No new craters. In fact, I feel a sense of relief and a sense that this is a truth I can deal with.

"So you divorced me because I was a complete asshole," *I sum up.*

Claudia smiles a little, but it's still a sad smile and my heart shatters. Such a good feeling. I still have a heart to break.

"That's pretty much it."

"I listened to you, you know. I'm a much better person now."

Claudia leans in and kisses me on the cheek. "I have to run. Good luck." She turns and clicks away down the hallway.

I take another long pull on the tequila. Another. To hell with rationing. In fact, to hell with this whole thing. If I leave now, I'll miss all the traffic. I'll leave a note with a PA for them to read in the unlikely event that I win: "Zack Fluett couldn't be here tonight because he is a recovering asshole, so I am accepting this award on his behalf with the hopes that it doesn't result in a major backslide." *I knock back the last of the contents of the flask with a vengeance.*

"Oh Mr. Fluett, I'm so glad I found you!"

I turn around. It is the kindly little PA from before.

"There's a problem with Wendy Harper's piano player. She's asking for you backstage. We need to hurry."

I sincerely wish I had not just finished the tequila.

CHAPTER 12

WENDY HARPER WAS, TO the best of my ability to discern, the most genuinely nice and normal person I ever met in the music business. I met her in a suite at the Little Nell, which is the type of place where a diva's worst behavior would be easy to spot, but there was none. My publisher called to tell me that Wendy was in Aspen for a long ski weekend with her husband and kids, had seen my name on a poster for an already past show at the Belly Up, and had asked if I would drop by for a cup of coffee one afternoon.

I was more than happy to accept, as this was the woman who had essentially ensured, so long as I didn't drastically alter my lifestyle, that I wouldn't have to worry much about money for a good long while. Her recording of "I Turned Around" stayed on top of the Country charts for twenty-seven weeks and was number one on the Hot 100 for six weeks. She sold millions of records and downloads, sang it on her HBO special as the final encore, performed it in stadiums around the world, and allowed it to be used in conjunction with a TV commercial for a big insurance company. Her version had also been used over the closing credits of a big Hollywood block-buster, which allowed me to buy a new pickup.

When I arrived at her suite at the appointed time, I was surprised that she opened the door herself, wearing ski togs. There were no personal assistants in sight. She immediately gave me a big, warm hug, like I was long-lost family. I didn't exactly know what to do, but it felt so nice that I hugged her back like I was family too. She invited me into the suite, which looked like a ski shop had exploded. Within seconds I was introduced to her three children: Alexa, age nine, Andrea, age eight, and Robert, age six. They were polite and rambunctious, pink-faced from an afternoon on the slopes, changing out of their ski attire and calling out for hot chocolate and for Dad to turn on the Xbox.

Wendy took me to the kitchen where her husband Jackson was making hot chocolate, dressed in jeans and a t-shirt, barefoot. He shook my hand, and I was surprised at how much taller he was than I had expected. I don't think of baseball players as particularly big guys, but he was at least Lark's size with another twenty pounds of muscle. I guess you need that kind of a body to hit over four hundred home runs and a thousand RBIs with a lifetime .348 batting average in center field for the St. Louis Cardinals for something like fifteen seasons. We shook hands and Wendy excused herself to get changed.

"How was the skiing today?" I asked politely, because I couldn't think of a single other thing to say.

"Oh, no skiing for me. I'm not really allowed, by contract," he responded, "But Wendy said it was great. I'm petrified of the entire idea of it, to tell you the truth. Are you a big skier?"

"I haven't been on skis in at least a decade," I admitted.

"How long have you lived in Aspen?" he asked.

"At least a decade."

"So you didn't come here for the skiing."

"Nope. I'm not sure I actually remember exactly why I came here, but it's worked out pretty well."

"So there's more to this town than the Colorado version of Rodeo Drive I walked down yesterday?"

I smile. "Yep. I live out of town in a little place called Woody Creek. Once you get out of Aspen proper and head down valley it gets a lot less pretentious. I especially love it in the fall. The colors are just spectacular and the air is crisp, but it stays pretty warm when the sun's out."

"I try to be too busy in the fall to pay much attention to the change in colors, but that'll change soon enough, I suppose," he said wryly. "Not many years left in these bones for October."

"What are guys talking about?" asked Wendy, returning to the room in a comfy looking pink sweat suit.

"How the World Series really gets in the way of a good hike," I responded. Jackson grinned and excused himself to take hot chocolate to the kids.

"Yes, it's just sacrifice, sacrifice, sacrifice for us," she said.

"Cry for me?" I grinned.

"I loved that song too, but it was no 'I Turned Around'," she smiled back.

Wendy poured us coffee. We sat at the kitchen table for an hour, talking about the business, how it had changed and how it hadn't, the terrible things about it, and how there was no other business we could be in. I told her that I was thankful to her for recording my song and making such great use of it, and how much I enjoyed her version of it.

"I'm grateful to you for writing it, and I'm just lucky I got to hear it before Faith or Shania or Carrie…. Jeez, there's a lot of versions of me out there these days."

"I couldn't disagree more, Wendy. You're one of a kind."

"Your song was what was one of a kind, Zack. It would have been a hit for anyone, and it'll probably be a hit for someone else down the road. It would have been a hit for Lark Dray, if he had gotten it first too."

"That would have been pretty unlikely."

"You two don't get along so well?"

"Not so much."

"That's too bad. It's like fighting with family when that happens."

"That's exactly what it's like, Wendy," I responded. "But I'm not sure that's how Lark feels about it."

"Well, it's still a great song," she said. Then she asked if I would be sure to send her any new songs I came up with that might work for her, and I assured her that I would. We traded e-mail addresses, and when Jackson came back into the kitchen to start putting dinner together, I took my leave, getting another big hug at the door. I was surprised a few weeks later when the first congratulatory e-mail I received for the Song of the Year nomination came from Wendy, even before I got the call from my publisher.

I responded, *Right back atcha! See you at the show!* Although I doubted that I actually would.

CHAPTER 13

5:47 p.m. PST

I AM REALLY SWEATING now as we run down the concourse of the Staples Center. I have got to shed a few pounds. Maybe I'll get the flat tire on the mountain bike fixed and ride it around Aspen and Woody Creek. Probably a good way to get killed.

The PA leads me through yet another layer of security, and suddenly we are backstage. The activity is frenetic. I stop to take it in. Roadies shove a massive champagne glass into place to go onstage as another crew rapidly dismantles a set piece consisting of a giant banjo, guitar, and fiddle. The cynicism toward the industry that I have been nursing all night dissipates as my appreciation for an actual live show returns, even if it is prepackaged bullshit for television. My problem has always been with the executives and agents and managers and lawyers and promoters and sundry hangers-on. It was never with the people who actually put on the show—the roadies, sound guys, lighting crew, carpenters, wardrobe, craft services, and, yes, even the musicians.

"We really have to go, Mr. Fluett," says the kind-

ly young PA, whom I begin to notice is rather pretty as she takes my hand. She has that sort of cute-librarian-with-glasses thing going on. It feels nice to hold her hand. She's less than half my age. The running has obviously increased the rapidity of tequila absorption. Don't do anything stupid, here, Zachary. You're out of drinking practice. Leave the nice girl alone.

We thankfully slow to a walk backstage, into those corridors of the Staples Center the fans rarely see, all beige cinderblock and fluorescent lights casting a chartreuse glow across the concrete floor. The PA leads me straight into a set of dressing rooms and calls out, "Mike, I've got him!"

I recognize him before he even turns around. Five-foot-five, spiky black hair, black t-shirt, long black shorts, worn Converse high tops, arms sleeved with tattoos. Mike Trask turns and grins and sticks out his hand.

"Nice to see ya, Blewit."

"You're looking well, Trash Bag," I respond, warmly shaking his hand. "What's going on?"

"Accident." Mike turns around, and I move next to him. Ben Felder is sitting in a makeup chair with a bloodstained towel wrapped around his right hand. He grimaces toward me in an attempted greeting.

"Ah shit, Ben," I blurt out. "What did you do?"

"It was an accident," repeats Mike. "They was just having a little toast and the glasses blew up when they clinked 'em. Ben's cut up some."

"Finger?"

Ben nods. "Pretty good slash right on the joint of my little finger. I'm afraid it might have got a tendon." He looks pretty scared. I don't blame him.

"Shouldn't you get him to the emergency room, like, stat?" I ask.

"We've got a driver ready for him, but Ben wanted to stay for a minute, in case you had any questions," responds Mike.

"About what?"

"The piano part," Mike says, not without irritation.

The Fear suddenly materializes, fully formed and menacing, from where it had been hiding behind the sweating and the running and the tequila. The obvious reason for my being here in this moment becomes self-evident.

"Oh, no. No, no, no."

"You gotta play, Blewit," Mike says, firmly.

"Why me?"

"You wrote the fucking song," Ben points out, annoyed and in pain, and I can't blame him.

"There have to be a million keyboard players around here. Drop a net! You'll catch one. Get him to do it!"

"We aren't using charts," Ben says.

"You wrote the fucking song!" Trash Bag yells at me, clearly getting pissed that this conversation has become a negotiation. Somewhere deep in my memory I am reminded that one of the reasons that Trash Bag is so good at his job is because he has a temper that goes from zero to sixty in a nanosecond.

"Look, guys, I'd love to help you," I lie. "But I've been drinking," I tell the truth.

"So what?" says a voice from behind me, the voice that made "I Turned Around" an international hit. "Weren't you a big-time rock star, with all that entails?"

I close my eyes. My head starts to hurt. I will myself to disappear, but I'm pretty sure I'm hung out to dry on this one. I turn around and open my eyes, and Wendy Harper looks at me expectantly. I stare at the floor, ashamed. I take off the goddamned Stetson, rolling it in *my hands. My throat goes dead dry. I feel the need to vomit.*

Wendy's look doesn't change. "I need your help," she says, simply.

I look her in the eye, holding her gaze for a beat, then two, and then I am staring at the floor, nodding.

"I've had a couple of vodkas myself, rock star," Wendy says gently, and I look up again to see the soft, friendly, long-lost-family-member eyes that I first met at the Little Nell. "We'll get through this together."

I breathe. Calming.

"Hell, this shit's gonna be fun!" says Trash Bag. "Let's get this cowboy into a rehearsal room. He's playin' tonight!"

PART TWO

CHAPTER 14

CULTURAL WASTELAND
<u>Waiting Here for Hours</u> ***1/2 (*Defiant Groove)*
<u>Their 15 minutes aren't over yet!</u>
OK, so maybe having a sense of humor isn't that bad of a thing. On this follow up to their stupid/silly smash hit "Cry for Me," one-hit-wonder wannabes Cultural Wasteland fire up a summer sing-along (and most likely drink-along) that's funny and catchy and, surprisingly, just downright good.

New Releases, *Blender*, April 1993

AT FIRST YOU'RE JUST "in a band." Then you've "got a following." Then you're "signed." Then you're "in the studio," followed by being "on the road." Then, one night in Pierre, South Dakota, Bobby Craft gives you a nod after you rescue a particularly bad start to the show by slowing things down and then absolutely nailing the trademark staccato triplets on his 1977 hit "Butcher, Baker, Candlestick Maker." Suddenly the whole band gets the groove and plays it exactly how Bobby wants it, according to Hoyle, and the audience goes wild. The promoter gives you your share of the gate, which turns out to be more than enough to get a couple of glasses of decent scotch, a good steak, and a respectable bottle of red wine, considering that you're in South Dakota. Then you're a "professional musician."

Then you're on the bus one morning in early November, and the bus driver pops out one mix cassette for another, and low and behold, there on the radio, somewhere between Flagstaff and Tucson, is "Cry for Me," by Cultural Wasteland. And you jump around and pound each other to pieces, and then Lark takes charge of the radio and starts scanning around, and there it is again! And you beat hell out of each other again.

By the time you get to Phoenix, the label calls and says you've got two more shows with Bobby, and then you're to come back to L.A. to get set up to go out on your own in the winter, first in the U.S. and, if things go well, maybe in Europe. Well, then you're starting to be something else. Then you get a treble clef tattooed on your neck.

The label chose the second single, "Waiting Here for Hours," a mid-tempo rocker that had a lot of the same sense of humor as "Cry for Me" but without the silliness and novelty. We (Lark, really) made another fairly stupid video, though not as bad as the first. Our Defiant Groove artist reps, along with our stylists and new publicists (we were still with C&C, but they had assigned us new people, far higher-ranking than Claudia), took us shopping on Melrose and set up new photo shoots.

We also met with a production designer who showed us a few simple props we could put on stage, including rugs, a big tapestry that hung behind

Huge's drum riser, and a couple of big, hinged, plywood palm trees left over from a late-seventies Pablo
Cruise tour that had nothing to do with Cultural
Wasteland as far as I could see, but I liked them
anyway. Lark said they represented L.A., but I
think we should have used the Hollywood sign instead, if that's what we were trying to say.

Lark insisted that we go back into rehearsal to get
in shape for the tour and to start getting some new
material together for when, we assumed, the label
would exercise its option and send us back into the
studio to record another album. We had spent so
much time on the road worrying about getting Bobby's songs just right that we had begun treating our
opening set as a warm-up jam before the real show
began. Now we were going to be the real show, so
Lark took on Bobby's role and began tearing everything we had down to the foundations and starting
over again.

This became quite a source of irritation to me because, just as they had been with Bobby, most of the
expectations for arrangement changes and nuance
came down on me. It was one thing to put up with
the petulant demands of an old-time rock star with
OCD, but it seemed another to get it from my partner. Deep down we all knew he was right, though,
so we just went ahead and got on with it, but I admit
to being somewhat pissy about it from time to time.

We were now infinitely better musicians than
we had been in the studio. We rebuilt our show so
that the songs would sound enough like the record
or the radio so the audience wouldn't be surprised,
but so that our performances were also denser and
more musically complex, more interesting to expe-

rience live, both for the ear and the eye. Lark and Peter's intertwined guitars became less of a series of tradeoff solos and more the delivery mechanism of a signature sound through chorus and verse alike. My piano grew ever more important in creating the actual bedrock of the melody, the part you could remember and hum, while continuing to contribute to the increasingly complex rhythm tracks that Huge and Chris were laying down.

For this tour, we would have a clean new bus just for us, another for the crew, and a truck for the equipment, which included both a Hammond B3 organ and Yamaha baby grand for me, in addition to the old Fender Rhodes electric and synths that I had taken on the road (and lugged in and out of venues myself) before. This time, there would be no lugging.

The label released "Waiting Here for Hours" on a Tuesday, and we kicked off the tour on Friday with a show at the Greek, an absolutely marvelous L.A. venue. There was an opening band, we had our own dressing rooms, and there was a terrific spread of food along with whatever you wanted to drink and just about anything else you might want, including, oddly enough, fresh underwear, both boxers and briefs. I changed skivvies on general principles.

Once announced, we took the stage in near darkness and kicked into "Baby All the Plants Are Dead" to what seemed to be polite applause and support, only to find, when the lights came up, that it was extremely enthusiastic support from an audience that less than half filled the venue. I had a momentary sense of terror, as if it were all just a twisted mind fuck, but then I caught sight of a pretty young girl down front, singing along at the top of her voice to words I had written, and I began to look around, and everyone was singing. There weren't a lot of them yet, but we were back in L.A., and our following of hundreds from the days in the clubs had swelled appreciably. I think we all sensed this at the same time, because suddenly Huge stomped the kick drum hard, twice, and we all took it up a notch, blazing through an hour-long set, encoring with "Waiting Here for Hours," all of three days old, and they knew all the words to it too and screamed along on the choruses. It was pure joy.

That night we all got hammered. I was so happy, I asked Claudia to marry me. She said yes. We announced it to all gathered, then climbed into the first available car and drove two blocks before we got pulled over and I got taken to jail. When she picked me up in the morning, rather the worse for wear, she offered that I could take back the proposal with no hard feelings. I politely declined, and she agreed to begin making preparations for a summer wedding in the Hamptons after we got off tour. Of course, by the time that happened, I would be a different person. By the time that happened, I would be a Rock Star.

CHAPTER 15

AFTER THE LONG AND terrible year of rehab on
the little finger I had destroyed on Lark's cheekbone on Grammy night 1997, I realized that I had
to start making some money. I had spent my share
of the advance from the third record and had been
informed by the label that I would not be getting a
share of the fourth, which was how I learned that
I was no longer a member of Cultural Wasteland.
Thus, I found myself auditioning before Daryl
Miller for the dubious distinction of becoming one
of the keyboard players backing up The Coreys, the
popular boy band.

Daryl was a well-respected producer, studio musician, and keyboard player in his own right. He had been musical director and the leader of the studio band for a late-night talk show until it was cancelled, and he had played on a hell of a lot more albums than I had. I walked into the audition a bit sulky because, after all, I was a rock star and this was a boy band, but Daryl knocked that shit out of me immediately.

"Look, Blewit, I know you think this is beneath you, and maybe it is, but I've been told that you're a damn good musician, so I'm going to let you try out anyway."

"Only my friends call me that."

"I'm trying to be your friend."

"Then call me Zack, and I'll let you know when your trying has succeeded."

Daryl allowed that that was fair enough. He explained that The Coreys had seen each of their first three albums go multi-platinum around the globe in less than two years, and that their most recent one was going to go Diamond in the U.S. (ten million records sold!) when their fourth record was released in a few months. It was also expected to go Diamond. This shut my trap. It doesn't really matter how much ego you have about your music, musicality, and musicianship—if you're in the music business, you can't help but be impressed by the sheer massiveness of those numbers.

Daryl further explained that The Coreys were going out for the better part of a year on a 147-date tour playing stadiums and arenas in more than a hundred cities all over the world, and that they were building one of the largest stage shows in history to do it. Management wanted to address criticism of The Coreys' prepackaged sound and rumors of lip-synching by putting together a first-rate band that would play live with them. That band was to help make it obvious that everything happening musically was happening live (which it was, I can honestly attest). One of the ways to help achieve this, interestingly enough, was to showcase a grand piano and analog organ in the band.

Because the show was so incredibly choreographed, each performance had to be almost exactly identical. The show would be successful because the special effects would be over the top, the dancing would be unparalleled, and the music would be loud, complex, and perfect. I pointed out this would mean that The Coreys would have to be perfect too, and Daryl told me they would be; that's why they had sold some thirty million records already. Daryl's job, as musical director for the tour, was to find the eight very best players he could to make the band as perfect as the boys.

To that end, Daryl had fired the original four members of the backing band from the previous tour and started fresh. He had since hired back two of them, drummer Sonny Kaye and guitar player Jorge Barr, and he had also hired a new bass player, a cat named Alexi Manray, who had three solo albums out on a well-respected jazz label. That, once and for all, put aside any ego trip I might have been on; this guy was a better musician than all of Cultural Wasteland put together, and we were pretty good!

Daryl was looking for another guitar player, a reed player, a percussion player, and the poor fool who would try to introduce piano and B3 into arrangements that had never heard of such a thing.

Daryl worked with me alone for about half an hour, and then brought in Sonny, Jorge, and Alexi, and we played through charts for about another half-hour. Daryl called for a break and told the other guys to go grab a smoke, and I knew I didn't have the job.

"You're really good, Zack, just like they told me. I've got some other people I have to hear, but you did a great job, and I'll get back to you."

"You can start calling me Blewit, now, if you want," I responded. That elicited a grin. "Look, how long before you have to make final decisions?"

Daryl looked at me with interest. "About a week, maybe ten days."

"Would you please do me a favor, Daryl? I know you don't owe me, but, believe it or not, I do want this gig. You're right, you guys are cats, and I want to play with you, even if it's in a circus. I'm out of shape. I'm still working on rehabbing my finger, and I didn't take this audition seriously enough. I can be a lot better than I was today. I know I can be the guy. If I go home and work on this, can I come back in a week or so and try again?"

Daryl eyed me again. "Sure. Same time, same place, one week from today."

"Same charts?"

Daryl looked thoughtful. "Now that you mention it, no. Have those ready, and these too." He turned and pulled out a large black leather folio, flicked through the contents, and then faloomped the entire thing down on the top of the piano in front of me. Me and my big mouth.

"See you next week, Daryl."

"See ya, Blewit."

CHAPTER 16

THE TUXEDO JACKET IS off and the air conditioning is on. My hat sits upside down on a chair in the corner. Ben is teaching me how to play my song. I have to give him credit; it is a pretty little line that he has developed to counter the melody when it moves to the guitars, or in the case of this evening, to the strings that will be providing additional support. It has a Rachmaninoff feeling.

I, for one, have always been a believer in using an orchestra when one is available. I realize that Ben has told me a small fib when he said there are no charts. Indeed there are—lots of them, for a whole orchestra—just not written parts for the band members on stage, all of whom have been to this rodeo before. I squint at the small notation for the piano part on the master chart. How do conductors read this stuff? I play a few measures here and there as Ben holds his bandaged hand against an ice pack and allows the pretty PA to pour Wild Turkey into his mouth from time to time.

"Exactly. That's it. You've got it. I knew you'd pick it right up," he says, slurring just a little.

"It's a nice arrangement, Ben. Did you do it?"

"It was a collaboration, but yeah, it's mostly mine."

"Good work. Now it's time for you to go get that finger looked at. You've done all you can here."

Ben hesitates just a moment. "You know, Zack, that whole Cultural Wasteland thing, I never wanted it to work out that way, you know. Sometimes things happen, you know?"

I smile at him. "I know, Ben. There are no hard feelings between you and me and there never were. I got what I deserved. And besides, there is no Cultural Wasteland anymore anyway, for you or me. Now get out of here."

Ben smiles, nods at the PA for another shot, and then allows her to help him up and lead him toward the car waiting to take him to Emergency. As he exits, the professional musician in him leaves the room, and the rock star returns.

"Trash Bag! I'll be taking this here pretty girl with me to the ER. Need help filling out the forms and such. She's through for the night anyway. Right?"

Trash Bag doesn't bother to look up—just waves them off and returns to his clipboard. "Get me another runner!" he shouts as they leave the Staples Center.

I turn back to the keys and begin searching the score. I noodle here and noodle there. I begin to play the part from beginning to end. It's a little tricky; Ben has absolutely massive hands, much bigger than mine. I have to rework some of the fingerings. The hard part is trying to relearn a song I've played thousands of times, hundreds of different ways, often on guitar and rarely involving more than one instrument.

I have also never played it drunk. A pint of tequila is still swimming around inside of me, and medical science *says that the last of it won't be gone until after the show is long over. I'm out of drinking shape. I'm nervous. What if I make a complete fool of myself? Worse yet, what if I make Wendy look bad?*

I'm also troubled. Something has always bothered me about this arrangement. It's the same arrangement from the HBO special and the big Hollywood movie, and it is, well, huge. It's magnificent and people love it. I love how much money it has made, but it really isn't to my taste, at least toward the end. I practice that part carefully. It is utterly foreign to me.

I can do this. I can hear the strings in my head sawing along and the big blocky chords as the melody soars for the last time. I can do this. I can do this.

I can't do this. I slam my fists down on the keys. Shit.

"What's the matter, hon?" The woman is like a cat.

I turn on the bench. "Not a thing, Wendy. Not a thing. Just a long time since I've been a gun for hire, and I'm not as good at sight-reading as I used to be. I'll get it though. Don't you worry."

"Bullshit, hon. I've been watching you for five minutes. You can play it. You just don't want to. What's the matter?"

"Really, Wendy, it's nothing. I just need to practice a little." I turn back.

I feel a hand on my shoulder. I stare at the page and rest my hands on the keys.

"I want you to think about what I'm going to say right now, Zack. I want you to listen. I'm nominated for Album of the Year tonight, mostly on the strength of your song. Your song is also nominated for Song of the Year, and I'm here tonight to sing it for both of us. Do you know what I'm not nominated for, besides Best New Artist anyway?"

I can't help but grin at that.

"I'm not nominated for Record of the Year. What would you have done differently?"

"Backstage at the Grammys is really no time to go into that. I'm happy as a clam. I just wish Ben were OK, but he's not, so I'm going to do my best."

"That's not good enough, Zack. I'm a big girl and a professional, and I'm asking you a question. If I don't like your answer, I'll ignore it, but if you don't tell me what you're thinking right now, I'm going to go all kinds of diva on your ass."

I can't handle that.

"I don't like the swell in the final verse."

"OK. Why not?"

"Because that's when you find out that it's just too late. It doesn't matter that he's learned his lesson, or that she's learned her lesson in your case. He's not just gone this time. He's dead, and it's just too damn late. I think the swell there is too operatic, too dramatic. It's supposed to be devastating, and my experience of devastation has always been a quiet one."

Wendy blinks repeatedly. "What should we do?"

"Nothing," *I think to myself. Stop this nonsense. There's an eighty-piece orchestra out there, a stage set, and lighting cues. Half the civilized world knows and loves this song—Wendy Harper's version of this song. It made her a crossover sensation. Do not fuck with her international hit on Grammy night!*

"It's easy," *I hear the tequila saying, or maybe it's me.* "You just have the orchestra rest from bars 144 through 168, then just the cellos come back in pianissimo at 168. I would leave the rest out altogether."

"What'll I do?"

"Just sing the last verse, maybe a little slower, may-

be a little looser, I'll put some feeling into the part and you follow me—it'll be OK if you're a little unsure. Just think of how you'd feel if somebody important to you just died, and sing."

Wendy smiles and looks away, maybe welling up. "That's why I fell for the song in the first place. I hadn't thought of that in awhile."

I am uncomfortable. I didn't mean to make her cry. What the hell is wrong with me? "Well anyway, you asked, and I answered, and maybe someday you can try it that way, but not tonight. Let me get back to work!" I spin back to the keyboard.

Her hand comes back down on my shoulder, but now it is not soft and kind and caressing. Now it clutches me insistently, powerfully. "Oh no you don't."

"Look, Wendy, there's lights and orchestrations and live TV and . . ."

Wendy cuts me off with a vicious glance. "Do you know what it's like to feel like a fraud, Zack?" Her eyes bore deeply into mine, and I realize that we are playing for keeps here. This is not about getting up on stage and knocking out your big hit before heading off to the af-ter-party, maybe with some hardware and maybe not, depending on the politics.

"Intimately."

"I don't want to feel that way anymore." She piv-ots and spreads her arms, encompassing the whole of the Grammy Awards and the Staples Center. "This used to be about recognizing and being recognized by your peers. It used to be about doing something special for them, and the folks at home who used to buy records and consider themselves our fans."

I nod, even though I had never known such a time. But I had known of it.

"Now it's about money and the labels and the politics of the industry and whatever else. And that's OK. That's the way it goes. Whatever. I can't guarantee that either one of us will take home a statue tonight, but we're going to play together out there. You and me. We're going to play your song. Our song. And we're going to give the best performance of the night. Not to show them or to prove a damn thing. We're going to do it because this is what we do. Do you get it?"

I swallow. I want to cry. I nod.

"OK, then. You get the changes to the orchestra; it sounds like they're pretty easy. Now what about lighting, and what should I do about my wardrobe?"

"Trash Bag!" I shout. He turns to look at me. "You can kill me dead later, but right now I have to give you a couple of minor changes for the orchestra and lighting on 'I Turned Around.'"

"No way, Blewit. Wendy's on in just about an hour. No changes."

"Make the changes, or I don't go on at all, Mike." And here she is. The diva. She is now six-foot-seven and carrying a Thompson gun. Trash Bag, being the professional that he is, recognizes a battle lost, grits his teeth, and walks into the rehearsal room.

"Anything you say, Ms. Harper," he smiles thinly. "Blewit, if there are no other last minute problems, I expect to be overseeing your death in the parking lot at nine-fifteen p.m. The orchestra and lighting crew will all be armed and in attendance."

"No problem. I've had it coming for years. But honestly, Mike. It's not that bad. Here's all I need you to do."

CHAPTER 17

Backstage Battle!
Several sources have indicated that there was quite a fracas backstage at the Grammys last week involving Cultural Wasteland front man Lark Dray and keyboard player Zack Fluett. No official word has come from the 'Waste camp, but our sources indicate that there was a lot of blood. And they said rock & roll was dead!

Entertainment Weekly, February 16, 1997

THE GOOD THING ABOUT breaking Lark's nose was that I really enjoyed it for about a second, and it changed his perfect looks for a lifetime. Unfortunately, most people would say that his perfect looks got even better.

The bad part of breaking Lark's nose was the "boxer's fracture" I simultaneously suffered. As described to me by a series of physicians, the knuckles of my index and middle fingers, supported by the highly stable radial tendons and larger second and third metacarpal bones, made short work of Lark's nasal cartilage. Unfortunately, the greater mobility of the ulnar side of the hand, which allows for all those fast trills in the treble clef, in addition to the smaller size of the fourth and fifth metacarpal bones, makes them less stable and more susceptible to fracture when coming into forceful contact with something solid, such as Lark Dray's left cheekbone. This is why the neck of the bone behind the first knuckle of my little finger on my right hand snapped like a twig when I punched the arrogant, lying prick. So when the doctors called it a "boxer's fracture," I got the gist of it even if I didn't fully understand the more detailed explanation.

Notwithstanding this diagnosis, I believe that I did not, in fact, have a "boxer's fracture." When a boxer snaps the neck of his fifth metacarpal, he winces in agony, they stop the fight, his ring manager cuts his glove off, and they take him to a hospital.

What I actually suffered (this is an after-the-fact self-diagnosis, of course) was a "dipshit fracture." This occurs, medically speaking, when the dipshit (that'd be me), gets all kinds of fucked up, gets pissed off at the lead singer in the band that he loves and is supposed to make him a fortune, sucker-punches said lead singer, breaks a finger vital to the dipshit's career, and then continues his bender for a couple of days before seeking medical attention because he's too drunk/stoned/wired/opiated to do much of anything but drink, pop pills, and attempt to convince his "girlfriend" to service him, all while keeping his hand in a bucket of ice. The bucket of ice probably helped a little, but not nearly as much as immediate medical attention would have.

After Phoebe, the "girlfriend," had decided she had had enough of this nonsense and left, the bender slowed down, primarily because there was no one around to bring me booze and drugs. At that point in time I got to looking at my hand, bluish from all the ice, and realized that I was in pretty bad shape. As I came out my self-induced anesthesia, I realized that the finger was really throbbing like hell.

As the doctors later described it, once again employing all that obscure language: the natural tension of the ulnar flexor tendons had caused the metacarpal to dorsally angulate at the fracture site, bowstringing the broken bone like another knuckle. In layman's terms, it looked like I had a fourth knuckle on my little finger halfway to the wrist. My whole right hand hung limp and lifeless. I decided it was time for a cab ride to the emergency room.

After sitting in the emergency room in Venice Beach for an hour, I decided it was time for a cab ride to the emergency room in Santa Monica. There a young French-Canadian admitting nurse named Nurse Gorné recognized me. My day at last began to improve, or so I thought. She sat with me and filled out the forms for me, because of my hand, then informed everyone that there was a very famous keyboard player in the house who needed attention for a bad hand injury. There had been several gossip column stories about the fight at the Grammys, and I confirmed them and was happy to hear that the story on Lark was that his nose was busted.

In fairly short order I was taken in for X-rays and then the emergency room doctor came in to get to work on me. He introduced himself as Dr. Sehdev, and he appeared to be a fourteen-year-old Indian (dot, not feather), but when he spoke he seemed authoritative and knowledgeable, explaining the injury to me as appearing to be a "transverse fracture of the fifth metacarpal with communition showing at least three separate pieces of bone." He commented that even with the icing I had done, the passage of time and inflammation was going to make reducing the fracture somewhat more difficult and potentially painful.

I suggested drugs. I was pleased when he agreed, but they turned out not to be the fun kind. I have always avoided needles. Never done heroin. He pulled out needles, big ones, and loaded them up with a nasty concoction known as Lidocaine. The first one went into my wrist. He called this an ulnar nerve block. It felt as if my entire hand were suddenly on fire and that the contents of my veins had boiled into the Alien creature's acid blood. The ulnar nerve block was to help prepare me for the next injection, which was the fracture block. If it did, I cannot imagine how painful the procedure would have been without it.

The fracture block consisted of inserting a fairly large needle into the middle of the break itself—right into the site of the injury! Proper procedure required that the physician actually bounce the needle off the various pieces of bone in an attempt to deaden the highly agitated nerves there to allow the subsequent setting of the fracture. Proper procedure should also have included restraining the patient, because when the needle struck broken bone, I screamed and took a swipe at poor Dr. Sehdev. Fortunately, I missed. Nurse Gorné held my left hand thereafter (it may have actually been more of a hammer lock), and the doctor continued his ministrations with less finesse than at the outset.

After the fire in my hand began to die down and my fingertips went numb, Dr. Sehdev (whom I was now mentally referring to as Dr. Sedative with something of a wry gallows humor, or so I thought) proceeded to reduce the fracture, which is the medical term for setting the bones back together as best as possible so they can knit. This is accomplished by a medieval torture practice known as "Jaeger's Maneuver." In my prior (and quite extensive) experience, a Jäger Maneuver involved projectile vomiting. When it comes to a dipshit fracture, the maneuver requires that the doctor pull apart the new, unwanted knuckle at the fracture site and push down hard with his thumb behind the fracture while yanking outward on the knuckle, essentially grinding the bone fragments back into place.

This is stunningly painful, not to mention an auditory nightmare. You can actually hear your bones grinding against one another. The pain made me cry, but the sound made me faint.

I awoke to blurred visions of fireflies and an auditory sensation equal to about a dozen hits of nitrous oxide. It took me a moment to realize that I was lying on an examination table. The poster of the inner ear hanging on the far wall swam into view and then into focus. Nurse Gorné cradled my head in her arms and lovely bosom, and she was still holding my left hand, just not in a hammerlock. She became quite beautiful to me in that moment. I felt no pain and in fact felt a mild and pleasant buzz. I noticed Dr. Sedative strapping a contraption known as an "ulnar gutter splint" onto my right forearm and hand to stabilize the newly set fracture.

"What happened?" I murmured.

"You fainted," said the doctor, matter of factly.

"Oh, I'm sorry."

"Don't be ridiculous. I'd say it happens two out of three times."

That was a nice thing to say, so I thought I ought to show my appreciation for his professionalism. "Sorry about taking a swipe at you there. It was a knee-jerk reaction."

"That happens about one out of three times. You learn to dodge."

What a fucked-up career choice, it occurred to me.

"I'm writing you a prescription for Vicodin to help with the pain for the next few days. Have you ever had Vicodin before?"

What a fantastic career choice, it occurred to me. "Pretty much every day for the past five years or so."

Dr. Sedative frowned at me.

"All right, then I'll give you Percocet, but don't drink with it or you'll regret it, rock star," he responded, crumpling up one prescription and writing a fresh one, which he handed to me.

"Make an appointment to come back in three days for X-rays so we can see how things are coming along. And don't punch anyone else." With that he left.

Walking out of the examination room on Nurse Gorné's arm I stopped and said, "Wait a minute, I think I left my ring back there." I hustled back, pulled the Vicodin prescription out of the trash, stuffed it in a pocket, and rejoined her in the hall.

"Stupid of me. I took it off the other night when I started icing my hand."

She smiled and walked me to the front desk where

she set up a future appointment for me, called me a cab, got my address and phone number, and agreed to drop by after work to check on my progress.

The next three days were really not that bad. I watched a lot of TV on a cocktail of Percocet, Vicodin, and Absolut that kept me fairly pleasantly zoned out. Nurse Gorné dropped by every now and then to check on me. She always felt that I wasn't taking good enough care of myself, so she would give me a sponge bath, a hand job, and cook something for me to eat. I nicknamed her Nurse Porné, or just Porny for short, and promised her that once I was up and around again, I would repay her kindnesses.

Based on Dr. Sedative's initial comments, I expected it to be no more than a week before she could at least be on top and two before I would be able to support some of my own weight with my right hand, so I could be on top. I realized that I had dodged a bullet and things really could have been much worse. In my more lucid moments, I realized what an incredibly stupid thing I had done and promised not to take my good fortune for granted when I got healthy and back in the band again. I'd also have to apologize to Lark when he got back from Europe, because, even though he was a jerk, it was still a very stupid thing I had done given the history we shared.

Unfortunately, upon my next visit to Dr. Sedative, I was informed that I had not dodged the bullet. New X-rays revealed that the fracture was not setting properly and the bone fragments were not knitting back together. He referred me to Dr. Price, a Beverly Hills reconstructive plastic and hand surgeon who worked with a broad array of celebrities, professional athletes, musicians, and suburban

weekend chainsaw users. Upon entering his sumptuous offices and seeing pictures of some of the stars
he had helped mend, I named him Dr. Pricey. He
reversed the original diagnosis of a transverse fracture and instead opined that what I had was a spiral
fracture, the nature of which prevented the bones
from knitting together on their own because they
simply would not stay in place. The solution was to
knit them together using the medical equivalent of
baling wire and chewing gum.

The procedure, performed by Dr. Pricey more
or less on the spot, involved more incredibly painful anesthesia, followed by the use of an evil device
known as a Stryker Drill. The Stryker Drill is a fancy brushed-steel screwdriver attached to a pistol grip
with Kirshner wire loaded through the back of it and
powered by compressed air, like a badass handheld
Black & Decker. Dr. Pricey drilled right through
the skin of my knuckle, past the ligaments and tendons, through bone and directly into the marrow
canal of my fifth metacarpal, sewing together three
steel pins he had stuck straight through my whole
hand around the site of the break. The pins and wire
held the bone fragments in place to allow them to
begin the process of knitting back together.

Why standard procedure allows that I should be
made to stay awake and without a blindfold during
such a procedure is completely beyond me. Perhaps
it's staying up on those twenty-four-hour residency
shifts that prompts doctors to take revenge on certain types of patients, such as rock stars with dipshit
fractures. I watched in complete horror as Pricey
rammed cauter pins through my hand and drilled
wire straight into my bone. In an attempt to distract

myself, I commented that the Kirshner wire looked like treble clef piano strings.

"That's because that's what it is," Pricey informed me, tying the wire onto a pin and snipping it close.

Ah ha. After all those years pounding on those keys, causing those hammers to wallop those strings, the strings finally got to have their day with me.

I was instructed to return in three weeks to have the pins and wire removed. Pricey gave me another prescription for Percocet, warning me once again not to drink with it. Of course I wouldn't, I replied, thinking to myself that someone in his position really should understand rock stars better. I returned home for a sponge bath, hand job, and lasagna in considerable pain, but confident that I had made it through the worst. Of course I was wrong.

On the fourth day after my visit with Dr. Pricey, Porny didn't show up. The night before, she had changed the dressing on my hand for me, which was bloody and crusty and, frankly, disgusting around the pin sites. I had promised Dr. Pricey that I would arrange to have this done every few days, but I had been something of a baby about it, I must admit.

Porny reminded me that she was doing this as favor to me. She got paid to change peoples' dressings most days, and she didn't generally have to give hand jobs to patients who wouldn't shower. Through a Percocet, Vicodin, and Crown Royal-induced haze, complicated by a high dosage of fear, disgust, and self-loathing for what had become of my hand, I informed her that there were thousands of women out there who would gladly lick my bloody hand clean for the opportunity to wrap their hands around my rock-star cock. I can see the excessiveness of this statement now and regret having made it.

As a professional, I suspect Porny saw the path I was going to go down and managed to get out of Dodge just in time. I can't say as I blame her, except for one thing: in her rush to get out of the house after my "licking" tirade, she left the medicine bottles capped. When I awoke to my throbbing right hand (not to mention unwashed body and penis) the next morning, I uttered the phrase I had been repeating to Porny that had at first made her laugh, then chuckle, then smile politely: "Well, better get goin', that bottle of pills ain't gonna swallow itself!" In fact it had. They all had. Childproof caps are also dipshit-proof.

Doing anything with my right hand—hell, my whole right arm—besides letting it rest gently on a pillow on the arm of my Barcalounger, was extremely painful, especially when the blood level in my Percocet stream got too high. Opening a childproof cap one-handed is tricky indeed, and most movements caused my hand to throb. I decided that starting with a general anesthetic was a good idea, to take down the overall pain to a level where I could then try to work with one hand, so I hit the Absolut. That did help the overall pain level, but, due to the phenomenon known as the "shampoo buzz," it also quite drastically and quickly reduced my overall motor skills, such that attempts to place the bottle between my knees failed utterly. A subsequent attempt placing the bottle between my feet ended in a fall that caused me to bang my bad hand, which was absolutely excruciating. This caused my frustration level to rise, prompting me to kick the refrigerator and jam my big toe.

Eventually I won the battle with the bottles by employing a hammer. This caused the pills to scatter wildly across the kitchen, but at least I could take a few with vodka to get my pain down to a reasonable level and even allow for a nice nap on the cool floor. I awoke several hours later in a small puddle of up-chuck lying, fortunately, on my left arm and hand, which had gone to sleep. I was, for a few minutes at least, essentially paralyzed from the waist up, which was something of a strange state of affairs.

Feeling eventually returned to my arm, and I was able to push myself onto my knees in the fading day-light. I then crawled around the floor on my hand and knees, collecting the various pills from where they had landed and brushing them into a fairly neat pile. Scooping them into a piece of old newspaper, I put them up on the kitchen counter. I threw a dish-towel over the puddle of puke, took a couple more pills, and retired to my chair in front of the TV with the half full bottle of Absolut. All in all, a fairly successful day.

I continued on in this manner for several more days. There were a couple of highlights, such as the time I finally felt well enough to clean up the mess in the kitchen. I picked up the dishtowel, prepared to clean up the puke, and about forty cockroaches scur-ried away from the site of their feast. I screamed like Fay Wray and stomped around in disgust. Later, af-ter I had finally cleaned the mess up and could think about it, I allowed as how tough a bug the cockroach really is to dine out on vodka and Percocet. It should have killed me, and I'm a lot bigger.

The other highlight was the visit I was paid, at my request, by Eddie, my coke dealer. He didn't normally make house calls, but I told him about my hand, some of which he had already read about in the gossip rags, and he took pity on me. I had noticed on about day seven or eight that the lasagna Porny had made me the evening after Dr. Pricey put the piano wire into my hand had not left my body, nor had the other meals she fed me before bailing out, nor had the package of Italian dry salami nor the jar of pickles I had been eating from time to time between soap operas and naps. My belly was distended, and despite repeated, focused attempts, I found myself utterly constipated.

I generally did not have a problem with regularity. Part of this stemmed from a diet that consisted of three parts liquor to one part food and part of it to the fact that I considered beer to be food. Another reason, of course, was the consumption of cocaine, which I had simply forgotten in the narcotic meadows of Percocet-land. I figured that a couple of beefy lines would straighten out the plumbing, as the first thing I always did after getting into the blow was to take a shit, which is why I was not allowed to do coke on the Cultural Wasteland tour bus. So I called up Eddie.

When Eddie arrived, he looked genuinely concerned. I have never known a coke dealer to look genuinely concerned about anything other than a strange face at a big buy or a request for credit.

"Dude, you look like shit."

"It's probably because I can't shit. That's why you're here."

"Dude, your eyes are, like, fucking yellow."

"That shouldn't be. I've been pissing just fine," I sassed back with a laugh. "Come on in and let's do some lines."

Eddie gingerly entered the house and followed me to the living room, where I pushed a pile of beer cans off the glass coffee table and onto a pile of Absolut and Crown bottles on the floor.

"Line 'em up, my man!" I stated grandly, sitting down on a couch.

Eddie looked around uncomfortably, and then took a seat across the coffee table. "Dude, this place smells like death."

"Sorry, I haven't had the cleaning lady in recently, but I will remedy that, indeed I will. Now, how about a little cocaine, hmmm?"

"No dude, this place doesn't just smell bad, it smells like fucking death. What is that smell?"

I leaned toward him, elbows on the coffee table. "I'm sorry for the state of my housekeeping, but I'm sure if you ram some cocaine up your fucking nose you won't smell anything at all."

Eddie reared back. "Dude, it's your hand!" He leaned in to study it more closely, and I took notice of it for the first time in some time. I had gotten myself on a pretty good constant buzz and, since I wasn't able to use it at all, had come to treat it like something I had to carry around but that was otherwise of no great importance. Indeed, the dressing was dirty and tattered, there was a fair amount of blood, pus, and crusting around the pin sites, and when I bothered to put my nose up to it and take a good sniff, I did have to admit it smelled like the Civil War.

"Oh, that's not too fresh, is it? Sorry about that."

"Dude. How long have you been cooped up in here?"

"Don't know exactly. I'm supposed to go back on the fifteenth to have the piano taken out. What day is it today?"

"Aren't you supposed to go in to have the bandages changed or something, dude?"

I thought about this for a while. This had indeed been discussed with Dr. Pricey, but there was a reason it was unnecessary. Now what was that again? Ah, yes.

"I told him I had a nurse."

"Do you have a nurse, dude?"

"I did. She gave me hand jobs and lasagna but now I can't shit."

"Where is your nurse, dude?"

"Went away," I sighed. "I fear I was cruel to her."

"All right, dude. Let's get you to the hospital."

Although I was now beginning to have a vague sense of unease about that thing on the end of my right arm, and although I was appreciative of Eddie's willingness to be of assistance to me in what I was coming to realize was a time of need, I remained steadfastly unwilling to move until I had done at least a couple of nice big rails. Eddie relented and allowed as how it did seem to help with the smell somewhat. Nonetheless, we drove to the hospital with the windows down.

We didn't go to see Dr. Sedative nor did we go to see Dr. Pricey. Hospitals, the real kind with people in white coats and ambulances and frequently police officers, made Eddie uncomfortable. Instead, we went to a little place on the edge of the walk streets behind Abbott-Kinney in Venice. There I met Dr. Thompson, whom I deemed required no nickname, being that he was essentially a gonzo doctor and, therefore, already had the right name. Dr. Thompson was an honest to goodness doctor, but he had been defrocked due to repeated problems with the very medicines he had previously been allowed to prescribe and now just bought from drugstore cowboys. He ran a little operation near the Venice projects specializing in gunshots, stab wounds, and blunt instrument trauma for those who shared Eddie's opinions of real hospitals.

Dr. Thompson cleaned and redressed my hand, commenting on Dr. Pricey's wire and pinwork with approval. He also informed me that Percocet caused constipation. Even with the snootful of blow, I still hadn't felt any rumblings below. He suggested that the only way to empty myself out was just to get off the stuff for a few days. He supported his recommendation by pointing out that the high Tylenol content in Percocet, combined with the booze that I had been ingesting, was undoubtedly raising hell with my liver, as indicated by my jaundiced eyes.

I responded that, as much as I wanted to shit and keep my liver, the Percocet was keeping me out of almost constant pain. He suggested that, at least until my next visit with Dr. Pricey to discuss other options, I get off the pills and go with a regimen of smoking a ton of marijuana and fighting off withdrawal by zoning out on a light dose of Methadone. I allowed as how that sounded like a pretty good idea, and he gave me all the necessities for pursuing this program, in exchange for which I gave him money, which seemed like a good deal.

Eddie took me back home, taking the time to get me situated with my new drugs, as well as opening up some windows to air the place out and taking a few piles of trash to the street. I was quite appreciative of all this and bought twice as much cocaine from him as I had originally ordered, to compensate him for his efforts.

As he took his leave, Eddie said, "Dude, good luck with the hand. I always liked your band. Take it easy, all right? And call up some friends to come over and keep an eye on you, dude. I think you need it."

I thanked him for stopping by and then did a couple of lines and smoked some chronic and sat there thinking and waiting to shit. And then I realized that I really didn't have any friends to call.

CHAPTER 18

I STAND UP FROM the rehearsal room piano and stretch. I'm a little stiff. I clasp my hands together, and then push them out in front of me, palms away. I can see the old scars on my right hand and little finger, and I think of Ben's cut. A chill runs through me; I've been where he is. I don't think his injury looked as bad as mine, but it's a bummer nonetheless. It's weird to be welcomed back-stage at the Grammys due to a finger injury rather than leaving with one. Karma certainly has the prerogative to change her mind.

I center my feet beneath me and clasp my hands again, this time palms together with index fingers pointed to the sky. It's time for a little bit of the old Fluett sun saluta-tion, my own form of Yoga picked up from Phoebe before she fled. I lift my arms high above my head, rolling my shoulders back and toward one another and leaning my head back as far as I can, getting a nice reverse stretch in my back. I get an upside-down glimpse of the funny lesbian on the silent monitor across the room. I let my arms fall to my sides, opening my heart chakra (at least

I think that's what I'm supposed to be doing), and then bend over at the waist, letting gravity create traction on my spine, fingers almost touching the floor. I have to get rid of this belly.

From force of habit, I step back into lunge position, then put my other foot back and go into a downward facing dog. Note to self: down dog is tough in cowboy boots. I fall over. The tequila is still making its presence known. Think I'll just sit down here on the linoleum floor of the Staples Center for a second. Take a nice deep breath. There. Feeling a little better.

I stand up and walk over to the flat-screen monitor bracketed to the beige cinderblock wall and turn up the volume. The funny lesbian has just introduced something. The stage lights brighten into a red, white, and blue wash, and silhouettes of palm trees, two with a hammock strung between them, appear in the background. What can this be? A familiar ditty, played by an orchestra, wafts out of the monitor, kind of a mush of strings with the melody carried by too many tubas.

The spotlight hits two youngsters I recognize from football commercials for that show where they take ordinary losers and change them into world famous losers by giving them a chance to become pop stars. American Idol. *I hate that show. No one gave me a chance like that, or Wendy Harper, or Bobby Craft. What bullshit. The losers are wearing sailor suits. Suddenly I recognize the tune. This must be my Song of the Year competition from Messrs. Menken and Rice, by way of that old codger Sherwood Schwartz, who created* The Brady Bunch *and a bunch of other shows I watched as a kid, including this one about a group of castaways. I just can't believe that Disney saw fit to make a film version of* Gilligan's Island.

I have to admit that the Idols aren't that bad vocally, but there's really not that much for them to sink their teeth into. As Claudia says, "bad input, bad output." Suddenly, a gospel choir surges onto the screen, clapping their hands and providing heaven-sent vocal backing to this sorry mess. Oh come on! This is ridiculous.

Every year the Grammy show blows off ninety percent of the categories and most of the genres completely, but the gospel groups are always all over the tube (even though their awards are rarely if ever presented on the telecast). This is because you can generally save any subpar performance by giving it gospel backing. It's downright un-Christian and un-American not to like a nice gospel choir, regardless of whether it makes a complete hash of the material. I sadly have to admit that, in this case, it's helping. I wonder if it's too late to get the choir to come help out on "I Turned Around?"

"Mr. Fluett?"

I turn around. A huge pile of shopping bags, supported by a pair of pink rhinestone encrusted jeans and silver slippers, stands in the doorway. I've seen this look before, and it doesn't bode well.

"May I come in?" *ask the bags in a voice straight out of* The Bird's Nest.

"Certainly," *I respond.* "Can I give you a hand with that stuff?"

"Oh no, no problem! Where do you want me to put them?"

"Uh, anywhere I guess." *What's going on here?*

The bags walk over to a long folding table near the monitor and deposit themselves gently. Up pops a friendly face wearing glitter eye makeup and a garishly striped dress shirt with French cuffs. He sashays over to me and extends a limp hand. I take it and bow reflex-

ively, which elicits a girly giggle.

"*I'm Alain,*" *he announces.*

"*Zack Fluett.*"

"*And don't I know it!*" *His laugh peels off the concrete walls.*

"*Uh, what is all that stuff?*" *I ask. It looks like Melanie, the original GDT, went shopping again. This is never good for the pocketbook.*

"*That's your Grammy gift bag! You're just going to love love love love love it!*"

Ah. The Grammy gift bag. For performers. Like me.

Alain leans toward me, confidentially. "They say that it's worth more than thirty-five thousand, but I don't believe it. It's nice, but it's not as nice as last year's, and they said that one was worth thirty. Some of the really good stuff isn't in it this time. It's the economy," he concludes, nodding knowledgably.

Ah. The Grammy gift bag. Thirty-five thousand dollars worth of taxable income in the form of a bunch of crap I am unlikely ever to use.

"*Come on; I'll show you,*" *Alain chirps, clapping his hands like a child at Christmas.*

We return to the huge pile on the table. Alain reaches straight in a pulls out a miniature plastic Les Paul with buttons where the frets should be and no strings.

"*Guitar Hero III!*" *he squeals. Hmmm. I've heard that's fun.*

Alain keeps pulling items out of the bags like a magician. It is unbelievable that all this stuff now flooding outward across the folding table once fit into those bags. I hope I'm not responsible for putting it all back.

"*And a set of Sonoma X high fidelity ear phones, and an iPhone, and a Nespresso Coffee maker, and so many products! Look! It's hair care from Hair Dr. Spela, and*

Kinerase facial products, and SkinMedica toner! Sunglasses from Solstice Boutique, nice, and, ooh, Esperanto!" He holds up a fancy bottle of what looks like about a fifth of Mexican perfume. I shake my head to indicate my lack of interest.

Alain will not be deterred. He pulls out an oversized camouflaged duffel. *"This whole bag is from Mossy Oak Apparel. Perfect for an outdoorsy guy like you,"* he winks and raises his eyebrows at me.

"Let me see that," I say, with interest. He hands it over and I open it and begin pulling out the contents. It is filled with T-shirts, vests, long-sleeved shirts, sweatshirts, hats, and caps, all designed for the outdoor enthusiast. It says so right on the tag.

"Pretty swanky, eh?" Alain coos. *"Just going through the bag will take you all night."*

It occurs to me that I don't have all night.

"I have to get back to work, Alain, but thanks for bringing this by, it's all very nice."

"Delighted. Oh, and don't let me forget, here's your Performer credential, just in case someone doesn't recognize you."

I doubt that anybody is going to recognize me back here. Probably a good thing to have. I take the laminate with the Grammy logo and the words, *ALL ACCESS – PERFORMER* emblazoned on it and hang it around my neck by its lanyard.

"Thank you, Alain."

"No problem at all, and if you need anything else, just ask."

"Now that you mention it, I could probably use a cup of coffee." I'm not sure if it's the overwhelming pile of merchandise in front of me or the tequila working its way through my system, but I'm feeling a little lightheaded.

"No problem. Back in a jiff." He skips out.

I review the contents of the table as the Gilligan *number concludes on the monitor. They cut to commercial, and I turn down the sound. There is a Heineken/ Krups beer tender. Davy would have loved that. There's a sack full of DKNY men's underwear and t-shirts that are very soft and nice. Here's a gold bracelet that might make a nice gift for Claudia, and a cool pair of jeans that look like they might have fit me a dozen years ago, when I was a Rock Star. But not anymore.*

Holding the jeans and thinking of Claudia, I am reminded of the spoiled-brat keyboard player who was backstage at the Grammys the last time I was here. I wouldn't have thought twice about this stuff then. Probably would have lost it in a drunken haze, and certainly wouldn't have cared much. Back then, of course, the gift bags were nowhere near this nice, and also back then, we didn't declare this kind of thing on our taxes, like stars have to now. Nonetheless, it makes me think about the free Roberto Cavalli jeans and Versace jackets and the nine-foot Yamaha concert grands that would appear anywhere I requested them for as long as I wanted them. I ponder that long-lost lifestyle, in which grand theft auto was met with a slap on the hand, women bent over backward (or any direction I chose) to be near me, everyone was showering me and the rest of Cultural Wasteland with free crap, enabling our addictions, feeding our egos, and supporting an ongoing sense of entitlement that we shared in a long suspended adolescence.

I know now that only I was to blame when the consequences of that lifestyle showed up and karma deservingly bitch-slapped me around. These are nice things, and if I have to pay taxes on them, maybe I'll keep some and give the rest to charity, but this time I think I have a better idea of what they really mean, which is nothing. Except maybe for that bracelet for Claudia. It is nice. I slip it into my pocket.

Time to get back to work. It looks like they've thrown a few coins at the old monkey and asked him to dance. Better get the changes ready for the orchestra. I return to the piano and flick to the beginning of the score of "I Turned Around," a blank sheet of music paper in front of me, pencil in hand.

CHAPTER 19

Sometimes Loud Is Good

Cultural Wasteland blew into the Roma Auditorium last night and blew away the sold-out Italian crowd with their musicianship, energy, and pure unmistakable volume. Usually this reviewer finds an excess of volume means a lack of talent, but Lark Dray's gang of crazies (including new keyboard player Ben Felder) rocked like it was the '70s all over again. This was the first stop on an extended European tour.

The Herald Tribune, February 27, 1997

I HADN'T REALLY THOUGHT about it before then, but all of my friends were in Cultural Wasteland or in the solar system around it. Because of the family-like quality of being on the road or in the studio all the time together, with security there to keep out the great unwashed, and with the lawyers, managers, and executives always poised to keep anyone new from coming in and messing things up or taking a bite out of the pie, none of us really met a lot of new people.

Despite the differences and fights that had arisen between us, Lark was my best friend, my best man even, with whom I had spent the better part of a decade writing songs, performing, chasing girls (Lark was the best wingman ever), doing drugs, drinking, acting high and mighty and entitled, and just sitting around shooting the shit. Before we stopped talking, we had been just about as close as two guys can get, I suppose.

Peter and Chris were an acquired taste for most, but I liked them. One time they took me to visit their mother during a three-city swing through South America (where Cultural Wasteland just never really caught on), and it turns out that they were, in fact, distant members of the Argentinean Royal family. Their maternal grandfather was the Duke of Earl or something and had been the British Ambassador to Argentina, and he had married their grandmother there, a countess or something like that. I recollected laughing myself silly as these two complete reprobates conducted themselves with the utmost in dignity over a sumptuous lunch in their mother's fantastic villa in Buenos Ares, retelling with some friends a funny incident from their youth involving a ski instructor in Gstaad. I finally understood why they eschewed tattoos.

In some ways, Huge and I got along the best of all. It's likely that each member of Cultural Wasteland would say this, except possibly for Peter and Chris, being brothers, but then, brothers often fight, and Huge never fought with anyone in the group. Huge kept it all together. That was his role as the drummer, and it was his role in life.

If Huge had a motto, it was "I've got your back,"

as long as you were someone in his loyalty group, which included the band and anyone the band decided to include in its loyalty group, which unfortunately changed from time to time. I liked spending time with Huge because we could not talk for hours. He didn't challenge me, and I didn't challenge him. And sometimes that's just what you need, especially when you're feeling low.

But Huge and Peter and Chris and even Lark were in Europe with Ben Felder on keys, along with the bodyguards, and the makeup and wardrobe girls, and the rest of the crew. And the groupies were out there too, the pros and the amateurs alike. Suddenly I began to realize that I had been at the center of a white-hot sun, but now I was past Pluto or Neptune or whichever one is farthest away these days, headed into space. Into nothingness.

Porny had gone away and Phoebe before her and Judy the Waitress before her and some other ones before them. Claudia had gone away and taken our friends (her friends, really) with her. August West didn't even exist anymore, and Shelly from college was God knows where, and I didn't like any of my friends from home, and my sister had gone Christian on me, and the Old Man was dead.

I called my mother.

She wasn't in.

I did a couple of lines, knocked back a Crown and Diet, and smoked pot and watched television.

On the third day after Eddie came by, the Percocet turned loose of my bowels. I was essentially going through Perc withdrawal, but the smoke and Methadone was keeping me from being too wracked up. Nonetheless, once the constipation stopped, the diarrhea started, just as any doctor would have told me it would (as long as he wasn't Gonzo).

Not to get into too much detail, but at first it was great. It was like flushing two weeks' worth of depression. Everything that had been backed up left in a hurry. I also noticed that my eyes were not nearly as yellow as they had been. I had only a few more days to go to get the pins out of my hand, and then surely everything would start to improve. Things were looking up.

Then I couldn't stop. My intestines proceeded to become a black hole that sucked in everything from the body and expelled it. I became dehydrated and chapped; I lost weight at an alarming rate; my bones and muscles ached mercilessly. I began eating as much as I could, but it just went through me like all the beer and even water I drank as well, when I didn't just throw it up as soon as I swallowed it. My face became covered in "chow measles," a particular form of rosacea caused by repeated, furious alcoholic vomiting. The diarrhea was much worse than being backed up had been. So, in a moment of ostensible brilliance, if not clarity, I decided to reverse the process by adding the Percocets and Vicodin back to the Absolut, Crown, cocaine, pot, Methadone, salami, pickles, and beer and tomato juice.

This was an ill-advised move. I recall staggering around the apartment in a scene out of *Liquid Sky*, and then my little part of the world retreated from Earth, the solar system, the Milky Way, and out into the far reaches of the universe and then into nothingness.

I awoke in the hospital. I looked around. Claudia was sitting next to me with a none-too-friendly look on her face. My hand had a fresh dressing on it, but the pins were still in. My mouth was dry. I blinked several times so she would know I was awake and then tried to smile. She did not.

"Water?" I croaked.

Claudia pointed to a pitcher and glass next to my good hand. The plastic glass was full. I reached out and got it and took a drink.

"Hi."

"I'm just here to tell you that I'm not going to do this, Zack."

"Do what?"

"Watch you die or watch you get better, either one."

"What are you doing here in the first place?"

"I got you here. Your mother called me."

"My mother?"

"Apparently you left some fucked-up drug-addled jabbering message on her machine about not being able to reach her and nothingness and all manner of shit that a saint like her does not need from an ungrateful fuck like you, and she called me because I'm the only person she knew to call."

"Oh. Shit."

"Yes, there was quite a lot of that. It's quite a thing to find your ex-husband lying in a puddle of his own piss and shit and vomit. Thank God you were breathing and I didn't have to give you mouth to mouth. I probably would have let you die. Instead I just had to call an ambulance."

So much shame.

"I'm so very sorry. Thank you so much."

"You're welcome. And now I'm leaving. I have arranged for a parting gift."

"Don't go."

"I'm already gone, cowboy. Try to get your shit together, would you Zack? And call your mother. I told her you had food poisoning. I don't think she completely bought it, so add something to it, but stick with the program."

She walked out the door. Before it closed, in walked Bobby Craft.

"Hello, asshole. Welcome to Rock Bottom."

I smiled. Finally.

Of course, I was wrong.

CHAPTER 20

Fresh Squeezed? No Thanks!
The concert rider for the The Corey's massive *POP-a-Razzi* tour includes a demand for 30 cases of canned Country Time lemonade on ice, not refrigerated. Maybe that's what makes TJ's voice sound so, so sweet!

Tiger Beat, May 1998

I HAD WELL EARNED the nickname "Blewit." Shattered marriage, shattered hand, shattered career, shattered life. All of this had been in the back of my mind during the week I prepared for my second audition for The Coreys. I was determined to give myself a fresh take on everything, and I was going to start with this audition and then by kicking ass for Daryl Miller throughout the tour.

When I returned to Daryl's studio to try again, I sat down in the waiting room and noticed a fellow reading *Billboard* in the corner. He dropped the magazine for a moment, looked at me levelly, and nodded. I returned the nod. He looked familiar, but I couldn't place him. Nonetheless, a sense of foreboding came over me. Private detective? DEA? IRS? Paranoid much, Zack?

After ten minutes or so, Daryl stuck his head into the room. "It's now or never, Blewit. You ready?"

I nodded and clutched the leather folio of charts to my chest.

"You doin' OK, Chuck?" Daryl said to the man in the corner.

"Chuck" looked up over his magazine and nodded slightly.

"Thanks for waiting," Daryl said to Chuck, while holding open the door for me.

The fist of doom punched me in the pit of the stomach. Of course I recognized him; I had just never met him in person before. Charles "Chuck" Manuel. Played with Clapton; played with Jimmy Page; played with Jeff Beck; played with the Black Crowes; played with fucking everybody! If he had just played for Daryl, then I had some boat-size shoes to fill. But he was waiting, so maybe he was going to play after me, in which case I could only hope that by some incredible stroke of good luck, on this one day, I might be better prepared than he, and perhaps I could set the bar higher than he might expect. It was my only hope. Most likely, I was fucked.

When I got into the big room, things had filled out considerably. Daryl had added a fez-wearing percussion player I had never heard of named Torquis, a guitar player I had met a few times named Sam Warren, and a label mate of Alexi's, multi-instrumentalist Paul Macalwaite, who was surrounded by an array of saxophones, flutes, and an oboe. The Coreys were also there, sitting around on couches, flicking through magazines or playing bloody knuckles.

In the far corner loomed their morbidly obese manager and Svengali, a man rumored to be of dubious moral character, but one successful sonofabitch. The shadow of Chuck Manuel settled on my shoulder as I shook hands with everyone, then Daryl moved to his keyboard, told us which song he wanted, and counted it down.

I hustled over to the Hammond. The stops weren't set in the right places. I began frantically pulling and pushing. I looked up to see Daryl watching me out of the corner of his eye, and then I turned to adjust the Leslie and looked back up just in time for my cue. I slammed my right hand down on the five-fingered seventh chord, the toughest reach for my little finger, but I hit it clean and let it scream for four beats before wiping down the keyboard with my left and readjusting the Leslie. Each of us looked into each other's eyes and frequently back at Daryl as we rocked the track. Sure it was pop, but it was tight and hard and clean, and, at least at that moment in time, there were no moronic lyrics to hear (not that "Cry for Me" was exactly literature).

The boys all jumped up and started dancing, and not their choreographed stuff, but individually grooving on the sound we were making, smiling broadly at each other and high-fiving. I realized that they were musicians too. They knew what they wanted to sound like live, and they were getting it.

We went into the second number, a ballad where the grand piano plays a solo intro riff and then the entire first verse alone with TJ. As I played, he walked over and sang with me. His voice, even though unmiced and without any reverb or compression, was rich and high and clear, and I couldn't help but smile at him. The rest of the band joined in, and the boys all gathered near the piano to sing the chorus. Daryl brought us down to almost a whisper (I'd never known an eight-piece amplified group could be so quiet) so the harmonies could be heard, and there they were, tight and beautiful. Then the Manager made an almost imperceptible gesture from the corner, and they returned to their couches to listen, all smiles.

We played for another half an hour or so, and it was great fun. Somewhere along the way the shadow of Chuck Manuel left the room. I just played my best because the musicianship of the rest of the band and Daryl's leadership required and deserved it. I played with joy that my finger worked again and that there was no pain anymore. I was reminded of similar moments—of the first audition with August West, of that night in South Dakota with Bobby, and of Cultural Wasteland's first show at the Greek.

The Coreys left with the Manager toward the end, waving as they went. When we were finished, Daryl waited while I shook hands with the rest of the band and then said he would walk me out. I picked up the leather folio and started putting the charts back inside.

"You can just leave those," pointed out Daryl.

Of course I could. They weren't mine. In fact, Chuck Manuel was probably about to sight-read them and kick my ass all over the studio. I put everything down, feeling a little naked walking out without them. I had gotten close to those charts over the last week.

When we hit reception, Chuck wasn't there. Daryl walked me up to the receptionist and asked her if she would take down my sizes—shoe, shirt, pants, and jacket, even hat. I looked around, bewildered.

"What's going on?" I asked.

"What do you mean, what's going on, Blewit? You don't think we'd let you dress yourself, do you? You're in the band. That's what you wanted the chance to do, isn't it?" Daryl responded, a tiny smile playing at the corners of his mouth.

"What about Chuck Manuel?"

"Great guy, Chuck. He's recording down the hall. What about him?"

"What was he doing waiting here?"

"Oh that. He was just waiting for you to come in. I asked him to. Great guy, Chuck."

I took this all in for a moment, and then faced Daryl.

"You can just call me Mr. Screwit from now on."

And so I went to Las Vegas. Not the Vegas of the Strip or even off the Strip. The Vegas of one hundred and ten degree heat and warehouses on the outskirts of town. The Vegas of Ramadas and Residence Inns, not the Luxor or the MGM. There, out near the airport, in a warehouse the size of a jumbo jet hangar, I watched the biggest stadium show I had ever seen being built and prepared: The Coreys' *POP-a-Razzi* tour.

I was not a novice to big shows. Cultural Wasteland's *The State I'm In* tour had certainly been big enough: fifty dates in the U.S. and twenty abroad, all in venues of twelve thousand or more, and occasionally with two nights. Almost all of the gigs were in arenas, though we did play a couple of soccer stadiums overseas.

On the other hand, The Coreys' tour was only

about one-third arenas. The rest of the shows were in stadiums from sixty thousand to one hundred thousand seats, and in towns where the stadium only held sixty thousand, there were at least two nights, and in big cities even with big stadiums, there were often three nights already sold out. To say that it was the same thing, only bigger, would be accurate, but that would be like comparing me to John Holmes. I've had no complaints, but let's face it, there's no comparison.

We were in Vegas because that's where The Coreys lived, for tax purposes, as I understand it. I think each of them had about four houses, including those that their parents and grandparents actually lived in, but they "resided" in Vegas because of nonexistent state income taxes and because that's where The Manager lived. Also, the tour was scheduled to launch in Vegas, move around the country for about five months, then return to Vegas for the final show. Then there would be a two-month break before heading overseas. Before that, though, the show had to be built.

From the looks of the thing, it could have been the launch pad and mission control for a trip to the moon. More accurately, for three simultaneous moon launches. There were three full stages, two for outdoor stadiums, and one for indoor arenas. That way they could really pack in the shows, never having more than a day or two off between them. The next stadium would generally be ready or almost ready once we finished in one city, and the arena stages could be set up and taken down over only two days for quick turnarounds in smaller towns between stadium concerts.

The *POP-a-Razzi* concert was astonishing in its

pure size. When we would come into a place, we were like a small city unto ourselves. We would show up with some seventy eighteen-wheelers, thirty-five carrying the steel stage and another thirty-five carrying the production equipment, along with twenty-eight buses for all the people. In addition to the band, dancers, choreography team, management executives, administrative and personal assistants, and The Coreys, a typical stadium show required the services of two hundred and sixty-five employees, including roadies, wardrobe and makeup personnel, accountants, cooks, truck drivers, security personnel, medical personnel, a couple of lawyers and, I believe, one Indian chief who acted as a spiritual advisor. There were two complete such villages for stadium shows and another skeleton crew of a mere twenty eighteen-wheelers and fourteen buses for the arena shows.

The stage was incredible. When we came into town, the local venue would remove its stage, and we would put up our own, which overwhelmed even the biggest stadiums. It took three days to get the stage, lighting, pyrotechnics, and sound systems ready for a show that would last three hours. The stage itself was ninety feet high (imagine an eight-story building sticking up from the middle of a football field), two hundred and six feet wide, one hundred feet deep, and flanked on all sides by ten towers of speakers capable of ruining the hearing of anyone over the age of sixteen not wearing ear protection. Which was why each entrance to the show held free ear plugs in various colors that you took from candy jars when you passed through security.

From the main stage, there was a one hundred and

eighty-foot runway sticking out into the audience that connected to a satellite stage forty feet high, the back of which served as the main sound and lighting control center for the whole show. The satellite stage was not that much smaller than the stage for a standard size Cultural Wasteland show, to put it in perspective, and it was much more interesting. In addition to being connected by the runway to the gargantuan main stage, there were also tunnels to the main stage under the runway big enough for an eight-person golf cart to travel down. These were accessible by side doors or by trap doors on the stages, so The Coreys could disappear from one stage and reappear on the other in a flash of smoke. Or, if they didn't feel like that, there were zip lines they could fly down from the main stage to the satellite and flying harnesses that would take them back up, flying over the screaming audience through the rockets' red glare. It was all pretty damn impressive.

The crew continually built and broke down the stages for practice throughout our rehearsal time in the hanger, and we moved back and forth between them. Daryl had our hands full putting in long days of practice on the music and making sure we understood every detail of the show. He worked with the boys and the choreographer on the arrangements, making changes to incorporate the dancing, special effects, and the patter throughout the show, while making sure that the meat of the songs themselves remained rock solid.

Then, he started working on contingencies. What do we do if Jorge breaks an E string while playing lead? Simple, Sam takes over and Jorge moves to rhythm. No sweat. We had all played in bands before and we all knew how to "fake it" if something went kerblooie. For Daryl, though, faking it wasn't good enough. The lights, the dance steps, the explosions and fire, all of these had to work perfectly with the music (not to mention the singing, let us never forget the singing). So Daryl came up with all manner of contingencies: amps that burn out, bass strings that snap, piano players whose fingers fall off, saxophone players who swallow a reed, musical directors who die of simultaneous heart attacks and perforated ulcers.

This was a sly approach. First, despite the best efforts of even the best crew of roadies and technicians, when you tear something down as fast as you can and rebuild it almost every day, and when that something is as complicated as the world's largest concert tour, things are bound to go wrong. Bass strings are unlikely to snap, but shit can still go wrong and most likely will, and we were prepared for it. Second, we moved from knowing and being competent with (extremely competent, even) our own parts, to knowing each other's parts as well, and this allowed for greater nuance in our playing, even though it remained extremely precise in terms of delivery. This was Daryl's genius, because even though we, as a band, played virtually exactly the same show every performance for five months, each one was different (just as The Coreys were a little different each night), and to the audience, it was palpably live, which was just what Daryl and The Coreys wanted. It was also never boring for us.

One thing Daryl didn't make us do was to rehearse with the dancers. He told me that he had learned this lesson in preparation for the last tour, when just one day of working with choreography that wasn't finished or learned yet almost soured the band on the music to the point where they couldn't get back into it, himself included. He likened it to doing aerobics to a song you liked; soon, you liked it no more.

Instead, Daryl got a soundboard set up, and we performed the show from start to finish on tape. The dancers who had survived the rigorous tryouts rehearsed to our recordings on their own until about a week before dress rehearsals. Hence, it wasn't until right before we went out on the road that the original GDT danced into my life.

Melanie Locke was, upon first glance, an extraordinarily beautiful young woman. She was upon second through ninety-eighth glance as well. When you looked deeply into her aquamarine eyes, there was an intelligence and sexiness that went beyond her mere good looks. She also had an absolutely killer bod, hard as a rock from all the dancing, and yet not overly muscular like some of her colleagues, primarily because she was tall for a dancer.

She had tremendous charisma that came across on stage even from the background. It was never any surprise to me that her charm would eventually come across on screen, although that wouldn't be for some time to come. On the day that I first laid eyes on her she was only twenty years of age, totally violating the time-honored "divide by two and add seven" rule (whereby you take your own age—which at the time was something over thirty for me—divide it by two, add seven, and thereby arrive at the age below which you should not delve in matters of the heart).

The nice thing about the "divide by two and add seven" rule is that it doesn't mean you can't look; you're just not supposed to touch, unless you're anywhere near a playground sign that says *All adults must be accompanied by a child*, in which case you must neither look nor touch and you probably need some therapy or some suicide if you do. It was, therefore, perfectly according to Hoyle for me to watch this lithe feline move about the stage in a leotard and loosely tied man's dress shirt.

I was promptly smitten in a fashion that rarely happens to me. I am as appreciative of a pretty girl as the next fellow. I have romanced, picked up, or pointed out to artists' reps plenty of very pretty girls with whom I have then had or attempted to have sex (depending on the witches' brew of chemicals and alcohol in my system at the time). To stir that spot in the pit of the stomach, to cause the mild arrhythmia and the seeming inability to look elsewhere or think of anything else, well, that usually requires an intelligent comment, a witty aside, a genuinely kind gesture, or an unexpectedly athletic act of sexual congress that bears repeating. But with Melanie Locke, simply watching her dance with the light in her hair was enough to bring her to my attention and catalyze feelings of puppy love. But how to bring myself to her attention?

"Blewit!!!"

The band crashed to a halt. I looked up at Daryl from my reverie and realized that I had not made the required eye contact with him in some time, perhaps more than a minute, perhaps more than an hour, and my fingers were still noodling around on the keys, despite that the stage had gone deathly quiet. I pulled my hands back and felt myself blush for the first time in well over a decade.

"What are you doing?" he demanded.

"Nothing," I stammered. This was clearly not a satisfactory response to Daryl, who continued to stare at me. The rest of the band was chuckling quietly at my discomfort, and I had grave misgivings that the public humiliation that had just begun had a ways to go if I didn't just get the rehearsal back on track.

"Sorry, Maestro," I said, "I just got a little spacey, I guess. First time watching the dancers do their thing. It looks great! Won't happen again, though." There. That was pretty good.

Daryl stared at me, at first with his imperious look, but then I could see a hint of mischief behind it too. "Yes, the dancers are very pretty, aren't they?" *Cut it off at the pass! Cut it off at the pass!* "Very talented. Very talented indeed!" I attempted to agree. Where have all the rock stars gone? Why was I acting like this? My band mates had gone beyond chuckles, straight through chortles, and were heading down the homestretch to guffaws.

"And very pretty indeed, don't you agree?"

"Well, who could disagree?"

"Precisely my point. Ms. Lamont? Where is Ms. Lamont?" The choreographer came out of the wings, grinning, but quickly adopted a formality commensurate to Daryl's. I realized immediately that this was one of the drawbacks of working with very creative people – they were liable to improvise something at the drop of a hat that was intended to make you look stupid.

"Yes, Mr. Miller? How may I be of service?"

"Ms. Lamont, it occurs to me that we may have been unintentionally rude. Although we do have rather a lot to accomplish in a short time, I'm afraid that does not relieve us from our duties to etiquette. My pianist, Mr. Fluett, has not met your young ladies, and it seems to be hampering his ability to perform. Perhaps, once we have arranged proper introductions and the parties have become acquainted, we might get on with the rehearsal?"

"Absolutely, Mr. Miller," responded Ms. Lamont. "Ladies! Please form a line, facing the rear of the stage. Mr. Fluett? Please come down and be introduced."

Fuck. Daryl gave me a toothy, expectant smile, like some demented black headmaster. The band was in hysterics. Alexi leaned against his amp, head in hands. Sonny beat his head against his floor tom. The only way out was to play along, as fast as possible. First rule of improvisation: always say yes to whatever is offered up to you.

I rose from the grand piano, flipped an imaginary set of tails like a concert pianist, and strode haughtily to the front of the band riser. I was pleased to see that this got a smile from the dancers, who had carefully lined up, and even a snort out of Daryl. Upon reaching the front of the riser, however, I realized I was in deep trouble, because there was no connection between it and the main stage. The laughter increased behind my back as various roadies and techs, intrigued by the lack of activity on the stage, began sauntering out of the wings to see what was happening. I thought about turning around and going out the back way and down to the stage, but that would only prolong the hilarity. I looked into the wings and suddenly saw my opening.

"Mr. Trash Bag! Oh, Mr. Trash Bag!" I called out.

Mike stepped out of the wings and pointed a thumb at himself. "You talkin' to me?" he sneered.

"I am, Trash Bag. You see, I'm supposed to introduce myself to that lovely group of young ladies, but I seem to have encountered an obstacle."

"Yeah? So what's that got to do with me?"

"A ladder, Mr. Bag. Do you have one? Something to get me from 'up here' to 'down there,' like, uh, pronto."

"I got yer 'down there' right here," responded Mike, but one of his crew was already hustling across the stage with a twenty-foot metal ladder. What pros.

As I descended, Daryl slowed the laughter by informing the rest of the band that they should join me, but to take the stairs backstage. As I heard them lumbering down, I was introduced to each of the dancers one by one. I shook hands and bowed politely to each, just like my mother had taught me when I was about five and it seemed cute. Apparently, my mother was right once again. Upon my introduction to Melanie, she curtsied, I bowed, and then she held onto my hand for a moment longer than necessary when we shook hands.

"Glad you made it down," she said, allowing me a long look straight into those mesmerizing eyes, indicating, it seemed, her full knowledge that it was she upon whom I had been fixated, and conveying, I felt sure, her encouragement. The look lasted two seconds, but it seemed that I could see years into the future all at once. Moments later the rest of the band crashed the stage and everyone introduced themselves to everyone else, the roadies removed the ladder, and, at Daryl's command, we all trooped back upstairs and proceeded to tear it up. I didn't feel the need to look at Melanie throughout the rest of rehearsal; the sense of wanting to drink her in before she disappeared was sated. There would be plenty of time, even though I knew deep down that it would never be enough.

While we were in Vegas, I didn't see Melanie except on stage during the remaining rehearsals and dress rehearsals. I didn't get a chance to talk to her one on one until after the first show. Even then, we didn't say much, as we were in a crush of people at the effusive after-party, but we did both comment on how much fun we'd had and how we were looking forward to the long tour. I gave her my cell number and told her that I would be delighted to take her out on our night off, which just happened to be in L.A. in two nights. She said she'd think about it, but I was pretty sure she was interested.

The show had, in fact, been fun. It was an almost totally different experience than a Cultural Wasteland concert. First, it was bigger. Second, the atmosphere and crowd noise were entirely different. Cultural Wasteland fans were, by and large, in their twenties and thirties; they were passionate about good music and enthusiastic about the band, but they were adults. The Coreys' fans were, by and large, girls eight to eighteen who screamed constantly and often cried. For many, I'm sure they weren't even sure what it was that they were feeling, but good God, they loved those cute boys. I have heard that the girls that screamed and cried for Sinatra and The Beatles were all plants by the PR departments of their labels, but after touring with The Coreys, I don't believe it. The sound of sixty thousand screaming adolescent girls is both deafening and unnerving, but once you get used to it, it provides a hell of a lot of energy.

Also different, of course, was the focus of attention. Even though Lark was the obvious front man of Cultural Wasteland, I was still in at least one of the spotlights. I was a member of the band, and the band was the star of the show. I had my own dressing room; my face was on at least some of the merchandise; I actually got more groupies than Lark (the same was true for the other guys in the band; Lark was kind of standoffish when it came to groupies); and I had my own security detail.

With The Coreys, I was support staff. I was the focus of attention and polite applause of perhaps one-half of the crowd for my ten-second B3 solo during band introductions at the one-hour-and-nineteen-minute mark of the show, but other than that, I was part of the stage dressing. This was quite freeing, because it did, indeed, allow for a considerable amount of fun. There was pure enjoyment in playing with a group of good musicians. There was the pure fun of watching a bunch of little girls just freak the fuck out. I even got a kick out of the lasers and flames and explosions and confetti cannons.

At the end of a good Cultural Wasteland show, I felt like I had a big dick and was deserving of the whole world stepping up to suck it, if they could get past security. After a good show with The Coreys, I felt like I'd just been to a top-notch amusement park, and then I could walk out without a bodyguard.

On the band bus late that night to L.A., I got a call from Melanie. Yes, she would like to see me tomorrow. The dancers were having a run-through in the hotel ballroom from two to five to clean up a few problems from the first show, but after that, she was free. All the girls had been informed that the quickest way to get booted off the tour was to get involved with one of The Coreys, because it wouldn't last long. Even though I wasn't one of them, she thought that being seen out with a member of the band, especially this early in the tour, might not be a good idea. I agreed. She asked if I had a suggestion for where we might meet up that would be quiet and where we could talk without worrying about running into someone from the tour. I certainly did.

"Why don't you just come on over to my house?"

CHAPTER 21

I AM ALONE IN the rehearsal room, sitting at the piano making final notation changes to the score of "I Turned Around" for the conductor. I still feel the effects of the tequila, but it's good to have something constructive to do, even though I have a sinking feeling this is not constructive at all, but yet another in a long line of stupid, self-centered, self-destructive acts. You don't just re-orchestrate a song for live television at the last second. That's like deciding to go straight for the moon instead of docking at the space station once you've already left the launch pad.

OK, maybe it's not that bad. No one is going to die or anything, unless Trash Bag and half the crew kill me in the parking lot. All the confidence I had a little while ago when I was talking to Wendy has fled. I am making a big mistake here. Maybe I can get her to change her mind.

"Oh, excuse me. I didn't know this room was taken."

A pretty girl stands in the doorway. Very pretty girl. She's carrying a guitar case and wearing a blue and gold kimono jacket over a loose, off-white hemp shirt and old Levis. She has bare feet. She looks for all the world like Michelle Phillips from The Mamas and the Papas circa 1967. Always had a thing for Mama Michelle, even if she was born a couple of decades before me.

"No, no problem," *I splutter.* "I'm just doing a little paperwork here. Come on in and make yourself at home."

She walks into the room and sets down her guitar case. I cannot help but give her ass an appreciative stare, despite the fact that it is probably illegal for her to drink. I want to try to say something witty, but I realize that I am a sweaty middle-aged fat man with a tequila buzz that is halfway to hangover and a job to do. I turn my attention back to the insert page I am preparing for the conductor's score.

I hear the latches of her guitar case open. I wonder what type of guitar she plays. Girls who play guitar are always pretty cool, but a girl who plays a certain kind of guitar...

Yep, there it is. I had a feeling. Probably subconscious from seeing the case. It's a Taylor. Doyle Dykes Signature model. Transparent black with the short-scale, grand auditorium figured maple body, "Chet"-style fretboard markers, Florentine cutaway, and an abalone white rose peghead inlay. She sits easily cross-legged on the floor and begins to tune it.

"Nice guitar," *I find myself saying.*

She looks up and smiles. "Thanks. I love it."

I find I once again have nothing further to say, and so I turn my attention back to the score. She tunes away in the background, and then begins softly to hum a pretty melody. I look up and watch for a second, and she catches me. She stops.

"You sure I'm not bothering you?" *she asks. I detect a*

slight accent. Perhaps British or Australian? Kiwi may-be?

"Of course not. Am I bothering you? I'm almost fin-ished here, but I can do this somewhere else."

"Not a bit. I'd just like to sing a little and get warmed up."

"Playing tonight?" *Stupid question.*

"Mmm hmm." *Intelligent answer.*

"Go ahead," I say. "I'll just finish up, but I hope you don't mind if I listen a little bit. Sort of hard not to."

She starts to play again, a little four-chord progression using simple cowboy chords to walk down from C major to A minor to G major to F major, then back to A mi-nor, to F major, and then to C. Incredibly simple and yet somehow new. The strings squeak sweetly as she moves her hand from chord to chord. She would do better with a guitar with a slightly smaller neck, but then again, it wouldn't sound like this guitar. She sings, her voice high and clear and unbearably sad, but without sadness. In-stead, it is the pure voice of hope and determination in the face of absurd obstacles.

I listen as she sings, and I know I am hearing a tru-ly original voice. She is probably only nineteen, but I can still relate. She sings about being born in the wrong time. She sings about being apart from your loved ones and missing them, and yet she sings about needing to be alone when you are home. She sings about watching the world go by from the rear window of a bus; she sings of long-distance love affairs and of one-night stands; she sings of noisy bars and empty halls and of trying to tell the deepest truths while those around you are telling the shallowest lies. She calls this life of music an "Insanity Salad," and she can't stop tossing it.

It's wonderful. I recognize in her voice the many

*nights she has had to sing over the chatter of the bar or cof-
feehouse patrons, trying to reach just one or two of them,
sometimes getting the whole crowd and sometimes getting
nothing. I have a vision of her listening to a lover on the
phone telling her a lie or else just the bad news, and I see
her hanging up and moving on with strength, although I
sense there will be a good long hotel room cry later. I see
her smiling to herself as yet another heartbreak or disappointment gets turned into a beautiful melody or a well
phrased lyric, and I feel as if it were my own, the satisfaction she takes from that. It is an addiction no less powerful than any other, and one that makes those of us who are
victim to it make choices that few can understand.*

*She cannot be more than nineteen or twenty at the
most, and yet she already knows and feels these things and
expresses them in a way that I relate to as a middle-aged
man who has made more mistakes than I can count.
Others will feel these emotions powerfully too, but none
of us will truly know what she feels. We'll just feel like
we do. This is an artist. I feel suddenly and powerfully
toward her as if she were my daughter. I feel like I want
to envelop her in a hug that will protect her and comfort
her but by which she will not be smothered.*

*She finishes and looks up at me shyly. I smile at her
broadly and feel my eyes well. Tequila didn't used to give
me the weepies. I must be getting old.*

"*That was a wonderful song. The best I've heard in
many, many years,*" *I say.*

She looks down at her slightly dirty feet. "*Thank you,
but this year will do.*"

*Song of the Year. I have to get these changes to the
conductor, and I have to sit down with Wendy. Shit. I
gotta go.*

"*Shit. I gotta go!*" *I say.* "*It was nice listening to you.*

Good luck with everything!"

"Thank you," she says, starting to get up. I wave at her to stay put. I am already halfway out the door, clutching the score to my chest. I stick my head back in the door for one last look.

"If you don't mind me giving you a little unsolicited advice?" I begin. She nods for me to continue.

"You're young and perfect the way you are, but some-day you're going to wonder if you should take it all so seriously, and when you do wonder that, that's the time to try not to take it all so seriously."

She is puzzled. So am I. I should take my own advice from time to time, but now is not that time.

CHAPTER 22

Broken In, Not Broken Down
New Cultural Wasteland keyboard player Ben
Felder refuses to play anything new, and by that
we don't mean he's copying Zack Fluett's chunky
riffs. Ben only plays used instruments in the studio that previously belonged to or were played by
guys like Al Kooper or Ben Tench, and he prefers
to play rigs that are older than he is. Not all artists are in it for the free new gear, obviously.

Keyboard Magazine, Notes, November 1997

ONE OF THE REASONS rehab hadn't really worked
for me the first time was because I didn't really go.
I was rehabbing my hand at the same time, and it
wasn't going well. I was still in the hospital recovering from severe dehydration when they removed the
Kirshner wire and pins from my hand. This they did
with no anesthesia, and it was quite painful.

Bobby suggested that it was a good way to get
started on my substance abuse rehab, because I needed to start feeling pain as part of my process of getting sober. I wasn't entitled just to numb out, so he
said. Unfortunately, as much as Bobby knew about

substance rehab, he didn't know anything about hand rehab and the new phrase my doctors would soon be teaching me: "reflex sympathetic dystrophy."

After removing the pins, my hand was essentially a stiff club. I had no movement in my ring or pinky finger, and surprisingly little movement in my thumb and other fingers, in part due to atrophy and in part due to the simple nature of the musculature of the hand. It's pretty hard to move any of your fingers without causing at least some movement in the others, and any movement of the little finger was still very painful.

I had assumed that I would be squeezing on a ball or something to rebuild the muscle, but that turned out to be quite a ways in the future. Instead, to begin with, they put my hand in a vat of hot wax. This was supposed to be helpful both in terms of reducing pain and adding some resistance as I attempted to wiggle my fingers. I would do this for perhaps ten minutes or so, then remove my hand from the wax and let a thin layer of it harden. It was then my goal to clench my fist hard enough to break the wax. The fact that this was incredibly difficult was my first clue that I was really going to have to work hard to get my hand back to where it had been, and this depressed me to no end.

In addition to being depressing, the rehab process was painful, and yet I had Bobby hanging around me all the time, making sure that I didn't take any pain medication. This probably seemed like a good idea to the attending physician who was overseeing my recovery from the incident with the opiates and alcohol, but I was discharged from the hospital on that count after a week.

After that, I was in outpatient rehab at Dr. Pricey's clinic, and he and his staff had no compunctions about using drugs to block the pain in my hand such that I could move the process of recovery along faster. I was ashamed of my behavior and of Claudia having to find me like she did, but I felt that the most important thing was to get my hand healthy again. The incident had arisen from an unfortunate combination of things. I was certain it would not be repeated.

Bobby, of course, did not share my opinions in this regard. When I got out of the hospital and got home, I discovered that he had de-drunked my house. There was no booze to be found anywhere, nor were there any medications, including aspirin or cough syrup. The place was completely cleaned up and aired out. I was appreciative of Bobby's attempts to help, and so I decided it was best just to hide my use of pain medication from him. I'd simply lie to him. I did allow as to how it would probably be a good idea to stay off the booze for a while, though.

I found that my body was still going about trying to fix itself and was doing a horrible job of it. My hand rehab proceeded achingly slowly, primarily because the pain was just too severe for me to do much. After two weeks I was still unable to make a fist sufficient to break dried wax, and the pain was actually getting worse. My hand puffed up and the skin grew hard and shiny. It looked like it belonged on a fat mannequin. The hair all fell out and my fingerprints disappeared. I felt as if my hand were literally on fire.

Dr. Pricey diagnosed reflex sympathetic dystrophy, and explained that there was no real explanation for it. My autonomic system—the "fight or flight" mechanism in the body—had decided that something horribly traumatic had happened to my hand and was therefore flooding it with adrenaline. This should have stopped shortly after the trauma occurred, and certainly shouldn't be happening now that the bones had knit. Instead, for some reason, my own reptilian brain, in combination with my adrenal glands, was causing greater injury to my hand and preventing me from rehabbing effectively.

As it got worse, the amount of pain medication that I took naturally increased, and Bobby, who was suspicious in any event, figured it out. We argued about it, with him explaining to me that I was an addict, that addiction was a disease, and that I needed to stay off drugs and alcohol. I explained to him that I had an actual physical ailment that was manifesting itself in extraordinarily painful ways, that I was becoming obsessed with the condition of my hand, and that I needed medication and treatment to try to cure myself. I then thanked him very much for his concern and asked him as politely as I could to fuck the fuck off, because I intended to take the advice of my physician. He left, informing me that he would only be a phone call away. Once he was out of the way, I was free to begin drinking again, which I did.

I was fortunate not to have a repeat performance of Rockstaritis. Probably even just the couple of weeks I had taken off helped my body from simply crashing again. I retreated to my Barcalounger with my pain pills and my vodka, and I rocked back and forth for hours, enduring the burning pain and flexing and unflexing my hand through it. Eventually, I began to notice a bit more movement, and I was able to break the wax more and more easily.

Then one morning I awoke to realize that my hangover headache hurt more than my hand for the first time in weeks. My longtime nemesis, the cymbal player in my head, was overshadowing the jackhammer operator that had more recently invaded my hand. I began drinking with renewed vigor and found myself taking fewer pills, and I worked harder and harder on my hand, following Dr. Pricey's advice to perform mundane tasks such as dusting or carrying a suitcase. I found that learning to hold a beer and, eventually, opening a beer without using my feet, was also good therapy.

Almost four months after the Grammys, the skin on my hand returned to normal and the burning sensation ceased completely. Dr. Pricey had no better explanation for why the RSD had gone into remission than for why it had started in the first place. I didn't care. I was just delighted to begin to teach myself how to play the piano again. Just playing a C major scale, slowly, once an hour at first was challenging, but the fact that I could do it at all was encouraging. I scaled back considerably on the meds, mostly because I was sick and tired of being so constipated all the time, and I even slowed down on the booze a little. I started to feel better for the first time in a long time.

CHAPTER 23

> **Obituary: Hunter S. Thompson**
> Hunter S. Thompson, the local journalist and author whose savage chronicling of the underbelly of American life and politics embodied "gonzo journalism," died Sunday of a self-inflicted gunshot wound at his home in Woody Creek. He was 67.
>
> *The Aspen Times*, February 21, 2005

"I TURNED AROUND" WAS not one of those gifts that come from the heavens or the universe or the subconscious or whatever. Every songwriter seems always to say, "It just came to me, and I wrote it in about five minutes," or "It felt like I was just channeling it," or "It was as if I were remembering a song that no one else had ever written." I have had these experiences from time to time. Sometimes they turn into hit songs, like "Cry for Me" did (though really most of the credit for it goes to Lark, but we did write it in less than fifteen minutes). Some of them become something else, like "Baby All the Plants Are Dead," which never made it onto an album, but was a staple of our live shows. The point is, "I Turned Around" was not one of those songs. "I Turned Around" took somewhere in the neighborhood of two and a half years to write to completion, and it constituted, in its own right, the best form of rehab I ever tried.

The process began when I moved out of the trailer in Woody Creek and into Davy's parents' house. Finally taking at least a paragraph from a page from Bobby's book, I realized the first thing I had to do was get rid of the booze. Even though Davy had been reasonably healthy his last few months in Woody Creek while he was working on *Snow Job*, there was still a huge stash from the old liquor store piled in the kitchen, the garage, and the unfinished basement. By my count, there were over five hundred bottles of booze and wine stored around the place, and as I lived there over time I probably found fifty more squirreled away in various hard-to-find places.

There was also a closet full of guns and ammo. This is not uncommon for Colorado in general and Woody Creek in particular. Apparently, Davy's dad was something of a gun aficionado, not to mention a friend (and delivery-making owner of the local liquor store) of a certain gonzo journalist who lived just over the ridge from Davy's place, with whom we occasionally shared a drink or twelve at the Tavern. I didn't want the guns in the place, and I really didn't want the ammo in the place, but I was also in something of a strange frame of mind, and so it came to me that shooting all the bottles to use up the ammo before getting rid of the guns had a certain logic and symmetry to it. So I did just that.

I had heard reasonably frequent gunfire from beyond the ridge and knew who was responsible. I must confess that once I started blasting away at the various liquor bottles I was somewhat curious if the man himself might appear to take stock of my addition to the local fireworks, but he never did. I suspect that it was just as well that way. Given the man's reputation, he might very well have shot me had he caught me murdering the better part of a liquor store. I did notice that once I started shooting, the sound of answering gunfire often came from beyond the ridge.

There was a big old stump in the backyard about twenty yards from the hillside, and over the course of several days, I tried out a host of guns. I began with the most fancy one, by my estimation, which appeared to be a genuine WWII Luger. There were fewer than a dozen bullets for it, but I guessed they were the right ones because the box was written in German and they fit into the gun, once I figured out how to open and load the magazine. I decided that the proper victim for the Luger was a case of Macallan eighteen-year-old, not out of any sense of using a German gun to kill Scotch whiskey, but rather using the most exotic gat for the highest-priced hooch. Likewise, when I finally got down to the rogue case of MD 20/20, I stopped using firearms entirely and simply took a sledgehammer to the bottles.

So the Luger took out all but one bottle of the Macallan. The .44 Smith & Wesson Special destroyed all of the Maker's Mark, and I used a snub-nosed police .38 with the identifying marks filed off to take out most of the equally elusive case of Crater Lake vodka. I warmed up for the rifles by destroying a few cases of Jack Daniel's and Gentleman Jack a bottle at a time with one of three .22s: a bolt action, a pump action, and a semi-automatic.

Then I went for the big game—all but one bottle of the Wild Turkey went down to a Remington .306 (no shotgun for this turkey—unsporting), and then I sadly assassinated all but one bottle of my dear Hornitos with a Winchester .270 with scope, shooting from the roof of the house. I dispatched the filthy Jose Cuervo with a series of blasts from a sawed-off double-barrel .410 of unknown origin. Finally, I killed virtually all of the wine, still inside the cases, with the Browning 12-gauge duck gun, making a most satisfying series of colorful explosions.

In this fashion, I spent almost a week practicing my marksmanship, destroying at least a three-year supply of booze while occasionally wondering what the man next door might be using for target practice. Eventually, of course, it was himself; it was the only time I heard a single shot emanate from over the ridge.

After cleaning up the mess in the backyard—picking up the spent cartridges and shells, raking and bagging the glass and torn cardboard—I put what remained back in the house: one bottle of Macallan in the cupboard above the stove; one bottle of Hornitos in the pantry; two bottles of Crater Lake in the freezer; and a bottle of Wild Turkey next to the sink in the utility room. I left a whole case of champagne in the garage just because somehow I didn't feel like shooting it and thought that someday it might come in handy for purposes of celebratory spraying, if not drinking. I put a bottle of white wine in the fridge on the off chance that I might have a female guest who might like some, and I kept a few bottles of various reds because it doesn't count as drinking if you add it to a jar of Newman's Own tomato sauce and eat it over spaghetti.

I remember when the Old Man finally quit smoking, way too late to do any good. He did it on his own, cold turkey, no patches or programs, and he always carried a pack of cigarettes with him. He did it because, if he were to fall off the wagon, he wanted to be able to do it right then and there, but also because it was evidence (for him, few knew he carried the pack) of his own willpower and ability to control his actions. Of course, he couldn't control the cancer spreading through his body, nor could the drugs or the doctors, but that was OK with him. That was just one of the vast mysteries of life, like almost everything else we have no control over. He could control what he put in his mouth, however, and he did.

I used the same approach with Davy's booze. It was always there if I wanted it or if someone else did as well. I just chose each day not to put any of it in my mouth, day after day.

I took the guns and the last of the ammo down to the sheriff. He accepted them with excellent grace and, in fact, recognized most of them from shooting parties he had attended with Davy's dad and the journalist, with the exception of the .38, which he was pretty sure was the missing weapon in one of Aspen's very few unsolved murders. He seemed confident that Davy's dad was not the killer of the transient from California found buried in a shallow grave in a bunker near the fourteenth green of the Aspen Golf Club, but he assumed that Davy's dad knew the identity of that killer and had taken that knowledge to liquor store heaven. We had a pleasant conversation. Probably my first ever with an officer of the law.

Then came the heavy lifting. Carpentry was not my long suit, but I did know a thing or two about recording studios, and one of the great things about the twenty-first century was the development of truly excellent digital systems that enabled one to record tracks in one's own home very nearly as well as in a big studio from back in the day, depending on what you were recording. So I set about building out the unfinished basement into a small but reasonably professional recording studio.

I started off with the soundproofing. Even though I was pretty far from anyone else, you still want to keep as much control over the sonic environment as possible. So soundproofing is not just about keeping the sound of playing the same guitar solo over and over in the middle of the night from annoying your neighbors, it's also to keep your neighbors' noise (or various chirping birds, barking dogs, or gonzo journalists with firing ranges) from getting into your recording. In addition, having soundproofing deadens the sound so you can control the amount of echo you want by using reverb and delay, rather than having to live with whatever ambient echo you have.

I built a hollow plywood floor supported by two-by-four joists on the concrete foundation, leaving trap doors here and there so I could run various cables without having them underfoot. This I carpeted in a hilarious deep orange pile I found. Prince Bandar bin Sultan had it installed in his twelve-thousand-square-foot "guesthouse" up the mountain when he built it in the seventies. One of the trust fund kids Davy and I used to drink with at the Tavern had purchased the place a few years earlier. He had lived there for a few years with it just as it was back in the day when deep-pile orange carpeting was apparently all the rage if you had a vote at OPEC meetings. We used to love doing blow up there. Something about that carpeting just made you feel decadent.

I had run into the trust fund kid at the hardware store, and he told me that he was in the process of doing some remodeling, including putting in new carpet, and he gave me the old stuff for free. It was fantastically ugly, but in a very cool way for a recording studio, especially given the amount of blow that had been done on it. Just because I was sober didn't mean I didn't want the place to have a rock-star feel to it. It was also an effective sound muffler. I had huge amounts of the stuff, so I put down two layers on the floor. It was deep and soft enough to nap on comfortably.

I divided the open basement into three rooms with walls of doubled sheetrock one inch apart so as to increase the decoupling effect on the sound waves. One room would serve as the control room, and the other two rooms were for recording, the larger one holding keyboards, guitars, and amplifiers, and the smaller one for drums and vocals. Over the sheetrock, I installed gray foam soundproofing. It looked like an egg carton built to hold about a million eggs, and I had to purchase it new.

The foam and shape really helped to deaden the

sound, but it was pretty unattractive, so I found some old rugs at a thrift store and hung them from the rafters here and there to break up the monotony of the egg crates. Because Aspen is such a rich community, you can find pretty amazing deals at the thrift stores, especially at the end of the season. These rugs were actually handmade in Iran with colorful vine ornaments on red or blue fields. They gave the whole place a bit of a psychedelic feel, especially when paired with the orange shag.

I built out the ceiling with professional-grade soundproof tiles and brought in a professional electrician to wire the recessed lights and to bring the electrical in the basement up to code, and then I installed a backup battery generator that should keep anything from being lost in the case of a power outage. It wouldn't provide me with the ability to keep recording, but I would be able to save everything and shut down properly.

I put in thick hardwood doors and a double-thickness glass window between the control room and the two recording rooms. I also replaced the glass in the outside basement windows with double panes, permanently sealing them shut. I then installed a simple ventilation system, using a big fan in the ceiling that would re-circulate air from the upstairs into the control room, keeping equipment and operator cool. The tracking rooms had no such ventilation, so I just put in floor fans and ran them with the doors open whenever I wasn't actually tracking.

The cost of the soundproofing wound up being almost equal to the cost of the rest of the equipment. I decided against going hog wild on lots of different kinds of electronics and instead just got a few top-notch pieces of equipment that would last. I got the newest Mac I could afford and hoped it wouldn't become obsolete too fast. I outfitted it with ProTools, a program that allowed for recording and mixing on the computer hard drive, eliminating the need for a large mixing board, so I was able to go with a smaller, used console for those purposes.

I bought a Korg keyboard controller I was familiar with from back in the Cultural Wasteland days. Then I got top-of-the-line Genelec 2029B near range monitors and some excellent, slightly used Alesis studio monitors with great bass that gave me a sound I was happy with. I purchased good mic pre-amps, two Neuman U87s (expensive, but there is no substitute), and an assortment of Shure microphones. Finally, I added a rack full of reverbs, delays, and compression. I had built a studio.

Overall, I found the process to be healing. I recommend building something to anyone if you are grieving for someone else or if your own existence has left you feeling at a loss. In my experience, it will not necessarily give you solace or cure the loss or allow for self-forgiveness or love, but it will buy you time. Time is what it's all about. Getting through the day.

You wake up in the morning (always a good start), do some exercise to get the blood flowing, put on a pot of coffee, and then get down to it. You work with hammer and nails, wood and metal framing. On some days you take a trip into town to the hardware store, have a little lunch, and check the mail, perhaps. You wrestle with the power saw, staple gun, sheetrock, and soundproofing. When the faint light from the basement window fades and twilight approaches, you head back upstairs for a cup of tea, reviewing the day's accomplishments and the schedule for the next day. Take a hot shower to get the sawdust and dirt off, and then fix dinner, perhaps a healthy stir-fry or a nice piece of fish with a salad. Anyone can learn to cook that kind of thing. Then a cup of chamomile and a few chapters of a good book, alternating fiction with nonfiction, and suddenly it's time for bed, secure in the knowledge of a day full of accomplishments, of forward movement, and a deep sleep followed by vivid morning dreams, clearing the brain's hard drive, and up for another day. Enough of these days buys you the time to put distance between you and whatever you need distance from—the deaths, the disappointments, the heartbreaks, the regrets, and the shame.

Day after day. Feel like a long walk? Take it. It's good for you and will make you more productive. It's not procrastinating. It's part of the process. Just get up in the morning and go to work and try to do something worthwhile, giving it your best, and try to be happy. That's all there is. And then one day the studio (or whatever it is) is ready. It's done.

For me, then came the tricky part. Throughout the finishing of the basement, the building of the studio, the home cooking, the tea drinking, and the reading, there had been an accompaniment. Davy's parents had a terrific stereo system, top of the line from the early eighties, and a truly wonderful collection of classical music. They had both LPs and reel to reel, but the tape player was broken. I decided to listen to all the records first, and then I'd get around to getting the reel to reel fixed, but I never did get around to it because I never finished listening to the records, and I probably never will.

I had something of a background in classical music, as anyone who has ever read an early biography of Cultural Wasteland knows. I am "classically trained" pianist Zack Fluett. In rock & roll parlance, this means, of course, that I can read music and tell Beethoven's Ninth from Mozart's Fortieth. This is not to say that I grew up loving or listening to classical music that much. I listened to a lot of Benny Goodman and Glenn Miller and Johnny Cash as a kid because that's what the Old Man liked, and I listened to a lot of Peter Frampton and The Eagles and Journey once I had my own money to spend on records, because that's what I liked. Everything Davy's folks had was classical, however, so I began listening to that. It was the perfect soundtrack, oddly enough, for building something.

Certain records I listened to once or twice. Others I listened to dozens of times. I spent huge amounts of time with Mozart, Beethoven, and Bach, but I also fell for the works of Tchaikovsky, Rachmaninoff, Chopin, Mahler, and Debussy, amongst countless others. I came to be able to discern the differences not only amongst composers, but also conductors, soloists, and especially pianists.

If I awoke full of grief or self-pity (which were really the same thing), a few hours with Glenn Gould's second recordings of *The Goldberg Variations* would set me right. On those few occasions when I began living in the future instead of the moment, starting to worry about how to get things that would "make me happy," I could listen to his earlier recordings of the very same pieces and be brought right back to the here and now. I actually came to think of the long dead genius as a close personal friend.

This may sound lonely and depressing, but I assure you it was not. During this time, I cannot say I was lonely. I was learning to love and forgive myself and, in times when I did get lonesome, I could go into town and see folks, have lunch, visit with whomever was around, and occasionally even meet a similar soul of the opposite sex with whom to spend a warmer night.

Once the studio was done, however, I knew I had to shut off the classical soundtrack. Now it was up to me to write my own soundtrack. Now it was time to build something using the tools I loved most and best but had taken for granted for far too long.

CHAPTER 24

I STEP OUT OF Wendy's dressing room, mashing my Stetson down on my head to keep from losing either it or my brains. Insanity Salad *indeed! Have I already lost my mind? What have I just done? I have just changed the arrangements, orchestrations, lighting, and costuming for a Best Song nominee, not to mention the piano player, less than an hour before the song is to be performed live to a television audience of some twenty million people!*

I tried to get Wendy to change her mind, but she wouldn't do it. Now look what I've done. If I didn't have twenty years in the music business under my belt, I'd just say that this time the show doesn't need to go on.

I lean against a cinderblock wall under a "No Smoking" sign and light up a Marlboro. With my All Access Performer laminate around my neck and the strain of the obstacles facing me apparent on my face, I doubt anyone is going to hassle me about a quick smoke. I review my mental landscape.

Trash Bag knows what we're up to and has notified

the director and the lighting guys of the fairly minimal changes. They are mostly taking things away, rather than adding them, so it's not a complete disaster for them, I guess. Trash Bag doesn't seem too much more angry than usual. I have gone through the arrangement with Wendy, and I made notations on the orchestration and delivered them to the conductor's assistant, who has assured me he will get with the maestro at next commercial break and notify him of the changes, giving him the chance to warn the musicians. I am actually least concerned about the orchestra. They are highly trained professionals and can react quickly to these types of last-minute changes. Playing whatever is on the page as edited and interpreted by the man on the podium is what they do.

I'm more concerned about the band. Wendy will get me together with them in a little while, but they're used to the old arrangement and won't be using charts. The changes for them are less significant, but the drummer and bass player are going to have to pay close attention. This is ridiculously stupid. Trash Bag should beat me up. What time is it? I'm thirsty. I still feel about half in the bag. There's the Talent Lounge. I'll go get a water or a Coke. I put out my cigarette and head on over.

I enter the Talent Lounge and immediately feel a bit more relaxed. I guess that's the point of this place, after all. Instead of the bare cinderblock walls, there are tall racks on casters with black pleated velvet hanging from them like soft shower curtains. The overhead fluorescents are dimmed, and there are lamps casting a far less garish light on the black leather couches and blond wood coffee and end tables scattered about the room.

There is a bar at one end and a table with peeled shrimp and other goodies on the other wall. Monitors sit atop stands throughout the room, allowing one to keep

*track of what's happening on stage from virtually any
vantage point. Madonna appears to be wrapping up a
"duet" with Elvis a la "Unforgettable" by Natalie and
Nat "King" Cole. It seems they have one of these every
year now. The sound is down, but unless I miss my guess,
they're doing "Viva Las Vegas."*

*I need something to drink. I turn for the bar and
stand face to face with The Boss. I am not entirely certain
I am past the stage of shitting my pants.*

"Zack Fluett?" says Bruce Springsteen, impossibly.

*I make a noise that makes him look at me oddly. It
sounds like, "Muflhumuhay." Instead I nod and smack
my lips. I really am thirsty.*

*Springsteen sticks out his hand. "Bruce Springsteen,"
he says, utterly unnecessarily. He looks fantastic, nowhere near his nearly sixty years, trim, dressed in his
traditional black on black, open- necked silk shirt, cowboy boots, looking, well, looking like a rock star.*

"Pleashameecha," I slur, gripping his hand.

*It doesn't matter how big Cultural Wasteland was
back in the day. There are certain stars that are just different, childhood heroes who you continue to treat with
awe despite how cynical you might get about the business.
Springsteen is one of them for me. I have all his records, although I admit that the first one was* Born in the
U.S.A. *I know it's not hip to love that record, but I do,
and more importantly, it introduced me to his music so I
could then go back and learn the brilliance of* Nebraska,
Darkness on the Edge of Town, *and* The River, *as well
as his earlier work and much of his work since then. Also,
my own piano style was heavily influenced by E-Street
monster David Sancious, especially from* Born to Run.

*The Boss seems to understand that I am at a loss. I
suspect this happens to him often. He puts his left hand*

on my right forearm and extricates himself from my grip. I let go immediately and feel incredibly foolish. He is incredibly kind.

"Let's go get a drink, can we? I'd like to talk to you."

I nod. I was going to do something, but this seems more important right now. What was it that I was going to do? That's it. I was going to get a drink. This is perfect!

We amble over to the bar and Bruce makes it easy for me, ordering two Cokes.

"You drink Coke?" he says.

"Sure. That'd be great."

He hands me a Coke. I feel suspiciously like I am suddenly in a Coke commercial. I feel a wave of emotion. Even the Old Man would be impressed with this. He always thought the Vietnam vets got a raw deal, and he would listen to Born in the U.S.A. *with me on the eight-track player in the pickup on the way into town on bleak winter mornings. It is the last album I bought on eight-track and the only one I have owned in that format, LP, cassette, CD, and MP3.*

Right now I miss the Old Man as much as I have since the moment of his death. He was my first hero, and he took it with excellent grace when The Boss became a new kind of hero for me, as we grew apart.

"I'm sorry I couldn't play on The Death of Fun," *says Bruce.*

"Me too," I agree, for no apparent reason other than that I don't feel like disagreeing with The Boss. His mention of The Death of Fun *makes me think of Woody Creek, which makes me think of sort of the closest I ever got to Bruce Springsteen, which was one time when I opened for Rick Springfield when he was at the Belly Up in Aspen, which prompts me to laugh.*

The Boss looks at me oddly. I shake my head to clear it. I'm not making sense here. Wait a minute. What did he just say?

"Wait a minute. You wanted to play on The Death of Fun?"

"Sure. Unfortunately, when your people asked, I was on tour. You know how that goes. I couldn't just leave, and by the time we got back, you were all finished. You didn't need me anyway. It's a great record."

I stand there stunned.

"Well," says Bruce, clearly growing a little tired of my lack of communication skills, "It was nice talking to you. Call me if you ever do another project like that one and we'll see. I gotta get cleaned up a little for the cameras now."

He sticks his hand out again, and this time I shake it properly and smile. "Thanks a lot," *I say.* "It was very nice talking to you. And good luck tonight!"

He grins. "I'd wish you the same, but you don't need it."

He heads off. I take off my hat and look down at my rumpled tux. It occurs to me that I am nominated for Song of the Year, and I am going to be playing that song onstage in just a little while. Perhaps I, too, should think about getting a little cleaned up for the cameras. I scan the room, catching a glimpse of pink denim and silver slippers. Alain. He'll be able to help me out.

CHAPTER 25

Bill Graham: 1/8/31-10/25/91
Bill Graham, the quintessential rock concert promoter and impresario, was killed last night in a helicopter crash near Vallejo while returning home from a Huey Lewis and The News concert at the Concord Pavilion. Also killed in the crash were Graham's girlfriend Melissa Gold and the pilot Steve Kahn.

San Francisco Examiner, October 26, 1991

PROBABLY THE BEST SONG Lark and I ever wrote together was "Rain in Her Eyes," which is another song that was never a hit single but that developed a life of its own. It was on the first Cultural Wasteland album, appeared on the *Live!* album, was in a well-respected indie flick, and was technically the only Dray/Fluett composition to appear on Lark's solo acoustic album. I'm sure it pained him to do it, knowing that I would get paid my song publishing royalties on it, but I think it's fair to say that we both loved that song more than we despised each other.

It was in the waning days of August West, in

the room I shared with a couple of hysterical med students on Cole Street. Who knew med students could be so much fun? In any event, Lark came by with his guitar one night and flopped on my futon. I had put the Fender-Rhodes in the apartment because it was just too heavy to schlep from gig to gig, and I liked having something to play if I got an idea in the middle of the night.

"If you run into Carol, tell her I was with you all night last night. We drank beer and Jägermeister and tried to write a new song until we passed out," Lark declared.

"OK." I was noodling around with a chord progression on the Rhodes, trying to figure out if I could rip off "Here Come Those Tears Again" by Jackson Browne without anyone noticing. I figured I could.

"What's that?"

"Oh, just a little something I've been messing around with."

"Sounds like something I've heard before."

"It won't when I'm through with it."

"What is it?

I turned around in annoyance. "It's just the basic chord progression from "Here Come Those Tears Again" by my man Jackson."

Lark flipped over on his stomach and pulled a pillow over his head.

"No, no, no! Make it stop!"

I kicked the bottom of his size-thirteen work boots. "Fuck off! Just because you think four chords in a song is one too many!"

Lark rolled back over and pulled the pillow off his face, sitting up resigned. "No man, that's not it. I'm coming over to the dark side on Mr. Browne. I just don't want to hear any crying songs right now."

"Does this relate to your 'passing out' here last night?"

"Uh, yeah."

I spun all the way around on my stool and gave him my undivided attention. "Who did you do?"

"Nobody important, just someone I met in Golden Gate Park the other day during the Bill Graham concert, but I spaced out on dinner with Carol, didn't call—you know the drill."

"So? You do that all the time. I do that all the time. So she hits you over the head with a shovel and you move on."

"See, that's just the deal. She didn't. I went by her place, and I stand there outside her door, and I tell her this obvious lie about spending the night with you, right? And she just stands there and looks at me with this look, I don't know, like she totally doesn't believe me but it doesn't matter because whatever I say or do is just fine with her, like some dog that knows you're going to kick it or some deer that knows you're going to run it down, but it isn't going anywhere. You know?"

"Not really."

"Maybe those aren't the best examples, but she's basically just listening to this line of utter bullshit, and she's smiling at me like 'Oh, you must be tired after your long night of drinking and songwriting, and I completely understand, and why don't you have a shower and a nap and we'll have dinner another time,' but she's got the old rain in the eyes, you know just glistening like, so you know that inside she knows exactly what happened. I just feel sick."

"Rain in the eyes?"

"Yeah, you know what I mean."

"I do. I totally do." I turned and began playing some chords, inspired by Jackson, but different in both key and progression. I began to hum a melody line, some nonsense words, then hit a simple three-chord chorus, one of those than can go on forever and you want it to, and then I sang out "Just standing there with rain in her eyes."

"What are you doing?"

"We're writing a song. Pick up your guitar."

"I just told you I don't want to hear about this stuff. I feel bad enough as it is."

"Bad enough to change your ways?"

Lark looked at me as if I had grown a third head, surprised and annoyed that I was not joining or at least facilitating his little pity party.

"Right. When we go to L.A., are you going to bring Carol along?"

Same look, slightly more incredulous.

"All right then. So you're an asshole, and you feel a little bad about it, but it isn't going to change your behavior, and you're going to break this poor girl's heart one way or the other, right? I'm not judging you here. I do the same things. We're going to be Rock Stars. We're going to break people's hearts and do things that we feel bad about. It's the nature of the game. Am I right?"

Lark shrugged.

"OK then, so we should at least have the common decency to write a song about it. We admit it! We're assholes and liars, but we do have feelings. And so, whether it's pity or apology, we at least acknowledge Carol and every other girl who's had the old rain in her eyes."

"I just got a chill."

"Yeah, I'm pretty proud of myself. That was good bullshit."

"What're the chords?"

Ironically, we actually did stay up most of that night smoking cigarettes, drinking beer and Jäegy, writing the song. My music and Lark's words. I give him credit; he poured his soul out. He spoke of the secrets we hold inside and the lies we tell rather than really communicating our true feelings. He actually really surprised me with the depth of what he was talking about. I changed a few words here and there, but most of what I said was, "Yep, that's true." I felt good about what amounted to a confession, even if there was no absolution to be found.

As we worked, I wrote down the music and the lyrics on blank sheet music, something few of our peers did and the other members of August West (none of whom could read or write music at the time) thought was pretty cool and put us above the other bands on our circuit. Mostly, though, it just meant that we didn't forget what we wrote in a blackout.

The next day, Lark had the decency to show up at Carol's again, this time honestly smelling of booze and three days without a shower, and he had the decency to just go ahead and break up with her. Carol had the decency to throw a potted begonia at him, apparently just missing the old melon, if you believe his version of the story, which I do, because Carol had been a college volleyball player and certainly could have kicked my ass. She then ran for the knife drawer. Lark ran for the hills. This being San Francisco, hills were abundant, and he escaped without injury.

I don't know if Carol ever knew that she was the girl with rain in her eyes or if she would have cared. For me, I had a girl or two with rain in her eyes, but I didn't do anything about it or learn anything from the process of writing the song because just admitting you're a self-centered asshole is only the first step. You also have to think about the consequences of your actions on others—something I failed to do. Just ask my parents. Or Claudia.

CHAPTER 26

Abba Icke Lek den här Högljudd
Amerikanen band Cultural Wasteland blåste in i
Stockholm Revisorn siste natt och blåste bort den
sålde - ute Svensk folkmassa med deras musiker,
kraft, och ren omisskännlig volym. Vanligtvis
den här anmälaren finnar en ut över volym me-
del en brist på talenten, utom Lark Dray's liga
av tokig raketen lik den var den 70s över det alla
igen. Den här var den tredje stopp på en utsträckt
Europeisk göra en rundresa.

The Stockholm City, September 5, 1994

THE FIRST EUROPEAN CULTURAL Wasteland
tour (and my last) was a gas. It was the height of
my days as a Rock Star, which turned out to be bad
timing and dangerously combustible. Touring the
U.S. had been great fun, but overseas was awesome.
One of the problems with touring the U.S. is that
you have to deal with Americans and the American
press. If you are an American band, you are pre-
sumed to speak and understand American English.
Hence, if you are leaving a club and someone shouts

out a question or comment, you can either answer, pretend not to hear, or ignore them. If you are in a foreign land, on the other hand, you get the added option of pretending not to understand (or actually not understanding), which then allows for the totally charming non sequitur.

For example, "Is it true that you deflowered our best hopes for a gold medal in gymnastics?" can be answered, "I love Luxembourg, especially the gardens of the royal palace!" This is incredibly handy.

Also, foreign groupies are better. This is not an unpatriotic statement. It is an opinion born of years on the road. American groupies fall into two basic categories: "Yeah, baby," and "Oh, dear." These categories can be summarized as the pros versus the amateurs.

By pros I do not mean to imply prostitution. Pro groupies are the ones that are into it because they dig rock stars in general and get off on being able to finagle their way backstage and then see how far they can get, the lead singer's hotel room being the Holy Grail. Pro groupies rarely fuck; they generally give hand jobs or maybe blowjobs. And pro groupies rarely care whether you get them off or not; that's not why they're there.

Pro groupies like the thrill of the chase, champagne in the suite, and a mouthful of rock-star they can tell their other pro groupie friends about the next day at lunch. They usually have jobs as administrative assistants, wear nice shoes, and like to compare and contrast the equipment, capabilities, personal hygiene habits, and other intimate details of various rock stars among one another. In short, "Yeah, Baby."

Amateur groupies, on the other hand, have a screw loose. These are the girls and women (and they do, in fact, come in all ages and marital statuses) for whom, no matter how they may pretend to deny it (or openly embrace it), there is a genuine fixation on a particular member of a given group (it's still usually the lead singer or guitar player, but not always). An amateur groupie sincerely thinks she is in love with the guy on stage. She thinks that, if only he got to know her, there would be immediate soul recognition, love at first sight, and then she would be spirited out of Des Moines to live happily ever after in a mansion in the Hollywood Hills.

It is a strange manifestation of this psychosis that the amateur groupie will not find it troubling that she may have to blow two roadies and a security guard and fuck the drummer in order to get to the moment of soul recognition with the target of her obsession. This is a good thing for roadies, security guards, and drummers. It's also good for the lead guitar player if he really wants to screw the hell out of someone or feel loved and taken care of, sometimes even for a few shows in a row. Unfortunately, unlike the pros who go back to their administrative assistant jobs, the amateur roadies are the ones that give rock stars a bad name, being as they are the ones left at the truck stop in Lodi or the ones that wind up bringing paternity suits even though the kid belongs to the high school boyfriend they left behind, or the rogue legitimate paternity suit that winds up costing a drummer an arm and a leg (something drummers cannot afford). In short, "Oh, Dear."

In any event, foreign groupies are not like this. Foreigners are, by definition, not American. By this,

I mean that, for the most part, they are not constrained by the religious and social mores of American culture prevalent for most of our history except for the period 1967 to 1981, during which period I was too young to be a Rock Star.

I am also not commenting on Middle Eastern, African, or Asian groupies. I'm talking about European and Scandinavian groupies. It is not a gross overgeneralization, I don't think, to state that both women and men from the old country have a more relaxed attitude toward sex. Hence, the acceptability of mistresses in French culture and weekend group sex getaways in Norway. Not to mention leather bars in Germany, but that's probably a different deal.

One of the major differences in foreign groupies is that they don't try to get a hotel room key from a roadie by showing their tits at the show, and they don't hang around by the backstage gate, trying to get through security. Instead, they somehow seem to know where the band is going to be having dinner after the show, and they show up there, usually in small groups, and they hang out, smoking and drinking and flirting with their eyes, until you notice them and send them a drink or invite them over. In this way, it's a lot like going to a club and picking a girl up, except that there isn't any competition. The foreign men recognize that there are rock stars in the room, and they just stay out of the way.

My theory on this is that it is a tacit deal they have with the women that allows the men to take female American tourists away from their boyfriends at the beach even as the foreign girlfriends look on, smoking, from the boardwalk cafes and bars. This seems a fair trade to me, as there are many more tourists than there are rock stars.

In any event, whether pros or amateurs, home-grown or foreign, the concept of the groupie is always the same. She wants to be close to you because you stand up there under the hot lights, doing something very few people can do and that even fewer ever get the chance to do. They don't know anything about you, in reality. They don't care if you're smart, or funny, or caring, or kind. They don't necessarily care if you're good-looking in person, just so long as you are well lit and cool looking on stage.

With the exception of the truly demented amateurs, your typical groupie has hung around a long time if she gets coffee. Usually they're gone before the hangover starts. They're filling an empty spot in their own lives, just for a moment, maybe a night or two a year, and that's all it is. By the same token, however, they're also filling an empty spot in the rock star's life, one night at a time, one town at a time, while out on the road for months at a time, family generally left thousands of miles behind.

You could very easily say that there was no excuse whatsoever to be knee-deep in a six-foot blonde girl in Stockholm when I had just gotten married three months earlier to a woman I truly loved. You could also say that it was a mistake to get married as quickly as Claudia and I did, especially given that Cultural Wasteland was just taking off. The odds of travel and groupies becoming a nail-studded two-by-four on the road to lifelong happiness were obvious. I should have known it. She should have known it. It was all a mistake. Maybe so, but after thinking about it for fifteen years, I have repeatedly come to the conclusion that if we had gone on vacation in Ibiza, she would not have wandered off with some guy named Pasqual she met on the beach.

I have no defense. I cheated on her when we were on the road in the U.S. Not every night, mind you, and only rogue blowjobs, but behavior that I knew would have pissed her off. I certainly would have been livid if I had found her firing up the old sno-cone on the pizza delivery guy. But at that time we weren't yet married, it was our first big tour, and everyone was having a ball, so I didn't want to act the prude or like I was being judgmental.

That's how I justified it to myself, anyway, but the simple truth is, when you're twenty-seven years old and you're up there under the bright lights and the chicks are throwing themselves at you, sometimes you just feel entitled to a little head. This is because being a Rock Star gives you a big head.

After that tour, and after the incredible wedding that followed it, you'd like to think that I would have it out of my system and that I would be thinking straight out there. And I did think about it; I did hit the road that time with the full intention of being good. Play the show, have some dinner and a few drinks, lay off the blow, hit the hay, and make sure to call Claudia every night. That was the plan, and I actually pulled it off for our two gigs in England, one in London and one in Manchester.

It was actually easy because we were used to the States and hadn't yet figured out the way things work in Europe. No groupies were waiting for us outside security, they weren't stalking us at our hotel, and our guitar tech Lars, famous for his abilities in this regard, had yet to find us a decent supply of coke. So we did the shows, went to pubs and drank gallons of piss, as they say, and then let jet lag take its natural course. I made my calls, and it all looked like it was going to work out fine. Very professional.

The second country we stopped in was Sweden. There, the wheels fell off in Keystone Kops fashion. First, Lars was from Stockholm, so he promptly got hold of a crapload of blow. Second, Lars was from Stockholm, so he insisted on taking us out to one of his favorite late night restaurants after the show. Third, Lars was from Stockholm, so he told everyone he knew that we would be coming, including his cousin Anita, whom he had promised to introduce to Lark.

This turned out to be both fortunate and devastating for me, because Anita was not very good-looking and promptly laid claim to Lark (he seemed to have no huge problem with this) fairly soon after we all began drinking together. This left me, wearing my wedding ring and all, as the logical choice when her friend Britt showed up an hour later. This was to be the beginning of my downfall.

Britt was, quite literally, six feet tall, and the most ridiculously stereotypical Scandinavian girl imaginable: Long, natural blonde hair, hard bod with big tits, perfect teeth, and bone structure that would have driven Hitler out of his mind. She also had these incredible ice-blue eyes that surveyed everything around her languorously but could bore into you in a moment once you started talking about something that interested her. She was pursuing her Ph.D. in Art, and her English was excellent, though delightfully accented. I thought she was smart and pretty funny, seeing as she laughed at my jokes. She drank and did a little blow, but was one of the few

Europeans I met who didn't smoke, which might account for the teeth.

Britt did not come back to the hotel when everyone was getting ready to go. Instead she asked me if I would like to take a walk and see some of her city, as I was scheduled to leave the next day to continue the Scandinavian leg of the tour. We walked around Stockholm for an hour or so, and then we stopped in a doorway, and she kissed me, and I kissed her back.

"This is my place right here. Would you like to come up and spend the night?"

This was my chance to say no. This was my chance to have a perfectly lovely and largely innocent evening with a nice lady who had showed me her town. I could then go back to the hotel and figure out if it was time to call my wife yet.

"I'd love to."

And so I did. And it was marvelous. Absolutely marvelous. When I awoke the next morning, there was the smell of coffee and eggs and the apartment was warm and soft with light. I pulled my jeans on and walked into the kitchen where Britt was wearing only an apron and panties, which somehow was just a massive turn-on. She turned the gas off under the eggs and we screwed quickly on the kitchen table. Then she turned the gas back on and we enjoyed a nice breakfast. I had to get back to the hotel pretty soon, as they'd start looking for me so we could get on the road. I almost didn't want to go, I was so comfortable there. I hadn't even thought of Claudia.

"You have to go now, yes?"

"I'm sorry to say that I do. I wish I didn't have to. I would love to spend more time with you."

"I can get a bag together in five minutes and come

with you, just for Oslo, Helsinki, and Copenhagen, if you want."

The first strike of terror. Suddenly I could see Claudia in my mind's eye, and I realized what I had done. I could see myself getting on the bus with Britt. Everyone, many of whom had been to my wedding, would be looking at me like stuffed wolves. I'm sure my facial expression displayed all of those emotions immediately, because Britt finished her coffee, dabbed her mouth with a napkin, and stood up from the table.

"Maybe not such a good idea," she said, then untied and pulled the apron over her head, set it on the counter, and turned back to the bedroom.

"No, no! It's a wonderful idea!" shouted out my penis, unexpectedly using my vocal chords. Did I mention her fabulous tits?

Her blue eyes bored through me, and then she smiled. "I'll get a bag. There's a new toothbrush on the sink. Wash your face and get dressed. We don't want to be late."

Getting on the bus was easier than I expected, except for the fact that it was crowded. There were already three Swedish girls there, each with what amounted to a tiny stewardess bag. I can only assume that the girls from Finland, Norway, and Denmark hate Swedish girls, because we never came close to meeting one of them during our time in Scandinavia. These girls were not amateurs who had fallen in love and would be left at a truck stop outside of Kotka. They were not pros about to return to work and dish on their big nights. They were, well, Swedish.

None of us boys on the bus really looked at one another except for Lark, who stared at me darkly

and looked pissed off. I wasn't sure if it was because I was with Britt or because he was still alone,
or maybe a little of both, but I didn't think much of
it. I just avoided his glare and took Britt back to chat
with the Ramos brothers and their dates for the next
week, and that was how it was left. Nothing much
needed to be said. It did, however, set the tone for
the rest of the tour, which for me would be a disaster.

CHAPTER 27

THINGS ARE LOOKING UP. Alain has found me a dressing room where I can get cleaned up. There are a dozen locker and dressing rooms at the Staples Center. The one I occupy was most recently used by the backup dancers for TJ Corey, but they are now about to go onstage to perform "I Love You Because I'm Lonely," the Song of the Year nominee from his breakout solo album away from The Coreys, Here I Come, *so it became available for me. I would have liked to have seen TJ's performance, just for old times' sake, but one look in the mirror made it clear that all the running and sweating and yoga falls had left me looking pretty rumpled. Best to attend to my own situation.*

I'm seated on a bench with the contents of my Grammy bag around me, along with a stack of towels that would pass muster at the Four Seasons. I had nearly forgotten all the amenities available to performers at a big show. I guess I'll be paying taxes on the hair care products, at the very least. I wonder what the taxes on Guitar Hero III *might be. That and the gold bracelet I stashed for Claudia.*

Alain has taken my tux and shirt to wardrobe to be pressed, and he insisted on giving the Old Man's boots a little shine, too. That was nice. I have to admit to having been a bit uncomfortable undressing in front of him, especially since I haven't purchased new underwear in a while, but he was polite and kept his eyes averted for the most part. I guess I could just bite the bullet and pay the taxes on the new DKNY underwear too and get a whole new fresh start. I wrap a towel around my waist and pad across the petroleum black dressing room floors with a bottle of shampoo in hand. I hang up my towel and step into the shower.

The water is instantly hot and feels incredibly refreshing. I could stand here for hours, but time is still of the essence, so I start lathering up quickly. I wish I had had the opportunity to take this shower before I met Springsteen. Maybe I would have been a little more responsive. That was a pretty poor showing for a first-time meeting with The Boss. I was definitely a little in the bag and had a lot going on in my head, but it was certainly a missed opportunity. I can't believe he was interested in playing on The Death of Fun. *Claudia never mentioned that, probably because she knew I would have been really disappointed if I had known about it. Nonetheless, the night is still young. Maybe I'll run into him again after I get finished trying my best not to wreck Wendy's entire evening.*

Rinsing the shampoo out of my hair I realize that the Stetson issue is now blessedly solved. No hat, but no hat head either. A fresh start, indeed. How many of those have I had? How many of those have I blown?

"Zack? Are you in there?"

Goodness me. This is unexpected. "I'm in the shower!" *I squeak.*

"Oh good. I haven't seen you naked in years."

Holy shit! I slam off the water, lather still sluicing down my body, and blast my way out of the shower, grabbing for my towel and realizing, an instant too late, that I have failed to put one down on the slippery Staples Center locker room floor. Wet, soapy feet meet damp, hardened petrochemicals. I am skating. I snap the towel across my belly and hold it across my back with my right hand, looking for something to grab with my left as I zoom toward the sinks and vanity of the vast dressing room bath.

I realize that I am acting stupidly and am headed for a hell of a wreck. I was willing to let Alain watch me get undressed, but I'm suddenly afraid to let Claudia see me? She's seen it all before! Well, there wasn't this much of it the last time she saw all of it. I really do have to get serious about working out.

All this flashes through my head as the door opens. Claudia gives me a bemused look as I slide past. I struggle to stop myself, but only succeed in turning from a forward slide to a backward slide, orbiting past her as the moon does the Earth, my front side always facing her, my back now to the wall.

"Hi," I say, nonchalantly, left hand raised in greeting like a vaudevillian about to take his final bow. Ha cha cha cha cha!

Blackness.

CHAPTER 28

Engagement: Fluett/Rankin
Burt and Cherie Fluett are pleased to announce the engagement of their son, Zack, to Claudia Rankin of Philadelphia. The bride-to-be is a graduate of Wellesley College. The groom-to-be is a graduate of Whitlash High School and the keyboard player in the rock act Cultural Wasteland. They live in Los Angeles.

The Whitlash Promoter, June 25, 1994

A MONTH BEFORE THE wedding, I took Claudia to Montana to visit with Mom and the Old Man and to determine if seeing where I grew up made her want to call it off right then and there. She probably should have. We brought along Lark and his girl-friend of the moment, a vegan flower child named Anastasia, and Huge, because I promised him there would be guns and alcohol, which was right up his alley.

Mom and the Old Man hosted a good old-fash-ioned country barbecue our second night there, and then they had the good sense to head into town for a few days, giving us the privacy to get wasted while looking around the ranch. The first day was actually a lot of fun. It was just the five of us, and I drove everyone around the place in the morning on mushrooms, then we came back and played some horseshoes and drank ourselves sober, then we shot a little skeet while the girls tried to nap, and when that didn't work out for obvious reasons, we all went up to the Pothole and went fishing.

Of course, Anastasia, the vegan, caught the biggest fish, so we had to throw that one back, but we made out all right and had a fresh fish fry that night, then watched a meteor shower, where we saw some forty shooting stars in just a few hours. The stars in Montana at night are pretty much unparalleled in the lower forty-eight, and everyone commented on how they couldn't believe that I could ever leave a place that beautiful.

The next morning, I suggested we take a turn around the meadows and hills on horseback. Claudia, of course, was an accomplished rider, but Anastasia announced that she didn't feel the need to be borne about by a noble beast. Neither Lark nor Huge had ever been on a horse, but both were ready for anything, so I went down to the barn to look at what we had in the way of horseflesh and was pleased to find that my old cutting horse, Sundee, was still around, as was Banjo, the Old Man's ancient but top-notch roping horse. Mom's Jingles, the one with the rocking-chair trot, was there too, as was another mount I didn't recognize. The Old Man's new foreman, Joe, was banging around down in the shop, so I ambled down and asked him about the new horse.

"Oh, that's Brandy. She's mine. Thoroughbred.

Used to be a race horse."

"I thought she looked a little different."

"Pretty, ain't she?"

I nodded.

"You oughta try her out. She's fast as the wind."

"Not much call for a thoroughbred up here, is there?"

"She ain't worth a shit as a cuttin' horse, but she's fast as hell. I just like to ride her when I'm giving things a looksee or ridin' fence. Otherwise I ride that old Sundee."

"My horse."

"If you say. Good cuttin' horse."

"Yup."

"You oughta try my Brandy, though. She's a fast one!"

"Well, that's just the thing, Joe. I got three greenhorn friends with me who want to go for a ride today. We'll go slow and they'll be OK on any of the Old Man's mounts."

"You oughta try my Brandy."

"You don't mind then?"

"You try her. I'll get her saddled up for you. You'll like her. She's fast."

"Well, we're probably gonna take it pretty easy, but I do appreciate the mount."

"No problem. Just mind you remember that she likes to take the lead when she's around the other horses. Guess it's the racehorse in her."

"Gotcha."

And so an hour or so later Anastasia waved good-bye to the four of us, Huge on Sundee, Lark on old Banjo, Claudia on Jingles, and me on Joe's Brandy, leading the way as we walked out through the east gate and up toward the high country. Huge and Lark both wore tennis shoes, torn jeans and t-shirts, but Claudia had on a split skirt and equestrian boots she had brought along for the occasion. I was wearing a pair of the Old Man's boots, an old pair of Levis I had found in a closet, a white flannel shirt, and my grandfather's ancient straw Stetson Roadrunner. I looked quite cowboyish, I reckoned.

We took it easy for the first mile or so, just walking along the Crick Field road, a well-worn two-wheel track made by decades of pickup trips to deliver cake and salt to the cattle in winter pasture. I myself had made the run many times, once pushing the blocks off the tailgate in thirty-degree below weather with a wind chill factor of ninety below. I shivered involuntarily at the old memory despite the beautiful day—sunny and low eighties with just enough of a breeze to keep the bugs down.

I took my friends across to a big open meadow and worked with Lark and Huge on how to post at a trot so as not to destroy their chances of having a family someday, and then how to sit forward into a canter to make yourself one with the horse. I taught them to lean back going downhill and to kick into a gallop going up, but mostly just to keep your center and let the horse pretty much do what it wants. This is a wise approach because the horse knows more than you, and also because it's pretty much going to do what it wants anyway. The trick is just to make sure you convince it that what you want to do just so happens to be what it wants to do too.

Claudia got along just fine, although the Western saddle did take her a little getting used to. I liked seeing the shine in her eyes as she watched me move Brandy around, forward and back, with the confidence and arrogance of the cowboy I had once been, and I liked the smiles and respect I got from Lark and Huge, both of whom were enjoying themselves and following my instructions with deference. So I added in a few little unnecessary cowboy tricks here and there, and I smoked and used phrases like "crow hop" and "slonchwise" and made something of a show of dismounting to open all the barbed wire gates and then spinning Brandy around in a tight circle as I mounted up. In short, I showed off for my friends, allowing karma an opportunity to show her bitchy little face.

We passed an hour or so up there and then walked the horses back to the barn on our way over to the lake. I explained to my cohorts how you never run a horse back to the barn and shared all kinds of other utterly useless insights with them. Everyone played along gamely. When we got back to the barn, Joe asked me what I thought of Brandy.

"Nice mount, Joe."

"She's a fast one, isn't she?"

"Aw we've just been hackin' around a little. I haven't turned her loose. You know, gotta keep an eye on the tinhorns." My friends smiled obligingly.

"Well, you oughta try her out when you get the chance. She's fast."

"We'll see. We're heading down to the lake now."

We walked away through the alfalfa field, tall and wet and green, then trotted the mile or so to the Pothole, where we got in a pretty good little gallop. We took a break to drink the cold, clear water of Fred & George Crick as it tumbled over rocks and into a small pool before flowing into the lake. Once on the ground, Lark and Huge immediately acknowledged that they were sore as hell in the legs, ass, and balls, so we lounged around for a while, chewing on timothy and watching perfect cotton-ball clouds float across the impossibly blue sky, before mounting up and turning for home again at a walk.

Halfway across the alfalfa field I saw Joe sitting and waiting on the barn fence. "Oh all right," I thought. "I'll turn loose your damn thoroughbred."

"Why don't you guys just keep heading back? I'm going to turn Brandy out and see if she's as fast as Joe says."

Everyone assented, and I called out a reminder to keep to a walk on the way to the barn. Huge looked at me as if I were an idiot. There was no way he was likely ever to gallop again.

I turned Brandy back into the alfalfa and put the spurs to her. She took off like a shot, and I had to tuck my feet back for a second to catch my balance. Then I set my boot heels low in the stirrups and leaned forward, rein hand and face low over Brandy's neck and right hand on my hip, just like the Old Man liked to see, and we flat flew through that field. My heavens, but that horse was fast.

We had cut a couple of wide S turns through the alfalfa when the combination of our velocity and a rogue cross breeze took my grandfather's Roadrunner off my head. I took Brandy on a wide, fast loop to the left and then turned back into the swath we had cut in the hay, pulled her up, and slowed down to a walk. I found the hat, dismounted, and picked it up. With the reins in my left hand and hat in the other, I turned Brandy around and put my left foot into the stirrup just as Brandy saw the other horses a quarter mile in front of her on the way to the barn. Instantaneously I was reminded: Brandy always has to be in the lead....

Too late. Off she went on a dead sprint for the finish line. I tried desperately to pull myself up, but despite my showing off earlier, I wasn't truly in riding shape. The hat in my right hand was preventing me from getting a grip on the saddle, and Brandy was just too damned fast anyway. We were headed for a hell of a wreck.

After about a hundred yards, I knew I had no choice and just gave up, letting go the reins and kicking myself out of the stirrup high and backwards. In my memory's eye, I can see Joe standing on the fence and pointing, and my friends all turning in their saddles to watch as Brandy broke hell bent for leather for the barn while I hovered in midair like Wile E. Coyote before cartwheeling through the wet green alfalfa at twenty-five miles per hour, turning my confident white cowboy shirt into a green and brown Jackson Pollock along the way.

The impossibly blue sky went black.

CHAPTER 29

LIGHT.

"*I think he's coming around.*"

I look up and see Claudia's face again, looking somewhat concerned.

"*Did I fall off the horse?*"

"*You are the horse, Blewitt. Put that thing away!*"

I look around. Trash Bag is grinning and pointing at my towel, which is no longer covering what it should be covering.

Claudia turns away with a giggle as Trash Bag and a couple of roadies help me to my feet.

"*You're just going to be the bane of my existence tonight, aren't you?*" *says Trash Bag. "You OK? I'm fresh out of pianists.*"

"*Yeah, I'm OK. Little fuzzy and headachy.*" *I touch a rising knot on the back of my skull. Definitely no hat now. "I just need my clothes.*"

On cue, Alain steps up, holding my fresh tux and shirt. He hangs them on hooks over my freshly buffed boots. I smile gratefully as the crowd returns to their various duties.

"Are you sure you're OK?" asks Claudia. "That was pretty spectacular."

Her smile makes me feel instantaneously better. "I just need to get ready. I'll be fine. You heard I'm playing?"

"I did. That's why I dropped by. To tell you to break a leg."

"It almost worked," I respond dryly. She laughs. "That's only for the theater, you know, not for television shows."

"Duly noted. Then I'll just wish you good luck."

"I should have just asked you to join me in the shower. None of this would have happened."

"Your luck's not that good," she says, but with a smile.

Claudia leaves and I don the new DKNY underwear, very soft and comfy, and then my shirt and tux. The trousers have a crisp crease again, and my white pleated shirt is starched and still warm from the iron. I sit down on a bench to pull on my boots. Goodness me. Alain has refilled my flask. Such service. I do so like it better backstage at the Staples Center.

I'm curious as to what he put in there. I open the flask and sniff. Definitely tequila. Good man, that Alain. I wonder if he even got the brand right? Well, only one way to find that out. But I've already had more than enough for one night, and I'm due on stage here pretty quick. On the other hand, the shower has sobered me up quite a bit, and my head is throbbing.

Alcohol is a general anesthetic. Might help the headache. I take a quick pull. Nope, not Fortaleza. Pretty good though, nonetheless. What might that be? Another pull. Heradura? Maybe. Just one more out of curiosity's sake. *Warmth begins spreading through my body, and my head does indeed seem to hurt less. This is definitely helping! It's smokier than Heradura, but I can't place it.*

Suddenly the light dawns and I look over at my pile of Grammy loot. There it is, the bottle of Esperanto, what I thought was perfume. It's half empty. It turns out that Esperanto is a very acceptable Reposado. Just one more hit out of respect for its makers and the Grammy gift-bag people.

The door opens and four lithe young women bound into the room, pulling off tight-fitting clothes and kicking off dance shoes, jabbering excitedly about how well the number went. That's nice. I'm pleased for TJ. He was always the nicest of the Coreys. Someday he'll come out of the closet, and I think he'll be a lot happier.

The scream snaps me out of my pleasant reverie.

"What are you doing in here, pervert?" shouts the brunette dancer, covering her breasts.

Suddenly in my mind's eye I see a middle-aged man slumped on a bench, holding a flask, one boot on, one boot off, staring pleasantly at a bunch of semi-nude girls in their bathroom. Eek.

"Sorry, sorry. My mistake. Wrong dressing room." I lurch to my feet and stagger toward them and the door. The Esperanto races straight to my head. I am off kilter, walking unevenly in one boot, stocking foot getting wet on the still soapy floor, other boot and flask gripped tightly in my right hand. I reach out my free hand to steady myself, but a young dancer cowers between anything that might help me regain my balance and me. I foresee an unfortunate incident and possibly a lawsuit, but she is an excellent athlete and ducks out of the way at the last second. I thump against the door jam and steady myself.

"Get the fuck out, motherfucker!"

I am kicked in the ass. I wheel out the door and back my way rapidly and apologetically across the vast hallway. I crash backwards into the far wall, whereupon I sit down. Hard. The dressing room door slams. I breathe and give my head a shake to clear it. Ow, that smarts!

"You, sir, are a menace to the Grammys."

Dandy. Lark stands over me, a rather amused look on his face.

"I'm a menace to myself, Lark. The Grammys just keep getting in the way."

He sticks out a hand.

"Hold, please." *I pull my other boot on, replace the flask, and pull my pant leg back down. I take a couple of deep breaths.* "Now, please."

He sticks out his hand again, and I take it in a handshake. He hauls me to my feet. I am reminded how big his mitts are, the grip still familiar even though it has been more than a decade since we last shook hands. I look him in the eye. Fuck, he looks at least ten years younger than I do. I let out a sigh and let go of his hand.

"Thank you."

"You're welcome. I hear you're playing tonight. That's good."

"I don't know. I'm a little the worse for wear. I'm not sure I'm up to it."

"Bullshit, Zack. You're indestructible."

I let out a cynical laugh.

"I tried to kill you every night for God knows how many shows and you're still kicking," *he continues.*

I can't help but smile at the memory. I point to the scar on my chin.

"You almost got me."

"You look better with it. Gives you that Harrison Ford thing."

"If it isn't Party Poopers, Incorporated." Claudia walks up, smiling. I am relieved that I have both boots on and am standing up. "Hello, Lark," she says pleasantly.

"Hello, Claudia," Lark responds, with genuine warmth. "I haven't heard that phrase in a long time. It's good to see you."

"It's nice to see you too, but I'm afraid I have to steal my ex-husband away from this lovely reunion. His meal ticket is looking for him."

"Sure. Have a good time, Zack. I'll see you later." Lark turns and heads off, which isn't a bad thing, because I can see the GDT headed our way.

"That was kind of a mean thing to say." I frown at Claudia.

"You're on in less than fifteen minutes and you smell like Mexico. Suck on this mint and get your shit together or everyone in this godforsaken arena will have something mean to say to you too."

I take the mint. I sincerely wish I hadn't given up cocaine.

CHAPTER 30

> アメリカン　囃子　文化的　荒野　烽火 Budokan 最終
> 夜分. 網羅 アト　壮絶 ギター スロー 又 把握 よ
> り 出し 荷馬車 付き キーボ Lark Dray 俳優 化
> 的 Zack Fluett.
>
> *Tokyo Shimbun*, July 3, 1996

THE GIBSON-THROWING STARTED off as a one-time angry, drunken, on-stage freakout at Budokan. Lark was in a shitty mood because the actress he had been dating at the time back in L.A. had just had a home video of her with a former Heisman trophy winner "stolen" from his place and made wildly public. The Internet was just getting going, and those grainy images of Lark's "girl next door" girlfriend with a big black cock in her mouth probably did as much for the NASDAQ and the dot-com boom as the invention of the modem.

In any event, someone from the label had FedExed us a copy of the video and we checked it out, kind of laughing at the poor girl's misfortune for a stupid mistake in her past, until Lark noticed that when the camera moved down for a lower and more impressive angle, in the background you could see a small statue of a bounding horse. Lark paused the video on the image, and each of us froze, because we remembered him showing the same horse to us backstage after he had purchased it in Kentucky while on tour there less than two months earlier. This video was fresh news.

Lark started drinking immediately. By the time we got to the pre-show question and answer session, he was already pretty loaded, and it didn't help that questions about the video kept coming up. Apparently the Japanese are polite, but very tech-savvy, and they were interested in Lark's thoughts on the Internet's ability to bring new forms of entertainment into our homes.

By the time we got to the stage, he was rotten and getting into Lark-drunk-aggressive mode. We made it through most of the show with Lark snarling like a wolverine the entire time, and the crowd was eating it up. Then, while playing a blistering solo on "This Is Gonna Get Expensive," he managed to break both his B and E strings at the same time. He yanked the guitar off his neck and made as if he were going to smash it on the stage, but he lost his grip and it sailed out of his hands and right at me. If I hadn't been watching him, it probably would have killed me, but I was, and so I stuck my hands up to protect myself and damned if I didn't just catch the fucking thing. Pure stupid luck.

Surprised as hell but damned pleased with myself, I turned to the suddenly hushed audience and held that Les Paul high above my head. Budokan absolutely exploded, and Lark pretty much screamed out the last verse and chorus as the rest of us pounded the living shit out of our instruments. The crowd stayed for at least a half hour after the house lights came up, still cheering what may well have been the most energetic show we ever played.

The next day Lark and I went into a hotel ballroom and began practicing tossing and catching a guitar. The Gibson Les Paul is one of the heaviest solid-body electric guitars going, so I was pretty skeptical. In the first place, I love my fingers more than any other part of my body, except my brain and its boss. A huge hunk of wood flying at me with enough velocity to sail across the better part of a big-ass arena stage raised the immediate specter of jammed or broken digits. A missed throw could also result in injury to either the brain or its boss as well. I suppose someone else could have gotten hurt too, but I honestly didn't really care much. Rock Star and all that.

Nonetheless, I was still pretty high from the events of the night before, especially because there was a photograph of me holding the guitar above my head in the entertainment section of the Tokyo papers that morning. The caption was in Japanese, of course, but I suspected that it said something like: "Cultural Wasteland keyboard player Zack Fluett catches flying guitar in astonishing concert stunt while crowd pays no attention to front man Lark Dray."

Lark and I started off about five feet apart, and he tossed the guitar to me gently. I caught it by the neck and body easily. Then we backed up and did it again. We did this over and over, farther and farther apart, and we learned some things about flying Gibsons. The first thing is, a Les Paul is actually not that hard to catch. Because it is so big, a reasonably accurate throw is unlikely to get past the catcher, and the key is just to make sure you get one hand on the neck and hold on until you get the other hand on the body. The second thing we learned is that this is most easily done if the guitar is sailing through the air on its back, as opposed to tomahawking at the catcher. Fortunately, you can generally throw a Les Paul farther and more easily by just mindlessly chucking it straight over your head than you can by trying to throw it end over end. The farther you throw it, the easier it is to catch, because you have time to get set up for it. It also looks much more impressive the farther it flies, which is a bonus.

So we began incorporating the throw into the concert. Word got around about the stunt, but the crowds still loved to see it, even though they knew it wasn't spontaneous. It just looked really cool and dangerous, which was the point. In fact, I went so far as to have a guitar with wings tattooed on my right forearm, to commemorate our signature concert moment.

Over time, however, Lark began to resent the attention the stunt focused on me. Rather than just let the whole thing fade away, he instead began coming up with new and creative ways to throw the guitar: one-handed from the butt, both hands backwards, both hands underhand like he was throwing it overboard, and so on. He began mugging for the audience on the throws, and suddenly I had to work a whole lot harder to make the catches, because the thing could wind up anywhere. I had to jump out from behind my rig way before he chucked it in order to get ready. Suddenly, I was starting to look like the dog end of a game of fetch instead of the star wide receiver in the back of the end zone.

Then one night in Sydney he threw it one-handed

from the neck and the sumbitch tomahawked straight at me. I should have just ducked out of the way, but in something like twenty shows I hadn't dropped it once, so I hung in there. I managed to reach up underhanded and grab the neck with my right hand, but I couldn't get my left hand on the body and it swung up and hit me flush on the chin. The Aussie crowd roared.

I stared at Lark, and he had this crazy fucking look in his eyes and was grinning that evil grin. I put my hand to my chin and pulled it away. It was covered in blood, and blood was dripping on the stage and down my front. This drove the crowd absolutely wild, crazy with bloodlust as Huge and the boys continued to pound out the powerful bridge riff of "This Is Gonna Get Expensive." Then, without really thinking, I took hold of the Les Paul like it was a battleaxe and hurled it right back at Lark.

His eyes opened wide, and all six feet five inches of him went straight to the floor. The guitar sailed over him and exploded against a Marshall stack. The crowd went apeshit. Although they loved it all, the Aussies, being Aussies, good-naturedly booed Lark for dodging, and when he looked out at the crowd and saw and heard that, he went straight into a white rage and came for me. I met him head-on and we were grappling on the stage and then Chris was trying to break it up and there were roadies pulling us apart and Huge decided this was a good time to go all Keith Moon and destroy his drums and Peter smashed a guitar and the concert ended in utter chaos.

We sold a hundred thousand CDs in Australia in the next week. It's still a record.

CHAPTER 31

My Hypocrisy Knows No Bounds
All right, I admit it. I used my credentials as a
writer for this magazine to score tickets to The
Coreys' sold-out *POP-a-Razzi* concert at Madison Square Garden for my 12-year-old twin
daughters. The many, many pronouncements of
gratitude I have received from them have largely
soothed the tinnitus inflicted on me by this absolutely massive spectacle of light, sound, pyrotechnics, and screaming children. Oh. There was
some music too. It was pretty good if you like
that sort of thing.

Blender, Live Notes, February 1999

I TOLD MELANIE LOCKE, future GDT, the story
of the flying Les Paul over Dungeness crab, a wilted
spinach salad with bacon, and a lovely Gewürztra-
miner in my home in L.A. on our night off between
The Coreys' Vegas and L.A. shows. She had asked
me about the scar on my chin, which she thought
was sexy. She was vaguely familiar at best with Cultural Wasteland, which I thought somewhat odd.

Sure, she was only seventeen when I got canned, but Lark had put out another Cultural Wasteland album after that before going solo, and we were, at least in my mind, pretty damn famous. Fortunately, she was only slightly more vaguely familiar with Lark Dray, referring to him as "that Adult Contemporary guy," which made me feel better.

It turned out Melanie had been sort of living in a cave for a while. Her father was a famous artist who was a complete and total jerk. Arguably a genius, certainly crazy, noncommunicative, passive-aggressive in the extreme, and utterly without a sense of self-examination, he was one of those people who should not have been allowed to have children. To his credit, he figured that out with Melanie and had no more, but that did her no good.

Melanie had no clear memory of her mother due to her mother's decision to put a hose in the exhaust pipe of the Range Rover and sit in the garage with the motor running until the maids came the next morning. Melanie was three. When Melanie was six, she made the mistake of asking Daddy the same question three times, not being satisfied with an answer that was just this side of "because I said so." Unable to deal with such a problem child, Daddy sent Melanie to the first in a series of European all-girl private schools, in which she would stay until she was eighteen.

The most recent had been a boarding school in Zagreb, Croatia, where Melanie had studied dance and art, primarily ballet and German postmodernism, with a minor in strap-ons and vibrators. Left to her own devices, Melanie had discovered masturbating by age eight, had figured out what an orgasm was by ten, and had charitably started sharing her discoveries with her classmates by twelve. As an exchange student in Berlin at seventeen, she had discovered sex shops, and she spent the better part of her final year of formal education fucking the shit out of very flexible, privileged Balkan girls.

Spending the summer after graduation at Daddy's house in Chicago's Evanston suburb, Melanie discovered boys. Specifically, pool boys. When Daddy came home one day to discover Melanie trying out her new tongue piercing on the pool boy he called Chico while another pool boy he had never seen showed her the joys of going organic in terms of dildos, he disowned her on the spot and threw her out of the house.

She made it to Las Vegas, where there is plenty of work for a very hot nineteen-year-old dancer happy to simulate eating pussy on stage every night while auditioning for legitimate dancing gigs during the day. She always had a clean, safe little apartment to herself, and she never hooked or even had to think about it. Her days were spent dancing and fucking, which wasn't all bad, but deep down she knew that someday she did want to get back to the life of high art, nice houses, and pool boys.

During my time in Woody Creek, I wrote a song called "Damaged Goods Magnet." It's about me.

Daddy didn't love you enough? Come to Papa. Mommy verbally abused you and called you worthless? Tell me all about it, honey. Uncle Eddie touched you there? I've got your back, my poor, sweet baby.

Wounded women flock to me. I'm not entirely certain why this is, but I suspect it's because, upon initial review, I seem a very safe harbor, when in fact I am more like any port in a storm. I chalk this up to my own mother. My mother raised me to be polite. I do not mean "please" and "thank you" polite; I mean nineteenth-century polite. I bow upon first meeting a woman. I rise from my seat upon her approach or should she rise from her seat. I open doors, including car doors even if I am in the driver's seat when she approaches. On the sidewalk, I walk to the street side of the lady and frequently cause mild consternation when I move from one side to the other. I pay for everything.

I also grew up in a remarkably stable, loving home to parents who remained married until death parted them, and I am reasonably even-tempered and patient. Although a drunk, I am generally not a belligerent drunk, but tend to be more on the "fun" side, if you consider stealing cars "fun." All of these traits, I believe, are attractive to women who have been mistreated or are in a spot of trouble, and so I appear to them as Prince Charming on his white steed, a role I seek out and relish for reasons that I really must address someday at length with a professional therapist.

Never mind that I am, in fact, utterly self-centered and, sometimes I fear, utterly cold at my very center. Never mind that, although I know I love my family very much, for most of my adult life I didn't call my parents more than once a month or so, I left the ranch without so much as a how-do-you-do concerning its future, I rarely visited, even when the Old Man was sick and dying, and I have not once remembered my sibling's birthday or those of her children, who idolize me.

The little things are solid. I've bailed girls out of jail, rescued them from bad situations, paid off their debts, held them at night when they were afraid, and introduced them to the joys of really great multi-orgasmic sex without fear or guilt.

I am also emotionally unavailable, disloyal on the highest levels, and an inveterate liar. But I'm working on it.

In any event, Melanie took to me.

Because we worked together, we felt the need to be secretive, even though about the worst thing you can do to doom a relationship is to try to keep it secret. There were no rules about fraternizing between band members and dancers, but we didn't want to take any chances that might get either one of us fired. As a result, we were able to keep the affair completely under wraps until just before the first show at the Rose Bowl, six hours after we got out of my bed our first morning together.

The first mistake we made was to show up last and together. We weren't exactly late, but everyone was there to notice us walking in together. Then, in response to raised eyebrows, we each essentially spilled our guts to everyone we knew, in our own fashions.

I imagine Melanie in the dressing room with the other dancers, none over the age of twenty-two, jumping up and down and wringing her hands and saying, "You can't tell anyone, but guess what I just did?!" I would hope that this announcement was followed by the use of the word "dreamy" at some point.

In my case, I was much cooler about the whole thing. I did intend to maintain at least plausible deniability over the affair, and my innate sense of politeness dictated that I not kiss and tell. Nonetheless, being a professional musician tends to place one in a permanent state of suspended adolescence, and so I felt a high-school-locker-room need to make it clear that, yes indeed, I did just screw our hottest cheerleader. I thought I handled the situation reasonably well, all things considered.

"Zacky, you got some 'splaining to do," started in Jorge.

"What?" I said innocently with a fake confused look on my face and a smile in my eyes.

"We saw you come in with that dancer, the one you been staring at and talking to on the phone in 'code'," responded Paul Macalwaite.

"What are you talking about?" I said, a small smile tugging at the corners of my mouth.

"You been hittin' the help," announced Sam Warren.

I believe I actually said, "Nuh-uh!" then followed that gem up with, "Besides, we're all the help!"

"Oh this is bad, this is really bad," said Alexi. "You're not supposed to mess with the dancers, man. You didn't give her any booze, did you? She ain't legal. This is bad, man."

Even though he was smiling, Alexi's comment caught me sideways. I had been thinking about the old "divide by two and add seven" rule, which is, like all rules, meant to be broken and then bragged about, as opposed to the "serving intoxicating beverages to minors" rap. I suppose I looked a bit concerned, so my follow up, "What?" came out differently than intended.

"Hey, don't listen to these guys, man. Nice work!

That's some hot young pussy you just hit and they just jealous," tossed in Torquis.

"What hot young pussy did Blewit just hit?" queried Daryl, walking into the dressing room.

"Old Zack knee-deep in tall-dancer groin gravy," growled Sonny Kaye. Drummers.

I whirled to face Daryl. "I am not!" I pleaded.

Daryl looked at me levelly. "Of course you're not. That would be stupid. Get your shit together and get out of high school, gentlemen. Lockdown in fifteen minutes." He left the room. All was quiet for a moment, and then Torquis silently walked over and bumped fists with me. The rest of the guys lined up and did the same. It was like being the winning pitcher at the end of a ballgame. Nothing more was said.

Once we were on the road and into a routine, things got easier. On show days and travel days, Melanie and I would pretty much stay apart, unless there was a solid three-hour block of free time in the afternoon. On those occasions, Melanie would break away from the other dancers to go do a little yoga, and I would claim that I needed to go do some therapy on my finger, and she'd sneak to my room for a little yoga with finger therapy. These were fast, feverish interludes during which we generally failed to get all of our clothes off.

On days off, however, most everyone went his or her own way. You spend endless hours of time with the same people locked up on a bus, in lockdown backstage, in hotel bars, and sometimes actually under the bright lights, and it's natural for everyone to scatter when you get some time off, no matter how well you get along. Actually, we had it easy as compared to The Coreys, because at least we could go out without disguises and security and fear of being recognized and chased all over the town in a real life *Hard Day's Night*. On days off, if you saw another member of the crew, unless you both waved each other down specifically, the unwritten rule was to nod politely and continue on with whatever it was you were doing. Thus, on days off, Melanie and I felt free to go out together and pretty much act like sixteen-year-olds, which, come to think of it, was not so much of an act for her.

On our day off in Oakland, we had lunch in Jack London Square and then roamed around Berkeley, checking out the hippies. In Seattle, we took a ferry to Bainbridge Island and hiked around all day in a mild drizzle. In St. Louis, we climbed to the top of the Arch. We held hands a lot or walked around with our hands in each other's back pockets, a practice I had previously disdained. We went to a lot of movies. We used the hotel gym together, where she would act as my trainer with exercises intended, unapologetically, to give me better strength, flexibility, and stamina for as much sex as I could stand.

Because Melanie wasn't old enough to go to bars, we didn't. She also wasn't a big drinker simply because she was keeping in such great shape. We'd have a bottle of wine with a room service dinner from time to time, and I'd have a beer or two out with the boys in the band every now and again, but that was pretty much it. There were no drugs on The Coreys' tour; there was no booze on the buses or backstage. Except for the matching tattoos that Melanie and I got, which I will not describe and which I no longer have, it was about the farthest thing from a Cultural

Wasteland tour that you can imagine. I was having an absolutely wonderful time.

For the first time in as many years as I could remember, I didn't need to vomit during my morning ablutions. I lost weight and got toned. I remembered things, like what town I was in and what I had for dinner the night before. We were playing really well, the *POP-a-Razzi* tour was ridiculously sold out, and The Coreys were the biggest thing in the world for the moment. More than that, though, I was in love and just flat giddy with it.

Daryl and everyone else on the tour were essentially cool with Melanie and me in a sort of "don't ask don't tell" way. We played by the rules. We were completely professional at all times when we were supposed to be professional, and then when we had free time, we spent it together out of sight from everyone else, who had the good taste to leave us alone. Honestly, I think everyone was pleased for us, because we were both happy and having a great time on the tour and with each other.

I was blind in love, and when my business manager called to let me know that my most recent publishing check had come in and was bigger than expected (in addition to my having saved a couple thousand dollars a week that I wasn't spending on booze and cocaine), I thought it would be a good idea to splurge a little when we had a day off in Dallas on her twenty-first birthday. I suggested to Melanie that, instead of checking out the stockyards or whatever they have there, we do a little shopping. We should have gone to the stockyards.

Dallas has good shopping. The reason this is true is because Dallas has rich people. In particular, Dallas has a lot of rich, bored housewives married to fat, rich, Texas oil men who largely ignore them in their pursuit of the next big deal, big cigar, big steak, big glass of scotch, and big-titted stripper. This frees the wives up to join the Junior League to discuss various ways of spending their husbands' money in between sport-fucking the local tennis and golf pros. Little did I know when we walked into Neiman Marcus that there was a dormant Dallas Junior Leaguer inside my sweet little Melanie, and that the GDT was about to be set loose like Godzilla rising from a nuclear witches' brew in the South Pacific.

It started slowly. We spent about five thousand dollars that day in Dallas, which I chalked up to it being her birthday and all and didn't think about twice. Hotel security came to our room that night on a noise complaint relating to Melanie's orgasmic screams. Her passion for me had apparently found new heights to which she gave voice. She also woke me up the next morning with a long, leisurely blow-job that ended rather explosively. This was a bit of a surprise, because although Melanie had no problem with oral sex (particularly when I was on the giving side), for her, giving head was a warm-up for the main event, which was always about how many times we could get her off before I finally came. I was quite fine with this, but it was fun to have the early morning be all about me. Usually that was the province of pro groupies, not girlfriends.

Over the ensuing weeks of the tour, we shopped in Minneapolis, Chicago, Boston, New York, and Montreal. Larger and larger sums were spent. Hotel security was duly called, and I assured them that no murders or rapes were occurring. Breaking our rules from the first half of the tour, during which we pretty well stayed away from each other except on days off, Melanie began sneaking to my hotel room at six a.m. to blow me and leave, whereupon I would go back to sleep for a few hours and dream of ice cream. Talk began of bringing another girl into our bed once the tour was over. "Wouldn't that be hot? Wouldn't you like to see me with another girl? Or she can suck your cock while you go down on me. Wouldn't you like that?"

During the years in Woody Creek, I chanced to meet a sportswriter from Fort Worth who listened to my tales of the GDT with some fascination.

"So the best you can reckon, this all started that one night in Dallas?" he asked.

"At the time, I just thought things were getting better and better, you know, young and in love and all that shit. But now I'm not so sure."

"I think you're right not to be sure. She caught the Junior League disease, all right, but I always thought it was genetic. Maybe it's a virus after all. Maybe she could just get it by walking into Needless Markups at the wrong time."

The sportswriter told me that increased spending (particularly on shoes and jewelry) with commensurate increases in vocal orgasmic output and blowjob input were classic symptoms of the onset of pre-marital Dallas Junior League disease, which, in addition to steep post-marital decreases in blowjobs or orgasms of any kind, has other symptomatic variants around the country. In Los Angeles, additional symptoms include marked increases in plastic surgery; in Atlanta, extensive and ongoing home remodeling often presents; Boston sufferers tend to fancy themselves art collectors, spending large sums on paintings so they can fuck the artists; and, in San Francisco, charity work on behalf of animals, usually abandoned pure breed lap dogs, is endemic.

Thus, by the time we got back to Vegas for the final show of the tour, I had burned through my publishing check and was already eating into my salary from The Coreys. I wasn't keeping very good track of this, of course, and neither was my business manager because the bills were running a month behind the spending, and he was further distracted by bitter divorce proceedings brought on when he discovered that his young second wife was fucking her plastic surgeon. I was still happy with Melanie, although I had noticed that the icy spot in the middle of my chest, the one that had seemed in full thaw for the first time since I scouted Mexican photo shoot locations for Cultural Wasteland with Claudia, had made its presence known again in the form of an "Oh come off it" during one particularly loud screaming orgasm. This made Melanie cry, so I bought her Manolo Blahniks, but I didn't feel great about it.

Nonetheless, my guard was still down during the end-of-tour after-party thrown for The Coreys by one of their biggest fans, a young billionaire who owned one of the hottest new hotel-casinos in town. He was actually a pretty fun guy who, unlike the boys, did like to drink (a lot) and do cocaine (a lot) and pop pills (a lot), and he was fully aware of my reputation from back in the day as the rock-star keyboard player for Cultural Wasteland. So he hung out with Melanie and me, treating us (and her especially) to life behind the velvet rope in the VIP section of the VIP section of a real-life Vegas casino.

We drank champagne and vodka and ate caviar and snorted coke and popped date-rape drugs like there was no tomorrow.

Which is how I awoke the next day to my first official blowjob by the second Mrs. Zachary Fluett; although, Melanie never did actually take my name, realizing, I suspect, what a hassle it would be to change it back later. It all took place, in typical music-industry fashion, in the Little White Chapel, with the billionaire serving as my best man and the Jessica Rabbit look-alike call girl who was with him serving as the GDT's maid of honor. In retrospect, the wedding pictures alone were worth the price of admission. The honeymoon consisted of a two-day Vegas bender after which our novelty wore off on the billionaire, and then two more days packing up Melanie's meager belongings and driving to L.A., where we set up household.

There were many things to buy, naturally. We certainly needed all new bedding and linens to make a fresh start, and she planned on cooking for me "all of the time," so we had to buy a host of new kitchen appliances, including Williams-Sonoma pots, pans, knives, blenders, Cuisinarts, a big George Foreman grill (I admit that was my idea), and a top-of-the-line juicer that I first took out of its box in Woody Creek two months after I moved into Davy's house.

After about two months, the blowjobs slowed down and the bills caught up, so when Daryl called and asked if I still wanted to go back out on the road on the European leg of the *POP-a-Razzi* tour with The Coreys, it was a welcome idea. When he noted that The Coreys didn't intend on asking Melanie back as a dancer, I allowed as to how that was probably a good idea too. Melanie made a big deal out of trying to convince me not to go, which was kind of cute but not very practical, so I gave her a credit card and headed off on tour, leaving her to her own devices.

The happenstance of Wendy Harper recording and making a big hit out of "I Turned Around" many years later made it possible that I not spend the rest of my life in crushing debt.

CHAPTER 32

I FOLLOW CLAUDIA THROUGH the backstage maze at the Staples Center. Even though the corridors are broad, they are crowded with artists, staff, and various hangers-on who have managed to procure backstage passes, frequently for no apparent good reason other than to get in everyone's way. There are also all manner of racks on casters lining the halls, mobile closets holding various costumes outside the dressing and locker rooms. There are also racks of equipment, computers, and folding chairs, and flight cases full of audio, video, and computer equipment.

The fluorescent lights cast a pale greenish glow on the beige cinderblock walls and linoleum tiling underfoot. It is not an elegant environment, although some of the artists do look glamorous. Claudia clicks along on her heels at an astonishing pace, as I try to keep up, huffing and puffing from too much gut and too many cigarettes. I don't want to break into a sweat again. I just got cleaned up for the show. I need a cigarette too.

"Claudia! Wait up, please." I weave to the right and

prop myself against the wall under a No Smoking *sign and reach into my jacket pocket for the pack of Marlboros. Claudia turns toward me with a dark look, and then retraces her steps.*

"I need a minute to compose myself," I say. I light up and inhale deeply.

"I hope you're taking this seriously, Zack."

"I am. I really am. That's why I need just a minute here. I know my body, and it doesn't like to run. When it runs, it sweats, and when it sweats, it looks terrible on national television."

Claudia frowns.

"There's no smoking here, you know."

"I know."

"The Rock Star doesn't care?"

"Oh, come on, Claudia. That's not really fair. I wasn't supposed to perform tonight. I was just supposed to sit politely in the belly of the beast, and I was willing to do that. Now I've got to get up on stage on national television in front of more people than I've played before in over a decade, and I just need a minute."

Claudia frowns, hesitates, and then lightens up a bit. "I suppose that's fair." *She checks her watch.*

I take another drag and look up at the ceiling panels. It's been a long time since I've been backstage in an arena, but they really don't change much. They didn't used to have flat-panel monitors hanging everywhere like they do now. Looking at one, I can see we're in commercial.

"We're in commercial, anyway."

Claudia sighs and takes her eyes off her watch. "OK. Just a minute, though."

I take another drag. I can feel the second round of tequila really beginning to get to work. I'm working hard to act sober. "I have something for you," I say, trying out my most charming smile and stalling for time.

"Oh?"

"Yes. I got you this." I reach in my pocket and hand her the gold bracelet from the gift bag. "As a token of my esteem and delight at seeing you here."

Claudia accepts the bracelet and looks at it carefully.

"It's very beautiful, Zack."

Way to go, Cowboy! I take another grateful drag.

"Re-gifted from the gift bag?"

Never, ever, try to put anything over on a publicist.

"Absolutely," I respond. "I'm giving the rest to charity, except the hair care products I used a little while ago, but I saw the bracelet and thought of you and wanted you to have it."

"What about Guitar Hero III?"

Damn it! "That too. I'm sure that would make a lovely gift for a needy child. It looks fun." Really fun.

"And the beer tender?"

"I hadn't noticed it."

She just looks at me.

"All right, I noticed it, but I don't need it."

"No. You don't."

Ow. That cut.

"Look, like I said, I didn't know I was going to have to play tonight."

"Yes, but that's not really the point, is it?"

I nod and crush out my cigarette. "No it's not. I made a decision and the evening turned out differently than I expected. So far it's better. I'm glad to see you, and even though I'm freaking out, I'm glad to be able to help Wendy. Also, the gift bag reminded me of a time when I was a guy that I'm not so proud of anymore, and I want to apologize to you for that guy and let you *know that, a little tequila tonight notwithstanding, I am doing better."*

Claudia smiles a sad smile and nods. "I know you are, Zack. I didn't mean to be too hard, and Lord knows I took the first drink with you."

"True. And I thank you for that. It was good not to drink alone."

"All right. Truce then, and thank you for the bracelet. It's lovely."

"May I help you with it?"

Claudia hands me the bracelet, and I carefully put it on her wrist, my hands trembling. She takes my hands and holds them. Hers are warm and I realize that mine suddenly feel like ice.

"Are you ready now?"

I nod, but I'm not sure. "At least I'm not expected to catch a flying Gibson."

"You never know. Lark's a Party Pooper from way back."

I'll watch my back.

CHAPTER 33

> **Cultural Wasteland Pianist Dans 'Ecraser**
> Cultural Wasteland pianiste Zack Fluett est
> allége étole un taxi, écraser en plusieurs luxe
> automobiles, ran une autobus tourné les voie, et
> écraser en une piscine dans Antibes hier. Il est
> dans prison en suspens charges.
>
> *Le Monde*, November 18, 1995

FRANKLY, I SHOULD NEVER have needed "I
Turned Around" to get out of the GDT mountain of
debt. The publishing royalties from "This Is Gonna
Get Expensive" should have been sufficient to keep
me in booze and the GDT in shoes for years to come,
especially given how short our marriage would turn
out to be. Only there was no publishing money from
"This Is Gonna Get Expensive," because Lark Dray
took sole writing credit for it.

We were not the first band to fight over publishing. Publishing is where the real money in the music business is. Publishing is the money paid to the
songwriter for the use of the song itself, as opposed
to a given recording of the song. Money gets paid

for putting the song on a disc and releasing it (mechanicals); for performing it publicly via the radio, TV, Internet, or live (performance royalties, generally collected by ASCAP or BMI); and for putting it in synchronization with moving images, such as in a movie or on a TV show or commercial (synch rights).

Publishing is one of the reasons Springsteen makes more money than the E Street Band. When "Blinded by the Light" by Manfred Mann's Earth Band gets played on the radio, The Boss, as songwriter, gets the performance royalties. Manfred Mann gets nothing and the E Street Band gets nothing. Publishing is why Mick Jagger and Keith Richards have more money than Charlie Watts.

Some bands, like REM or U2 or The Doors, split the publishing evenly amongst the band members, but most, like The Eagles or The Rolling Stones, don't. Cultural Wasteland didn't. I shouldn't be heard to bitch about this, because I was the beneficiary of this distinction when it came to Cultural Wasteland. We never released a single song written by Chris or Huge. Peter was a co-writer on occasional songs. Lark and I wrote virtually all the music Cultural Wasteland recorded, either individually or as a team. Thus, for a brief period before I lost it all, I made quite a lot more money than three of my band mates.

We are not talking about small dollars here. When you have a monster hit like "This Is Gonna Get Expensive," which played on the radio all the time, was used in TV commercials and movies, and sold a whole bunch of records, the dinero begins to pile up. Unlike artist royalties, publishing is not subject to recoupment of the costs of recording or touring or the like, so you actually get the cash in your pocket, which is one of the real tricks of the music business. Hence, a big hit song for a songwriter makes a huge difference in one's standard of living.

Now, I am going to allow that reasonable people can disagree about this, but I honestly think that I should have been a half writer on "This Is Gonna Get Expensive." If that had happened, everything would have worked out differently, which most likely would have been bad anyway, come to think of it, but it's really the principle of the thing that got to me.

"This Is Gonna Get Expensive" arose out of the unfortunate denouement of the first Cultural Wasteland European tour, the one that had started out with the shenanigans in Stockholm. We played London, Manchester, Stockholm, Helsinki, Oslo, Copenhagen, and Amsterdam. We hung around for a while in Amsterdam (I got a hunk of smoking hash tattooed on my left ass cheek) while the crew moved the show east to prepare for our performances in Berlin, Prague, Munich, Rome, and Milan. After those shows, the tour moved west again, where we would finish up with performances in Madrid, Barcelona, and Paris.

Along the way we had collected a variety of groupies, and most of us had collected at least one of a variety of social diseases, except for Lark, who had decided to get pissed at me about cheating on Claudia with Britt and had moved out into his own bus. I didn't really blame him, as my conscience had somewhat gotten the better of me too, but I also didn't think it was cool for him to act like he was better than the rest of us. So I stayed with the boys and continued to party like a rock star, while actually managing to avoid technically cheating on Claudia by getting loaded every night and either passing out or suffering the indignity of rock star impotence. In the interests of full disclosure, there were a few successful blowjobs in the former East Germany and the Czech Republic. When you have had to stand in line for food, I guess you just learn how not to take no for an answer.

We all agreed that Milan was our least favorite European city, and so we bolted out of there and headed for the Cote d'Azur for a few days of R&R before our last three shows. I was particularly looking forward to the final swing, as Claudia was going to join us in Madrid, tag along through Barcelona and Paris, and then we were going to take our second honeymoon, this time in Greece and Turkey.

Our first honeymoon had been a relatively short one. Cultural Wasteland had to get back into the studio to start the next album, and then we had to go off on our European tour. We did have a nice time in St. Barth's looking at all the beautiful naked people and spending fifteen dollars for a cup of coffee, but we recognized too many people from the music business and a few too many of Chris's ex-girlfriends. The second time around, we agreed to go someplace where we could enjoy a little culture, such as looking at old things while still spending quality time on the beach.

Claudia arrived in Madrid two days after the Milan concert, as scheduled. Unfortunately, I had been on the road and drunk for over a month and had lost track of date, time, location, and plans. I knew I would see Claudia in Madrid; I just didn't think of having to get there at a given time. I would get to Madrid when the band got to Madrid, and then I would see Claudia. It seemed that simple.

For Claudia's part, when she learned that the band had taken a small detour and stopped off in Antibes (Juan les Pins, actually) on the way to Madrid, this came as no surprise to her, so she just hopped the first available bird to Nice and grabbed a cab to come join us. This would have been great had Chris and Peter not tempted me out of the hammock at The Morea Beach Club in Juan les Pins, where I was happily eating shrimp and drinking rosé, and convinced me to go with them to have drinks at the Eden Rock down the road at the Hotel du Cap in Antibes. Lark was being a little bitch at the time, however, and so I decided to let Huge put up with his shit for a while and go act like a rock star and piss off rich people with the Ramos brothers.

This wouldn't have been a problem had Claudia not assumed that we would be staying at the du Cap, being the rock stars that we were and reportedly (though mistakenly) hanging out in Antibes. It also wouldn't have been a problem if Chris did not have a certain faculty with models, Peter didn't have a certain faculty with French women in general, and the models and stylists for a swimsuit layout in *French Vogue* hadn't been staying at the du Cap. It further wouldn't have been a problem if I didn't have a penchant for being in the wrong place at the wrong time and, instead of recognizing the wrong place and the wrong time when it shows up, instead went ahead and drank a swimming pool of Crystal and snorted a ski slope of blow, winding up, impotent as usual, in a pile of naked bodies in the *French Vogue* suite.

More importantly, absolutely none of this would have been a problem (except in the abstract, of course) had Claudia not walked into the du Cap just in time to see Chris heading upstairs and then followed him to what she reasonably assumed would be the Cultural Wasteland suite, managing to catch up just in time for him to open the door so she could see the aforementioned pile with her husband's brand new smoking-hash tattoo sticking straight out of it. Before Chris even knew she was there, Claudia had barged past him and, without uttering a word, begun throwing things, primarily champagne bottles, but also buckets, telephones, and small, expensive tschotskes.

This being the du Cap, there were many expensive things to hit and destroy with such handy missiles, including artwork, mirrors, large glass tables, windows, *French Vogue* models, and members of a certain rock group. She gave Chris a fat lip when he gently tried to restrain her, she hit me in the kneecap with a crystal ashtray, and Peter simply ducked back into the bathroom and hid when a vase hit the wall next to him. Like the shootout at the OK Corral, it was probably over in less than a minute, but an incredible amount of damage had been done on a whole host of fronts and the story would live on forever. Then she was gone like she had been shot out of a cannon, having not uttered a single word. But I'd seen the rain in her eyes.

I yanked my thousand-dollar jeans over my bleeding knee and limped after her, calling out in my most persuasively apologetic voice over the clanging of the cymbal player in my head. By the time I managed to get down the stairs and to the front door, I could see her taxi burning gravel down the elegant front drive of the du Cap. Fortunately, another cab was sitting right in front of me, engine running, as the driver assisted a bellman with another departing guest's bags.

I was in the cab in an instant, slamming it into gear. Sadly, it was the wrong one. I backed over the guest's bags, destroying, it turned out later, many thousands of dollars worth of clothing, jewelry, and wine, and just barely avoiding the dogslaughter of her Pekingese. I was able to halt the backward dash of the cab by slamming it into a parked Lamborghini (why do these hotels always insist on leaving the expensive cars up front?), and then I managed to grind it into first (why do European cabbies insist on manual transmissions?). The tires spit gravel everywhere, forcing the cabbie, bellman, and screaming little old lady to leap for safety. I then slammed into the left front fender of a Porsche that scraped down the side of the Ferrari parked next to it, before blazing away down the driveway of the du Cap in pursuit of my wife.

By the time I got to the end of the drive, Claudia's cab was out of sight. I chose to go left. I don't know if right would have been any better, but left was definitely wrong. I immediately found myself careening into the path of a tour bus full of Swiss birdwatchers. The driver slung the wheel left and drove straight off the road and along a rock fence. I heard the shriek of metal on old stone as I, at least from my point of view, skillfully swerved the car into a ditch, then back up onto the road in time to make a hard right at what turned out not to be a corner, but a private drive, whereupon I crashed through the closed wrought-iron gates, across a short expanse of highly manicured lawn, through a pair of blessedly empty cabanas, and directly into a tasteful, kidney-shaped pool that was too small to hold an entire car, but just large enough to ensure that I could not scamper away.

Several minutes later Peter and Chris arrived, following the trail of destruction. Peter tried to calm down the screaming French couple; I recall being thankful that most Europeans don't own handguns. Chris waded into the pool to see about helping me out. I looked around and back on my busy morning.

"This is going to get expensive," I reasoned.

Chris couldn't help but laugh.

The attorneys for the Paris promoters couldn't get me out of jail in time for the Madrid show, which I missed and the band just played without me. Apparently there were no demands for refunds or riots in the streets of the Spanish capital incited due to my absence, which should have given me some pause. I did make the show in Barcelona, which was a wonderful city I couldn't appreciate due to my remorse over not being able to get a hold of Claudia and having let down the band. Already by then, however, Lark was working on "This Is Gonna Get Expensive." On the bus from Barcelona to Paris, he kept revising lyrics and working on the chord structure (a slightly transposed version of "Baby All the Plants are Dead" with a reversed bridge and only a two line chorus) much to my extreme annoyance, until I finally got sick of it.

"If you can't show any fucking sensitivity to my

plight, at least get the fucking song right!"

"What do you mean?" he asked innocently, while grinning evilly.

"She hit me with an ashtray, not a telephone; it wasn't a Diablo, it was a Kountache; the tour bus was Swiss, not German; and the French couple was gay!"

Everybody laughed. "And furthermore, that walk down in the chorus is lame. You always do that. Just go with the repeating triad and leave it at that, then you can solo on it forever."

And that's the story of how "This Is Gonna Get Expensive" came to be the song that it is. In fairness, there's more to it than just a run-in with the French judicial system. Most of the song is about the divorce. And, in fairness, that part wasn't actually expensive at all. Claudia never took a dime from me. She just disappeared for about three months, and then the papers showed up one day, along with a handwritten note from her that said if I had ever had any true feelings for her at all, would I please do her the one, single kindness of simply signing them and returning them to her attorney in the enclosed self-addressed stamped envelope. I did so without comment and without seeking her out to try to explain or apologize or anything else, having figured out that she simply didn't want to hear it. It was one of the most emotionally painful things I ever did, to just let her go.

Also in fairness to Lark (the thieving one), I got my own song out of the whole fiasco, "Monte Carlo Blues," which I wrote after the Paris show was over and while still on the Riviera wrapping up my legal woes, when I should have been frolicking in Greece. I personally think "Monte Carlo Blues" is by far the superior of the two songs, but then again, I think "Bell Bottom Blues" is superior to "Layla," and we all know which song made more money in each instance.

In any event, by the time I got back to L.A., Cultural Wasteland had already recorded most of the tracks for "This Is Gonna Get Expensive" except for my half-hearted piano accompaniment and brief B3 solo. During live performances, my part would expand exponentially (as would the length of the song), and Ben Felder gives an absolutely amazing performance on the *Live!* album, but I have to admit that I didn't have a hell of a lot to do with the track on the original hit version, the version that determined ownership of the publishing.

Perhaps if it hadn't been for how everything subsequently went down, and perhaps if it hadn't been for the song arising out of such a painful moment in my life, I wouldn't have objected. After all, there were several other compositions that Lark and I each took individual songwriting credits on, although the vast majority of our efforts were Dray/Fluett. But seeing it go to number one, then playing it every night on our U.S. tour, then getting guitars flung at me during our Austral/Asia tour, and then finally watching Lark collect a Grammy by himself while the rest of us sat around with our thumbs up our asses, not being thanked, well, it brought out the worst in me. So I broke his nose and my hand. I've learned to live with it.

CHAPTER 34

ONCE AGAIN I FOLLOW Claudia down the hallways of the Staples Center, sucking on another mint. She's cruising along at a reasonable speed, and it's easier to stay close behind her now. God, she still has a great ass. I feel OK. Warm inside but not sweating. I'm definitely about half in the bag, but I think I can handle it. Just need to stay in the moment. Glad to be rid of that hat for the time being. It is a nice hat though. Have to remember where I put it later. Don't want to lose it. My guess is that terrific little Alain probably put it with the gift bag. He's everywhere you need him to be.

As we near the stage, the lighting gets dimmer, less fluorescent, and the green hues give way to a steely blue light. I begin to feel a thrill of adrenaline, and the sloppiness I exhibited with those poor dancers is definitely beginning to wear off. People are looking at me with interest, kindness, and enthusiasm. The word has apparently gone out that the broken-down old wreck who's nominated for Song of the Year is actually going to play. I'm going to play! How awesome!

Oh, Jesus H. Christ, I'm supposed to play. I don't know this band. I don't know this part. I'm going to screw up "I Turned Around" on its biggest night. I'm going to make a mess of everything for Wendy. Wendy. There she is. She looks great. Simple black dress, no adornments. Perfect for the spotlight. She's holding hands with her band in a circle. Always hate that prayer circle stuff, but have done it hundreds of times.

"Wendy?" *Claudia murmurs.*

Wendy looks over her shoulder at me, a bit crossly I can clearly see, and quietly opens up the circle for me. I step in, head bowed, and take her hand in my left and an unknown hand, smooth, wiry, probably a saxophone player, in my right. Wendy continues.

"Let us be grateful and joyous for this honor and for the opportunity to play together tonight and to share our music and this beautiful song with our peers and this audience and the world. Let us be filled with passion for music and give everything we have to it and one another on this special night."

This is nice. No mention of any particular deity. I can get behind this.

"Does anyone have anything else before we say amen?" *asks Wendy. I hope she's not talking to me.*

"Let us be grateful that Zack Fluett is here with us and looks reasonably sober," *growls an old familiar voice.*

My head snaps up and I look directly into the smiling eyes of Hugh "Huge" Howell.

"Amen!" *says Wendy.*

"Amen!" *says everyone else.*

"Amen," *I repeat with wonder.*

CHAPTER 35

BELLY UP
Saturday 9:00 pm
BOBBY CRAFT
Zack Fluett (Cultural Wasteland)
Monsterville Horton
Tickets $40

Aspen Times October 21, 2005

"I TURNED AROUND" STARTED off life as an attempt to write an angry song. It started off meaning "I turned around and left," instead of "I turned around and came back." It started off with the visual image of entering my home in L.A. after The Coreys' European tour to discover that all my stuff was gone. Not as in gone due to a robbery or fire. Gone as in replaced by new stuff.

Not that my stuff was that great, mind you, but the Barcalounger that had sustained me during my hand and drug rehab was now a velvet love seat, and my vintage movie posters were now vintage French absinthe advertisements. My house had been utterly transformed into, well, Melanie's house. If my key hadn't fit into the lock, I would have assumed that I had walked into the wrong place. Perhaps she should have changed the locks, because then it would have been less likely that I would have been standing in the middle of the living room when the naked man walked out of my bedroom. Suddenly, in my mind's eye, I could see myself lying in a pile of naked French models, and I understood for the very first time the meaning of the phrase "karma is a bitch." It would not be the last, by a long shot.

I took a page out of Claudia's book by walking away without saying a word, but I forgot to throw things, which is probably why I was still harboring a grudge several years later when I at last sat down in my new studio in Davy's house. The sad thing about it was that I should have been well over it, but I just wasn't.

The loss of my relationship with the GDT was pretty devastating, and not just because of the huge pile of debt. After fucking up with Claudia, then fucking up with the band, and then fucking up my hand and the rest of myself, I had gotten to a place where I was not at all certain that I would ever be happy and in love again. I also wasn't too in love with myself. That had all changed when Melanie came along, but it was for a very short moment— it was if the doors had opened up to the Promised Land and then just as quickly slammed shut.

In reality, I had known even before I went out on the European tour that things with Melanie were not going to be perfect or probably even work out. I had discovered that she was fucked-up and self-ish. I already knew that I was fucked-up and selfish, and I was aware that those traits do not generally work in harmony in a relationship. After it was over, though, I could only remember those halcyon days hiking around Bainbridge Island and screwing like we had invented the concept. I felt like a scumbag, even though she was the one who did the cheating.

I spent several months perched on various bar stools around L.A., half expecting to hear from Melanie and wondering what I would do when the call came. When the call did come, it wasn't from her; it was from Daryl Miller, informing me that my services would not be required for the next Coreys tour. I had gone back to my old drunk-every-night ways on the European tour, and it didn't sit well with him or the boys. Also, they were paring down the size of their tour, as the boy-band phenomenon was beginning to run its course. So now I had no gainful employment along with a rising tide of debt, courtesy of the GDT and my drastically increased cocaine consumption. I felt like a loser. For good reason.

This feeling chased me into and out of a host of Los Angeles watering holes until I could simply no longer afford the cheap hotels I was flopping in, and then it followed me when I ran away to Woody Creek, where I continued to obsess about my lost love while drinking with Davy and learning to play the guitar and playing college venues around the West. It was still there when I sobered up and went into hiding in the studio, and so I determined to drive it away by writing a song about it, visualizing that moment in my own living room back in L.A. But the anger wouldn't come. I just kept feeling bad about myself.

So slowly "I Turned Around" became about that

feeling, that sick in the pit of your stomach sad feeling, that heavy heart. That feeling of knowing that it's just too damn late, and there's not a thing you can do about it.

It started with how I had felt at the loss of the GDT, to be sure, but then it really became about Claudia and Davy and the Old Man, and then it finally became about me. That's when I think the song became the best song I have ever written and probably ever will write, because that's when I got honest, something that was essentially a foreign concept to me all my life prior to that and that has remained hit or miss ever after. I think most people can relate to the feeling of loss, and I think that's why people relate to the song. That and the fact that Wendy Harper is a big star who sings it beautifully.

What actually got me over the GDT was seeing a picture of her on a tabloid cover in the supermarket one day walking the red carpet at the Emmys on Lark Dray's arm. That did it just fine. That's when I wrote "Gold Diggin' Tramp" in about fifteen minutes, which, although it will probably never be a big hit, is a big crowd-pleaser at my live shows.

CHAPTER 36

OUT AND ABOUT
Seen: Cultural Wasteland front man Lark Dray
with TV's hottest judge, Melanie Locke, dining
at Crustacean. Word is that they got cozy after
meeting at the MTV Movie Awards.

People, June 21, 2005

MELANIE, THE GDT, WAS made for L.A. If I haven't made it abundantly clear already, she was rather
good-looking. She also lacked anything like a moral
center or a sense of ethics.

Don't blame me for not noticing up front. The absence of these traits is remarkably easy to overlook if
you spend all your time playing naked baby-oil Twist-
er. It has been my experience that these traits are
also essentially unnecessary and possibly even detri-
mental to a career in Hollywood. Agents don't have
them. At all. Record business people cultivate an
intentional lack of morality and a strong ethical code
requiring that you screw everyone as frequently and
as viciously as possible and simply accept the fact that
from time to time you'll get it sans lube as well. I met

an entertainment attorney once who had morals and ethics, but he was poor. He was the George Bailey of the music business, but without the bushel of money at the end. Actors do not have morals or ethics until they make over ten million a picture; then it is *de rigueur* that they cultivate a set of them and make them quite public and annoying.

Melanie had not bothered to cultivate any fake morals or ethics to speak of. Then again, she was just a TV actress, albeit a popular one. Melanie's willingness to tip over the casting couch was not the only thing she had going for her. I have heard, however, that her willingness to do so with the lesbian head of scripted series at one major network did lead to her getting her first recurring role.

In fairness, however, Melanie actually had the pure looks, along with the ability to knit her brows and seem concerned, that made her perfect for medical shows (hot doctor) or procedurals (hot forensic investigator). She was also a hard worker who had made the most of the $75,000 worth of acting classes I had unknowingly paid for before my return from Europe. She hit the ground running before we even broke up and never looked back.

I didn't recover as nicely or quickly as she did, obviously. Even though I knew the answers deep down, I still kept asking myself why it couldn't have all worked out. I actually asked Melanie once during the divorce proceedings why she had cheated on me and ruined my life, and her answer was astoundingly simple and, I think, honest: "You went away, Zack."

Well, OK, Ms. Damaged Goods. But only for a few months and only to keep us in top quality footwear. Maybe that's not entirely true. Maybe I knew she was troubled, and I was troubled, and the whole thing was bound to end in tears, so I went and hid out on the road, where I often go to hide. So one would think I could get to a place where I am happy for her success and willing to look back on our brief time together with some nostalgia but mostly with an understanding in hindsight that it was fun but just not meant to be. You would think I would get past it and move on. Then I am reminded that she's fucking Lark Dray, and I get testy again.

The story from the tabloids (and, yes, I do punish myself by reading them, but I try to follow them up with a little Kafka or Dostoyevsky) is that the GDT and Lark met at the MTV Awards a couple of years back. This struck me as typical, because the MTV Awards are a publicist's dream. The publicists often play matchmaker at such events, and MTV is especially good because there are usually all different kinds of celebrities there and everyone drinks, remarkably unlike the Grammys.

There are actually two MTV Awards shows: the MTV Video Music Awards (the "VMAs") and the MTV Movie Awards. The only significant difference between the two shows is the appearance of the actual award: a Moon Man for the video awards and a box of popcorn for the movies. At each, the same artists perform and the same people introduce the categories and accept the awards; they're just swapped. Everyone wears really cool clothes and acts really cool and gets drunk and stoned and often there are fights and usually everyone hooks up. I loved them.

On our first visit to the VMAs, we were nominated for Best Alternative Video, which was about the only place I guess they thought they could stick us with a

novelty number like "Cry for Me (This Sucks!)." We
lost to Nirvana, which was perfectly OK with us. That
year Claudia conspired with the publicist for that Icelandic electronica dance group to hook Lark up with
their lead singer, despite her having been engaged in
a very public affair with the Polish enforcer for the
New York Rangers. It was all over the New York papers the next day. Funny how the photographers just
happened to walk into our dressing room at the right
time to see her handing Lark a towel, fresh out of
the shower. The hockey player with the vowel-chal-
lenged last name was quoted as saying he was going
to cross-check Lark across Manhattan the next time
he saw him. Fortunately, before that could happen,
we were already headed back to L.A., and the singer
mooted the point by being seen a week later with the
striker for the Brazilian national soccer team. She got
around, I guess. In any event, MTV appreciated the
scandal and increased the plays of our second video,
"Waiting Here for Hours," considerably.

The next year we were nominated for Best Group
Video, as we clearly weren't alternative, for "Waiting
Here for Hours," and we actually performed our new
single, "Graveyard Shift," during the show. We lost
to TLC that year, but then again, so did the Rolling
Stones, so we didn't feel too bad. By then, Claudia
and I were married, so we pretty much just hung out
in the Green Room and drank and did blow. I got
drunk and belligerent by the end of the show and
wound up stealing Kid Rock's limo and crashing it
into Ricky Martin's tour bus. Claudia managed to
get me out of there without the need to post any bail.

Claudia's publicist replacement managed to hook
up Peter and Chris with the then-seventeen-year-old

Hudson twins, which made the scandal sheets. Also, Lark spit in the face of one of the Meat Puppets over some real or imagined slight, which started a brief scuffle, but all the rappers got edgy and pulled their gats, and everyone chilled out after that. Luckily no one was shot.

A year later Tupac wouldn't be so lucky just a few days after we won our Best Group Video for "Graveyard Shift." By then the edginess had gotten completely out of control. I'm actually glad that we weren't even at the VMAs that year because we were out of the country on tour. Lark graciously took the time to appear on a video link from Kuala Lumpur accepting the award without bothering to tell any of us that we had won. Granted, we were all getting happy-ending massages at the time and probably couldn't have been bothered, but it would have been nice to be asked. It also would have been nice had Lark used the words "we" or "us" during his speech rather than solely depending on his favorite words, "I" and "me." MTV did have the good taste to send five Moon Men to us, the award being for Best Group Video, after all. I later traded mine for an eight-ball shortly before moving to Woody Creek.

We won the big one the next year, Video of the Year for "This Is Gonna Get Expensive." That victory presaged similar appreciation for the song at the AMAs, the Billboard Music Awards, and, at least for Lark, at the Grammys. It was also another dragging-anchor event for me. It was the night of the WIHF, an acronym I invented and pronounce, "whiff," as in a missed golf swing or a swing and a miss, but it is, in fact, just the opposite. I should just fess up right now and admit that WIHF is a take-off on MILF (Mother I'd

Like to Fuck), but which instead stands for "Wish I Hadn't Fucked."

Claudia and I were divorced (or soon would be, it was just a matter of awaiting the return of the paperwork from the court after the statutory waiting period). Claudia had left L.A. and moved back to the Hamptons, where she was healing. She had gotten an old friend's niece, Camille, a job at her old place of employment, Calloway & Carrington, in Manhattan. Claudia had known Camille all her life and babysat her from time to time growing up; they were almost as close as family. Camille was working her first VMAs.

I had met Camille during various engagement parties, and she had attended our wedding. She spent most of the reception sitting with Mom, while the Old Man roamed around the fringes of the party, smoking and drinking boot bourbon, and I essentially ignored them all. My mother adored Camille. This comes as no surprise, as Camille was a very bright and beautiful young lady, having just completed her freshman year at Bryn Mawr. She was quite adorable. In fact, she was quite hot. This did not confront me at the time, but by the time we were nominated for Video of the Year, she was twenty-two, a graduate, and sitting in Cultural Wasteland's dressing room in a clingy little black dress, smoking cigarettes, drinking champagne, and catching up with me. She was scorchingly hot, and she knew it.

Well, we played "This Is Gonna Get Expensive" live, and the crowd went wild for the flying Les Paul, which had not been seen in the States yet, and then we won the big one and *we* all went on stage, and Lark made a nice speech about how *we* were all so grateful and how *we* all appreciated the hell out of our fans. Then we went backstage and drank some more and started doing drugs, and then we went out for a night on the town, and Camille just tagged right on along with us. We had an honest-to-God terrific night, the whole band, and it felt just like August West again except for the champagne and the limos and the good blow and the supermodels and the Moon Man I had in my hand. That one I kept.

Camille was fun and smart and ridiculously beautiful and ever so young. As a result, when I awoke the next morning on the couch in my suite with my clothes on, I felt pretty darn good about myself. I remembered most of the evening. I was safely ensconced in my room, rather than in a jail cell (I always do better in Manhattan, fewer cars to steal). My hangover was no worse than I would expect it to be. Finally, although the incredibly hot girl that my ex-wife babysat was in my bed and appeared not to be wearing her clothes, I felt certain that we didn't have much of anything to be ashamed of. I ordered up coffee and eggs, and she awoke while I was on the phone. By the time room service arrived, we had plenty to be ashamed of.

We were both to blame. We both felt bad about it. There was no question in either one of our minds that Claudia would have thought our hooking up to be a complete betrayal of her—her ex-husband and just-as-good-as-family getting together before the rubber stamp was dry on the divorce decree. In order to assuage our guilt, we came up with a list of all the reasons why, even though her feelings of betrayal would certainly be legitimate if she knew, what had happened was not, in fact, such a terrible thing.

One, whether the rubber stamp was dry or not, Claudia had left me and we were divorcing without chance of reconciliation. Two, just-as-good-as-family is not actually the same as family, because that would have made me her family too, and we both agreed that that would be creepy. Three, this thing happened well after and was not the cause of the break-up. Four, Camille was twenty-two, a college graduate, and capable of making her own adult decisions. (She added that one on her own. I had quietly done the math and knew that I had violated the old "divide by two and add seven" rule by at least a year, which canceled out the "capable of making adult decisions" argument. Not to mention that I was incapable of making adult decisions, which also canceled out that argument.) Five, it wasn't like we were going to tell Claudia about it or anything!

We put together this list not only to assuage our guilt, but because we both knew good and well we were going to do it again. Hell, we did it all day. This was not something that, if it ever needed to be explained, could honestly be explained away as an unfortunate and regrettable night of drunkenness that took a bad turn. Nope. This was a sober morning of passion between two people who were really into each other.

Camille was also damaged goods. Her father died when she was five, her beloved big brother ODed when she was twelve, and her mother had been in and out of various institutions for the better part of her entire life and was generally zwacked out on Thorazine. Magnet and steel.

Camille and I were doomed from the start, and we both knew it. We both knew that deep down we were never going to be able to be honest about this thing to ourselves or to anyone else. Secrets kill relationships and so does guilt. We just happened both to be a smidge (OK, maybe a lot) more selfish than we were caring when it came to Claudia's feelings, and the secrecy of the whole thing helped with that, while bringing in the element of doom, which also gave the thing a natural, if indeterminate, timeline.

Camille and I were not fuck buddies nor did we ever really fall in love. We really liked each other, however, and we were passionate. We talked on the phone a lot and wrote each other dozens of e-mails, something to which I was relatively new. I had gotten a computer to begin working at home on Cultural Wasteland projects (my first flirtation with home recording), and I quickly became addicted to the simplicity of communicating through e-mail. We were actually good for one another.

Camille was way smarter and darker and more troubled than most of the people her age. She couldn't relate to many aspects of modern American society—the materialism, the pop culture, the emphasis on success—and yet she was far from a hippie, exhibited a materialistic side, worked in the pop culture world, and was obsessed with "how she was doing." My musings on some of these matters, although undoubtedly not earth-shattering by Deepak Chopra's standards, were new and slightly more mature ideas than she had heard. I think she took some of them to heart and acted on them. She had also never had good sex in her life and needed to get in touch with her body.

As for me, I wanted to get in touch with her body. I also needed someone to talk to who could understand what a wonderful person Claudia was, and how I regretted what had come between us. When you think about this, it really is quite odd, because Camille was probably the one person that Claudia would have hated finding out I had slept with. At the same time, she was probably the only woman who could talk about Claudia with me without getting jealous or upset, and she could do so while lying naked on my back. She was honest with me about my obvious failings as a person, but she reminded me that Claudia also set extremely high standards and could be a little tough to get along with if you didn't achieve those standards all the time. Claudia was, after all, the one woman in my life (other than Mom) who wasn't damaged goods.

Most of all, Camille made me feel young and attractive when I was starting to feel old and wasted and beaten down by the road at only thirty-two. She helped me to start standing up for myself again, which probably led me to punch Lark Dray in the nose. I felt good when I was with Camille, whether it was on the phone or reading an e-mail or tangled up in a hotel room bedroom someplace, and so did she.

We felt good until we thought about Claudia, and then we felt bad, and slowly the good feelings faded and the bad feelings became pre-eminent, and then Camille moved to Hong Kong to work in the fashion industry. The whole thing just faded away quietly. I started dating Phoebe, a hippie chick who was not into materialism, pop culture, or success, but who did like cocaine and pot and making fun of Lark Dray, so I took her to the Grammys where she shrieked with delight at the sight of blood spurting from his nose and then helped me ice my broken hand while feeding me coke and Vicodin. Then she left too.

In any event, Lark and the GDT met not at the VMAs, but at the MTV Movie Awards. Lark had won Male Artist of the Year at the previous VMAs for his solo album, so he was introducing Best Female Performance, which went to some underaged coked-up little slut menace to pedestrians. Because that potential hookup was even too much for the publicists, a few of them got together and decided that Melanie, who was at the Movie Awards that year to stand around and get her picture taken as one of the stars of the hit new law drama (hottie judge) but otherwise had nothing to do, was a very good height for Lark in terms of publicity photos and the paparazzi, so they got them together.

Now, Melanie knew good and well who Lark Dray was by then. She knew the whole story of Cultural Wasteland, and him stealing "This Is Gonna Get Expensive," and how that cost her a bunch of shoes, and my broken hand, and my broken heart, but she went for it anyway. I have always assumed that she did it simply because she felt she was owed the "This Is Gonna Get Expensive" shoes, and she got them.

On Lark's side of the ledger, I can't say to a certainty that he knew immediately that the GDT was the second Mrs. Zachary Fluett (it's not like we invited him or anyone else to the wedding), nor that she had Riverdanced on my heart in Manolo Blahniks. We hadn't spoken in quite some time. But he had to figure it out pretty quick. Of all the people in the world who could hook up, none could have caused me a more intense sense of horror and betrayal.

Ah, karma. You fucking bitch.

CHAPTER 37

I AM STANDING WITH Claudia and Huge. We are watching the roadies haul a half-size replica of a Black-hawk helicopter and a Goliath-sized three-wood off stage, to be replaced with a riser for the band, a mic stand for Wendy, and a nine-foot concert grand for me. The Grammys have just gone to commercial. We're on after they return. We have maybe five minutes. I'm nervous. I look around and see Lark and the GDT standing in the wings. They are going to watch this performance. I am going to shit my pants.

"Of all the people in the world to get together, how could they have done it?" I muse to make conversation, quiet my nerves, and get some pity from my old friend and ex-wife.

"I set them up," says my ex-wife.

I make a noise like a squirrel that has just been intro-duced to the business end of an electric cattle prod.

"Beg pardon?"

"I set them up. It was strictly professional, and I thought she would be good for Lark at the time. It's

obviously worked out famously."

I am dumbfounded. I am hurt!

"Did I ever tell you that I slept with your niece?" I am really getting good at this "being honest and in the moment" thing.

Huge smacks me in the back of the head, pretty hard, hitting the lump from the dressing room Ice Capades.

"Ow!" Maybe too good.

"Mind your manners, Blewit."

Claudia grins at us. "No, Zack, you didn't, but Camille did. Quite some time ago. At first I thought it was pretty shitty and hurtful."

"It was. I'm sorry," I say immediately and with fervent honesty.

"Well, we were no longer together at the time, and you didn't do it to hurt me intentionally. Besides, she isn't my niece, Zack."

"All true, but still shitty."

"I'm with him," concurs Huge.

"Thank you both, but Camille made it quite clear to me that, while she was sorry as well and while what might have been something kind of special never got off the ground because you both felt guilty, it was still a very important relationship in her life and you were good for her. She's grown up a lot, Zack, and right or wrong, she credits you with a lot of it. So I forgave her and I forgive you. Now, can you forgive me?"

"For what?"

"We were talking about Melanie and Lark, remember."

I do remember now, but suddenly it seems far away and in the past.

"Of course I can forgive you. I guess a little payback was due anyway, now that I know you knew."

Huge smacks me in the back of the head again.

"Ow!"

"Don't you know when to just shut the fuck up, Zack?"

"Thanks, Huge," says Claudia, "But I would be lying if I said there wasn't a little payback involved." *She grins, and so do I.*

"Look at my side of things, Zack. First, Melanie is a horrible person. Second, Lark and you weren't even friends anymore. Third, I had a client I had to help out, and hooking up Lark with Melanie was the perfect solution. So I get a little payback as part of the whole thing. Bonus."

"You had a client to help out?"

"Confidential, of course, but let's just say Big Movie Star got caught giving Lark a blowjob—career in jeopardy, marriage destroyed, that sort of thing."

"That sort of thing happens all the time in this town."

"Big Movie Star got caught by his wife."

Egad.

"Important that gay rumors surrounding Big Movie Star and Lark Dray get quickly squelched. Big Movie Star gets caught instead with young starlet, gets her pregnant, gets divorced with a big, big settlement to silence the ex-wife, and then remarries. Lark Dray immediately begins a hot and heavy relationship with Melanie Locke, TV's hottest judge. Rumors subside."

Trash Bag steps up. "OK, boys, you're on. Get on up there."

"Run that by me again," *I say to Claudia. She just smiles.*

"I said you're on, let's go," *repeats Trash Bag, shoving Huge and me toward the stage.*

I look up at Huge. "I'm stunned."

"Shit, man. You didn't know Lark was gay? You are the most egocentric sumbitch I think I have ever met in my life. You probably didn't even notice he was in love with you, did you?"

The lights swirl before me.

Huge puts his arm around my shoulder and gives me a big squeeze. "Focus, baby. Play a good show."

We walk into the lights, and I can see the audience at the Staples Center.

PART THREE

CHAPTER 38

Fun and Games

"People don't take us seriously because they think all our songs are silly or funny," complains Lark Dray, front man of zeitgeist rockers Cultural Wasteland. "We're like everyone else," continues co-writer/keyboard player Zack Fluett. "We just write about our lives. Our lives happen to be more fun than everyone else's, but I'm sure that'll change and you'll see a more serious side of us in the future." I should point out that Dray and Fluett conducted the entire conversation with this interviewer in fake nose and glasses.

Songwriter Magazine, February 1993

PARTY POOPERS, INCORPORATED STARTED life at a party in Los Feliz hosted by Kevin Addington, the very cool and ahead of his time music supervisor who placed two tracks from the first Cultural Wasteland album before it even came out (but after "Cry for Me" was released as a single). He put one in a movie and one on a TV-drama about rich, angst-ridden teenagers. This helped us get our music heard and helped us get recouped on our publishing advances so we would actually start to see some walking around money when the royalty checks came in. We all thought very highly of Kevin and his new girlfriend, Zahavit, a former Israeli army intelligence officer and recent arrival to our shores.

Lark, Claudia, and I showed up early at Kevin and Zahavit's late one Saturday afternoon to help out with the preparations for the party. Claudia had brought avocados and various other vegetables, and she joined Zahavit in the kitchen for a glass of wine where they started chopping and mushing and doing whatever you do to make fresh hummus, salsa, guacamole, and some Jewish things I didn't know the names of. Lark and I went down to the yard with Kevin to help him move some speakers outside and then left him to set up a keyboard rig for one of the artists he managed on the side to play for the gathering that night. At his request, Lark and I took the VW and Kevin's credit card to the nearby Liquor Barn to pick up a keg.

We decided it was a good idea to get stoned. After toking up some nice Humboldt purple haze, we ventured forth into the vast carnival that is the Liquor Barn. We walked around for about twenty minutes looking in awe at everything they had, sometimes giggling at the idea of bringing certain things back to the party. Then we decided that we were truly the funniest people in the world and the party would be so much better if we in fact did bring back some of those things. Kevin almost surely didn't have enough booze anyway, so we also felt we should fill his larder being as how we had his credit card.

We browsed the wine section and bought a few

reds, a few whites, and some champagne. Everyone needs that. Then we headed for the liquor aisles and purchased, in alphabetical order, bourbon (three kinds), brandy (for our homies), gin, mescal (with worm), rum (both Barcardis), scotch (expensive), tequila (cheap and cheaper), and vodka (several flavors). Then we hit the mixer aisle and realized that we had been acting quite crudely. We had no plan. No theme. We had to rethink the entire thing. So we abandoned our cart and got another one from outside, but once outside, we thought it might be a good idea to take another hit. So we sat in the car and smoked another joint and rocked out to the radio for a while, and then we went back into the Liquor Barn.

It was even bigger than before. We roamed around again, somewhat lost but enjoying ourselves, until we came upon our old cart, still full of booze. It looked lonely.

"It was a good head start. Maybe we should have stuck with it," said Lark.

"I concur," I concurred. "We might have been a bit hasty."

"And stoned," Lark pointed out. "Why did we bail on it again?"

"Lack of thematic adequacy," I responded.

"Yes. Right. That was it," Lark agreed. "What if instead of matching the booze to the theme, we match the theme to the booze?"

"It would save us starting all over again."

And so we re-acquired our cart and launched back into the mixer aisle that had so flummoxed us before, but this time with a plan. Find a theme for each booze. We both liked this approach, and fell to it with a certain amount of creativity and recklessness.

There were some obvious choices, of course. The tequila became margaritas almost immediately. No sense messing with that. But what kind of margaritas? Frozen or on the rocks? Both, of course, so we bought a blender and four sets of Mexican sombrero marg glasses, along with a gross of limes and special margarita salt. Then we decided it was wise to purchase some shot glasses for later after people got tired of drinking margs but still wanted tequila, and then we got those little clay lime and salt receptacles.

The vodka was also pretty straightforward. As we already had Triple Sec for the margs, we bought some Roses Lime and were immediately set for kamikazes. We figured that this wasn't some frat party, however, so we also got a shaker, a stirrer, and plenty of olives for dirty martinis, and I insisted on getting cocktail onions for Gibsons as well.

"I thought a Gibson was just a kamikaze with gin," said Lark.

"Shows what you know," I said. "You, sir, are attempting to describe a Gimlet, only a Gimlet has no Triple Sec."

"Oh really, college boy. Then what is a Gibson, precisely?"

"A martini, either gin or vodka, with cocktail onions."

"That's it?"

"That's it."

"The cocktail onion turns a martini into a Gibson?"

"Yes it does. Do you want to know why?"

"Not really."

"It's a good story."

"OK."

So I proceeded to tell the story of how, during World War II, there was this guy who worked for the defense department and was always going out to lunch with the defense contractors, and this was back in the day of the three-martini lunch, and this fellow couldn't hold his liquor so he was always getting taken to the cleaners by these guys from Northrop and Lockheed and Hughes and such, and he was sure he was going to lose his job because he was an incompetent drunk. So this guy conspires with his local bartender to prepare his martini with water instead of gin, but to put a cocktail onion in it so the waiter will be able to distinguish his from those of his lunch companions. So this works for awhile, but eventually one of the Lockheed guys asks why he has a cocktail onion, and our guy just says he prefers the taste of it, so the Northrop guy says, "That sounds interesting, waiter. I'll have what Mr. Gibson's having."

"That's it?" asked Lark.

"Yes. That's the story of how the Gibson got named."

"That's not funny."

"I didn't say it was funny. I said it was a good story."

"It's not a good story either. It's not funny."

"It is too a good story. It's replete with commentary on human nature."

"I declare a party foul, doubled for having been committed before the party even started. Drink half of this bottle of Jose Cuervo."

I did not drink half the bottle of Jose Cuervo. But, being a little parched, I agreed to take a few large slugs, insisting that it was not a party foul but just to start the party. To make peace, and probably because he was a bit parched as well, Lark joined me. We then remembered that the party actually had not started and that we should probably get back to Kevin's and get it started, so we continued our work.

The scotch took some thinking, until we figured we would just save it for the last and drink it ourselves with Kevin to congratulate ourselves on a super party. So we bought the most expensive cigars they had to accompany it.

Probably feeling a little guilty about that, we decided to kill two birds with one stone by getting a lot of mint so as to be able to make Mint Juleps with the bourbon and the new drink that Lark had heard of, the mojito.

"The mojito is not a new drink," I pointed out. "Ernest Hemingway invented it in Cuba in something like 1954."

Lark gave me a look. He picked out a muddler, and I turned my attention to the brightly colored straws and sword picks and threw several bags in the cart. We proceeded to the register, where we remembered to ask for the keg that Kevin had ordered, our original task. They brought us a pony keg of some microbrew from Santa Barbara, along with a tap. We both studied the pony.

"I'm not feeling good about this," said Lark.

"Too brown," said I.

"Too small," said Lark.

We traded it in for something lighter and larger, more in keeping thematically with what we liked to drink. As the sullen, acne covered checkout kid rang up our various purchases while the young Mexican fellow retrieved the thematically correct keg, my eyes alit on an item on the shelf behind the counter.

"Do you know the sine qua non of a classy party, Lark?"

"I do not know what that means, college boy. Sir, may I please have that bottle of Cuervo back, so I may administer another pre-party party-foul shot?"

Acne Boy handed the bottle over without comment.

"Hear me out," I insisted. "A truly classy party has fresh soda water." I waggled my eyebrows and flicked my eyes toward the shelf. Lark's eyes shone.

"WhipIts."

"I think we owe it to ourselves."

"I concur," Lark concurred. (*Concur* was our new favorite word at the time.)

And so we rolled out of the Liquor Barn with a half-keg of Bud with ice and tub, several cases of booze and mixers, a little wine, thematically appropriate barware, hundreds of plastic cups and glasses, and a canister with three hundred cartridges of nitrous oxide, all several hundred dollars of it charged to Kevin's credit card without any comment from the spotty-faced kid behind the counter.

The Mexican fellow helped us load our purchases into the back of the camper van. We then decided to test the WhipIt maker to ensure it was operational.

"Turn up the fucking music!" snarled Lark, screwing his seventh nitrous cartridge into the otherwise empty canister and then sucking on it like there was no tomorrow. I complied, as I agreed that loud volume was a major component of a nice nitrous buzz, working as it did with that enjoyable Leslie-speaker auditory "whoop whoop whoop" that was the main reason for killing brain cells by the spoonful.

Once we noticed it was dark, we decided the

WhipIts worked perfectly well and that we should probably be getting back to the party. We cruised back up the hill with the volume on high, smoking another doob and finishing off the first bottle of Cuervo, which left us with only seven.

When we pulled up Kevin's driveway, it was clear that the party was already underway. People were standing around in the front yard, smoking, and folks were gathered on the front porch. Kevin raced out of the house.

"Where have you assholes been?" he screamed. "People are drinking cooking sherry!"

We looked at each other and it dawned on us that we probably had been gone a long time.

"Not to worry, Kev," enthused Lark, "We got the party right here with us. It's gonna be epic. Zack, make up a pitcher of kamies and get everybody started while Kevin and I get the keg set up."

I saluted. We opened the back door of the bus and the keg rolled out and landed on Kevin's foot. He screamed bloody murder, but it turned out to only be a glancing blow to a big toe. Looking back on it, he could have broken a metatarsal, probably called something like a "punter's fracture."

The keg bounced down the short drive and into a juniper bush. Lark and I got it rolled back up onto the front lawn while Kevin hopped around on one foot, swearing like a sailor. We decided it was best to set it up right there in the front so everyone could get a beer immediately upon arrival. I quickly helped Lark dump the keg into the tub and pour ice around it, and then I left him to tap it while I carried bags inside to set up the bar. There, Chris Ramos met me, looking at our purchases with appreciation.

"I'll be right back," he said, as I began filling a tall pitcher with ice, vodka, Triple Sec, and Rose's Lime. He returned a few minutes later with his dates, two Hooters waitresses. He had found one of Kevin's t-shirts and torn it into strips, then gotten busy with a red Magic Marker such that he and the girls now wore rising sun headbands. They grabbed the pitcher and a stack of glasses and began pouring booze down every throat they encountered.

I prepared a backup pitcher of kamies and then turned my attention to filling drink orders for the growing crowd around the makeshift bar I had set up on what turned out to be an antique credenza, the patina of which was particularly susceptible to margarita stains. Peter found extension cords and plugged in the new blender, joining me behind the bar. He blended margaritas, and I made mojitos. This turned out to be a major pain in the ass, because all the muddling takes time and effort and a certain amount of focus that I was rapidly losing because of all the dope and tequila. Also, I was blasting nitrous hits about every two minutes.

Around this time Huge came in from the front yard and told me that Lark was having trouble with the keg, so he was calling for help from "college boy." I turned over the mojitos to Huge, who resolved the muddling issue by bagging it and giving people rum-and-cokes or just handing them a shot of bourbon and a sprig of mint to chew.

I found Lark flummoxed by the keg. He was drinking from a bottle of Maker's and studying the situation. I handed him the WhipIt canister, and he fished in his camouflage short pockets, jangly with nitrous cartridges.

"It doesn't seem to fit," he muttered while holding his breath, eyes closed, nitrous working.

"We're dumbshits," I said. "This is the tap for the microbrew. It won't work."

"Ah fuck. Well, we better get going before this party craters."

"Let's borrow Kevin's Porsche," I suggested, realizing that it would be faster for the fourteen blocks down to the Liquor Barn and back.

"Good thinking."

We went back through the house, pulled Kevin's keys off the hook, and ran into him, now limping in flip-flops.

"Hey guys," he said. "This party is sort of an introduction for some of the studio people I work with to a couple of my artists and to Zahavit, you know? Maybe your boys could chill on the kamikazes a little? I was figuring just beer and wine and kind of a mellow time, you know."

"Absolutely, Kev," answered Lark. "We'll call them off just as soon as we get back from the Liquor Barn. We accidentally got out of there with the wrong tap, so there is no beer yet, but we'll be back in a jiffy."

"Well, hurry then, I don't want everyone getting all fucked up before the entertainment, you know?"

"We're on it. We've already determined that speed is of the essence." Kevin limped off to see how Zahavit was enjoying herself. I waved to Claudia, who was exiting the kitchen with her, both of them carrying bowls of dip and various chips and crackers to be set on the dining room table.

"This is going well," I said to Lark, heading to the garage.

"Be careful of the door," he pointed out. There was a hand-lettered sign on it declaring, *Don't let Bullshot (dog) into the house.*

"Right," I said. We slipped carefully through the door, closing it quickly so as to make sure Bullshot (dog) didn't get in, then hopped in Kevin's Targa, hit the garage door opener, and made it down to the Liquor Barn in record time. This time we were focused and made sure we got the right tap as quickly as possible (along with some cigarettes, a novelty dribble cup, and another couple of cases of nitrous cartridges, just to be sure).

When we pulled back up to the house, people were walking all over the street calling out, "Bullshot! Bullshot!"

Lark and I eyed the wide-open garage door. Oops. Well, at least he wasn't in the house. We pulled the Targa in and slunk out of it and over to the keg. There was a distinct whiff of vomit in the air, which was troubling this early in a party. We quickly tapped the keg, but it would only spew foam, having been dropped on the driveway and rolled into and out of a juniper bush. As we looked at the stream of useless white bubbles, we both began to get the giggles.

"This hasn't gone so well," remarked Lark.

"Well, we're better off than that guy." I pointed to the apparent source of the vomit, out cold in the begonias.

"True. I think that's Kevin's artist who's supposed to be playing later."

We began to laugh in earnest. Lark sprayed foam around, and we laughed harder.

"Just call us Party Poopers, Incorporated," I said,

and then we began to laugh until our sides hurt. People were still wandering around calling out for Bullshot. We heard the sound of something glass and probably expensive breaking in the dining room. Peter and Chris could be seen groping the Hooters girls through the living room window. The noise level indicated that the cops would soon be called, and everywhere we looked there were spent nitrous cartridges. We howled and sprayed foam again.

Then the paramedics arrived. We followed them in through the garage, noticing a bulldog with absolutely huge testicles hiding in a corner under a motorcycle. Good. At least Bullshot was OK. We closed the garage door behind us and, upon entering the kitchen, found the paramedics kneeling over Zahavit. Claudia stood near by, wringing her hands. She saw us, and ran over.

"I think she might be allergic to avocado," she said. "She was all excited about the guacamole because she'd never had it before. She took all of two bites, and then her face and lips puffed up something awful."

We guffawed. As the paramedics administered epinephrine to Zahavit, Claudia dragged us out of the kitchen. Kevin followed us darkly with his eyes as he held Zahavit's newly pudgy hand.

Fortunately, Claudia was sober enough to drive, and so we were able to make a fairly rapid exit, wheezing and gasping for air, sides splitting, heads ringing, unable to stop laughing. Claudia was not that amused. So we pointed out that, while we were, in fact, rock-star wannabe assholes and our participation in the party had included probable alcohol poisoning, a broken toe, a temporarily lost dog, certain damage to personal property, possible unwanted pregnancies, and foamy beer, only she had been able to cause the need for immediate professional medical attention. At that point, she also began to grin. God, I loved her.

CHAPTER 39

BOBBY CRAFT
The Death of Fun (*****)
Woody Creek/Warner Bros.
<u>Gallows Humor of the Highest Order</u>
This is the best record of the year. Go out and
buy it. Please, for pity's sake, do not download
it illegally. Go out and buy it and buy one for
everyone you love for Christmas. Trust me on
this one.

Album Reviews, *Spin*, November 2005

WHILE BOBBY CRAFT WAS living with me in
Woody Creek and dying, he regaled me with tales
from his rock-star days in the seventies. Someday
I'll write a book about it. When the chemo was really bothering him or he otherwise just wasn't feeling well, I'd tell him stories of the August West days
or the high times of Cultural Wasteland. He had
been clean for years, of course, and I was clean too
back then, but he still liked to hear the stories, just
like he enjoyed watching me enjoy a cigarette or ci-

gar on the back porch. I didn't let him get anywhere near the smoke, but he could watch it belch out of my mouth into the crisp Colorado air and remember what it was like to have lungs.

Bobby especially liked the Party Poopers, Inc. stories. He decided that he wanted to work with me on a song about it, so we took some ideas out of rehab, some tales of woe from the Party Poopers, and some of his stories from the Seventies, and then we took a phrase from my recently deceased gonzo journalist neighbor and wrote "The Death of Fun," which became the title track of Bobby's final album.

I have been given many gifts in my life, but the opportunity to produce *The Death of Fun* was among the very greatest. Bobby was crazy as a bedbug, but he had helped me to become the musician I was, had tried to get me clean after my brush with death, and had never given up on me when I went back down into the dark places. He was an AA guy, but he recognized that I wasn't really the type, and so he had sort of a side gig with me, which I referred to as AAA, for Alcoholic Artist Annoyance, as there was nothing even vaguely anonymous about my issues.

The simple additional truth was that I had learned to enjoy playing with Bobby. He was a great musician, and as he got older he became an even funnier and darker songwriter. He gave me hope for maturing into a better songwriter as well. I credit him for much of what came out of my best days in Woody Creek.

Bobby usually did a couple of gigs a year at the Belly Up. I would open for him and play with him on a few songs as well. The last time he came up I had been sober and living in Davy's place for almost two years. I had recorded a bunch of my album, and I was pretty happy with the space I was in. The Belly Up was Bobby's last gig on that swing, and so I convinced him to come on down to Woody Creek and see the kind of life the old AAA had made for himself. And so he did.

Bobby stayed for almost a week. We took walks and messed around in the studio and generally hung out like a couple of recovering alcoholics, smoking cigarettes and finding things to occupy our time. He listened to what I had been working on and made some welcome comments and suggestions, and we enjoyed one another's company.

Six weeks later Bobby called to tell me he had terminal lung cancer. I was shocked. When I asked if there was anything I could do, he told me that, actually, there was. He told me he had a whole bunch of songs that he had been working on for years with the intention of getting them on wax someday, but now there was a time crunch. He had no label and no money to speak of, and he could play live like nobody's business, but he wasn't an engineer or a producer. That was as far as he got before I suggested that he move into my guest room and we get started laying down tracks immediately.

Bobby told me he didn't want to get in the way of me making my album, which I appreciated. I informed him that I felt confident now that I was going to finish it, so I didn't think taking a little time off would be any problem. I also figured that any time spent working with him could only make my own work better in the future. I didn't tell him that I felt I truly owed it to him, the music business, the world, and the universe to make sure that every note

of music in him that we had time to get out could be
shared. He showed up two days later with a duffel,
his twelve-string Rickenbacker semi-hollow body,
and his six-string Martin.

Despite its obvious overtones, *The Death of Fun*
is not a sad or morbid record, although few people
I know who know anything about Bobby Craft can
listen to it without crying, and lots of people who
know nothing about Bobby Craft but who have ever
cared about another human being in their lives and
lost that person cry like babies when they hear it.
My belief is that beautiful things can cause us to cry
every bit as easily as sad things, and the work that
Bobby did on *The Death of Fun* is flat-out beautiful
and touching. It is also, like all of Bobby's work,
darkly funny and intelligent, with outstanding musicianship.

It helps that he didn't have to do it alone, and by
this comment, I am not breaking my arm off at the
elbow patting myself on the back. I do not under-
estimate my contribution to the album. I produced,
engineered, mixed, and played on every track on it,
and I co-wrote about half of the songs and all of
one song in particular. I also cooked every meal
for Bobby, made a million pots of tea, and held his
hand when the pain got too bad. Probably my biggest achievement was never stealing any of his pain
medication. That's not why the album is great, however. The album is great because so many of Bobby's friends, and he honestly didn't know he had any,
made the pilgrimage to Woody Creek to lay down
backing vocals or a signature guitar line or harmonica part.

It's also how Claudia and I became friends again.

It started with Huge. We had kept in reasonable touch over the years. He was just too good of a peacemaker to stay mad at, and besides, Lark essentially kicked everyone out of the band by going solo a couple of years later anyway, so that made it easier to talk. Huge didn't carry a grudge against Lark; he always figured that he was just lucky to have had the run he did. He moved to Nashville and did some studio work. He began pursuing his passion for woodworking, making fine artisan tables, chairs, and dressers. He would call me up from time to time, when he could track me down, and we'd catch up and talk about the old times and any news we might have about folks from back in the day.

He called me up one day in Woody Creek, about a year since we had last spoken, and I told him about Bobby's illness and the record. Huge asked me who was playing drums, and I allowed as how we were just getting started but that I was and that we were using a machine for the time being. Huge pointed out that I was a shitty drummer and that no proper Bobby Craft record could ever have a drum machine on it. I agreed but pointed out that what we were doing here was more in the way of therapy than really trying to record an album for release. Huge pointed out that that was a moronic comment and got on a plane two days later to come join us.

Huge's arrival fundamentally changed our approach to the record. At first it had been about getting songs recorded so they didn't go to the grave with Bobby, probably more for posterity than anything else. It was a couple of beat-up former rockstar recovering alcoholics doing something to fill their days in a constructive way while one of them went about the business of dying faster than the other one. That was perfectly OK with both of us. But when Huge showed up, all of a sudden I had to start acting like a real producer. Huge had been playing sessions in Nashville, and a couple of raised eyebrows and one impromptu nap on the orange shag floor of the tracking room prompted me to step it up and stop wasting time.

Suddenly, I was Leon Richard, the producer of the first Cultural Wasteland album, without the weed. I would get up in the morning, make myself some breakfast and something easy to digest to take to Bobby in his room. Then I'd go down to the studio and make a list of what I expected to accomplish that day, then get everything set up and prepared for the first downbeat. Huge didn't stay at the house with us, primarily because there was no room but also because he wasn't an alcoholic and so he could do things like go out in Aspen and have a few cocktails and chase cougars, which I am informed he did with alacrity. But he would show up on time in the morning (at least eight hours earlier than Leon would have had us show up) and lay down his parts.

Unlike Leon, I didn't make the record a song at a time, because I wanted to use Huge's time with us to best advantage. Bobby and I had already decided on about fifteen songs we wanted to get recorded and the order of importance for those songs in case he didn't live long enough to finish them all. So the first thing Bobby and I did was to record live versions of each of those songs with just a click track, acoustic guitar or piano, and vocals, so as to preserve the song and to give us someplace to start. By the time Huge arrived we had almost all of the songs recorded in that fashion, and we knocked out the rest of them during his first days there, including, at Bobby's insistence, a version of "I Turned Around," which he had taken a liking to on listening to the early tracks from my intended solo record.

For a week or so Huge hung out with us, recorded real drum tracks for the album, and cracked Bobby and me up a lot. Then, without telling either one of us, one day he showed up with Peter and Chris Ramos.

Bobby never liked Peter and Chris. Hell, almost nobody did (except girls), because they were too good-looking, too talented, and insufferable snobs. I don't recall them ever being too fond of Bobby either. In fact, I recall them making a shitload of fun of him back in the day when we were on tour with him, but then again, all of us (except for Lark) did that. But there they were, standing in my living room in Woody Creek, and when Peter asked Bobby, with great dignity and respect, for permission to play on a track or two on the album, Bobby cried.

That was the moment when I knew that Bobby and I were going to make a real record, and I cried too. Bobby cried a lot in those days, and I often cried with him, but like the album itself, it was always because of the beautiful moments, the moments we would miss once he was dead, and not because of anything sad. Whatever minor leftover tension there had been between the Ramos brothers and me was instantly forgotten, and we set about catching up with one another and creating a plan for their participation.

Peter and Chris were retired from the music business. I had been vaguely aware that they both settled down and had families. In fact, their mother had died and left them a boatload of cash, and then they had the good sense to marry well. Chris lived in Rio de Janeiro with a Portuguese shipping heiress and telenovela actress. Peter married the high school sweetheart whose father is the senior senator from either Iowa or Idaho, I can never remember which, and moved to Miami. Karma, being the bitch she is, blessed them each with two daughters who will undoubtedly grow up to be fabulously beautiful and hang around with degenerates like us, most likely getting involved in drugs and having group sex in art galleries.

The boys couldn't stay long, and none of us intended to try to make a Cultural Wasteland album with Bobby sitting in for Lark anyway, but they each played on a few tracks over a couple of days, and in the evenings we sat around and shot the shit. It was good for Bobby. Hell, it was good for all of us.

I took Huge aside and thanked him for what he had done. I told him I thought he was kind and brilliant and had really kick-started the album. He told me that he had put a call into what he called his "rolodex" person and that I should expect a call myself with any news of other folks interested in coming to Woody Creek.

Huge had been with us for almost two weeks when he left for Nashville along with the Ramos brothers. It was pretty quiet around the house for a few days, which was all right. All the company, as welcome as it had been, had worn Bobby out. He took some time off, and I got back down into the studio and cleaned up a bunch of tracks and laid down some keyboard parts. I was pleased to see that the structure of the record and of the individual songs on it was beginning to take shape. There was a lot of work to be done, but it was definitely becoming an actual album.

I was drinking tea in the studio late one afternoon and feeling reasonably satisfied when "the rolodex" called.

"Hey, it's Claudia."

All the air rushed out of me.

"Hello?" she repeated.

"Uh. Hi."

"Is this a bad time, Zack?"

"Um, no. Not at all. It's just that I haven't heard your voice in about a decade, and it, uh, sort of caught me off guard."

"Oh. Didn't Huge tell you I was going to call?"

"Huge?"

"Yes. He called and told me all about your project with Bobby and asked if I might check around to see if there are other folks who would be interested in helping out."

Duh. She's not calling to talk to you, moron. "You're the rolodex."

"Beg pardon?" I could actually see her arched eyebrows in my mind's eye.

"Never mind. Yes, Huge did tell me that someone would be calling, but I guess he neglected to tell me it would be my ex-wife."

"Oh. Would you rather not speak to me?" Her voice was suddenly icy.

"Oh, no no no no no! That's not it at all. I would love to speak to you! It was just a little unexpected."

A pause. Then a softer voice. "I'm sorry. Let's try this again." Pause. "Zack? It's Claudia speaking."

"Hello, Claudia. It's nice to hear your voice," I responded warmly.

"Huge tells me you're doing really well, Zack."

"Well, we've got a long way to go, but I think we've got the makings of a really beautiful album on our hands here if Bobby can just hang in there for a little while."

"I'm glad to hear that, but Huge told me that you were doing really well."

"Oh. Well, yes. I guess I am doing pretty well right now."

"I'm really glad to hear that."

"Well, thanks."

"Anyway, I don't want to spend a lot of your time, but I called a few people, and everyone I reached wants to be a part of this. Bobby has a lot of fans. Could I e-mail you a list of people and contact information so you and Bobby can discuss it and let me know what you want to do?"

"Absolutely. That sounds like a swell idea."

"*Swell*? Did you just say *swell*?"

"Of course not. Nobody says *swell* anymore. I said that sounds like a hell of an idea. A hell of an idea. Damn straight."

She laughed and my heart took flight. My God, how I had missed that laugh. We agreed to talk again after Bobby and I reviewed her e-mail. She signed off by telling me she was looking forward to catching up with me on all the events of the last decade, in addition to trying to help out with the album. I said that would be fine with me as long as she had just gotten out of a convent, and she laughed again.

Bobby and I were pretty much astonished by the

list. There were a couple of A-list actor wannabe musicians, several big stars from the Seventies who were still relevant, a couple of young kids with actual credibility as more than just pretty faces, and a whole bunch of really, really good players and singers who weren't household names, but then again, neither were Bobby and I. At least not anymore. At one point I did the math, and when you added up the number of Grammys that Bobby and I had at the start of the project, which was zero, and then added the Grammys of the other players on the album by the time it was finished, the total rose to twenty-eight.

They came and went in ones and twos over the course of the ensuing three months. Some of them caught Bobby on good days and some on bad, and some on both. The pain had started to get to him, and so Bobby was taking quite a bit of medication. Since he was on his way out anyway, he started drinking again some too, but not always. Pretty much if he started, then he drank until he passed out, but if he didn't get started, then he was OK.

I didn't try to do anything about it one way or the other. I didn't facilitate, but I didn't judge, either. After he ran me out of my booze, he'd either get himself together well enough to go shopping or he'd convince one of our visitors to bring him a little "somethin' somethin'."

For the most part, it was better when we had guests. Bobby had one, maybe two, good hours a day when he could muster enough energy to sing or play. Some days he didn't even try, but that was generally when it was just the two of us. Some days he tried and we just didn't get much. But generally when we had a guest in (and the more famous the guest, the better Bobby worked), I would try to make sure that they actually got to watch him do some work in addition to whatever I might have them doing in the studio. Because it was so heart-wrenching to see this sick, courageous, crazy musical genius pouring the very last of himself out, the performances we got from everyone else were just amazing as well.

At the end of the day, I actually wound up with way more material than I could use. I had to apologize to a number of artists because some (or even all) of their work didn't make the final mix. I found that sometimes once I put in all the background vocals and extra instruments that we had recorded on a given track, it lost the plaintive quality of Bobby's ravaged voice and breathing, and as a result, some truly wonderful performances will remain forever on a hard drive. To a person, not one of the artists to whom I apologized ever complained about being left on the editing room floor. Each of them stated that being part of the process was all that mattered, and I believe them all.

Throughout, I spoke with Claudia on the phone every few days, at first to help with arrangements for folks to come out and record, but later just to tell her how things had gone or were going or to talk about her day. Despite what we had said on the first phone call, we really didn't talk about the past. There was no discussion as to what was and wasn't OK to talk about; it simply didn't come up, and that seemed fine to us both. We sort of just started over. It was a new friendship between two people who got a kick out of the way each other talked, but with a certain ease and economy borne of having known one another intimately a lifetime before.

The one exception was when she broached the subject of inviting Lark to provide some background vocals.

"I don't think that's too swell of an idea," I said.

"Did you just say *swell*?"

"Actually, I said it in the negative, as in 'not *swell*,' but yes, I admit it. I do say *swell* from time to time."

"Did you used to say *swell*?"

"I don't think so. I guess it's a new thing. Things do change, you know."

"I know. Maybe things have changed with Lark, Zack. I haven't talked to him, but his people let me know that he would really like to be involved and pay his respects to Bobby."

"Well, see, the problem with that is that I would have to let him into my house, and he's not welcome in my house. If he wants to take Bobby to Disneyland or something like that, well, you'd have to take that up with Bobby, but as far as walking through my door and sitting on my chairs and singing into my microphones, I think I'll be the decision guy on that, and I don't want him here."

"He could be good for the album, you know. He's doing really well these days."

I hung up on her.

The next day I got an e-mail from Claudia that started off with a heartfelt apology. She had thought about what she had said and realized that she had overstepped her bounds. She recognized that I was the producer of the album and would make the decisions about whom and what was best for it and that I didn't need to listen to advice from some publicist (even if that publicist was my ex-wife who was helping to get the album made and had been instrumental in getting all the other folks to play on it). She also allowed as to how I was entitled to my opinions about my former band mate and best friend, and that I didn't need to listen to my ex-wife tell me about how well said former band mate and best friend was doing, and she apologized to me for her insensitivity in that regard. She then wrote that, notwithstanding the foregoing, if I ever hung up the phone on her again, it would be the last time I ever heard her voice.

I called immediately and apologized genuinely. She accepted promptly and without the need for me to grovel. Nothing more was said about it or about Lark participating in *The Death of Fun*.

Bobby lived longer than his doctors expected. He lived long enough for us to finish the record, and long enough for our biggest guest star to inform his label that it was coming time for him to renegotiate his deal, and if they didn't release *The Death of Fun*, he would most likely be headed across town to another label for the next ten million records he would sell. They promptly pointed out that they absolutely loved the album anyway, and of course they would put it out, although they'd have to start it in a limited run and see how it did. Bobby lived long enough for the reviews of the album to come out, and I know he enjoyed very much how every music journalist in the country fell all over the place in praise for the record and for his lifetime of work.

It was probably just as well that he didn't live long enough to learn that this acclaim and being named to almost every critic's "year's best" list generated about forty thousand lonesome units of sales. It was downright sad that he didn't live long enough to pick up his first and only Grammy for Best Contemporary Folk Album, but had he been alive, they probably wouldn't have made such a big deal of it and remembering him on the actual Grammy telecast. Also, the A-list actor who accepted the award made a much wittier and touching speech than Bobby ever could have.

The Death of Fun was a good record, and I was proud of it irrespective of either sales or awards. At Bobby's insistence, I kept "I Turned Around" on the album, even though I didn't think it exactly fit with the rest of the songs, all of which featured Bobby's dark humor or just plain darkness, whereas "I Turned Around" is pretty starkly sentimental. Nonetheless, Bobby insisted that it was the best song on the album, so we compromised and put it at the very end as a bonus track, after a fairly lengthy silence (so not everyone even knew it was there), and we left it with an unfinished sound, just Huge and me and Bobby, with his original raspy vocals.

The idea was for the record proper to end, but then for there to be a brief reprise, as if from the grave, for those special folks who had listened to the record as a whole and were still sitting there contemplating what they had heard. And that's exactly how Jackson Harper heard it one night lying around his hotel room after a loss to the Phillies. So he called his wife Wendy and played it for her over the phone.

CHAPTER 40

I SIT DOWN AT THE nine-foot Yamaha concert grand. I have not played a concert grand in over half a decade, and I am grateful that it is a Yamaha. They sponsored me back in the day, but even if they hadn't I would have chosen one for tonight, because they all tend to play pretty much identically. This can be important if you are playing a different piano every night. I tinkle a few keys and play a few soft chords as the cameramen get in position. I try to ignore the one standing right over my shoulder, shooting my hands on the keys. I feel my nerves stretching tight, the locusts beginning the rumblings prior to taking flight in my stomach. I'm going to puke.

"You've been to this rodeo before, Zack," I hear myself say aloud.

"Fifteen seconds," I hear the stage manager announce.

The funny lesbian comes back out on stage with a microphone. Behind her I can see twenty thousand dimly lit people, hoping for a life-altering performance by Wendy Harper. Well, at least hoping to hear something special, for once, at the Grammys.

What am I doing here?

The lights come up. The funny lesbian begins talking, but I can't hear her. She's not in my monitor. Is she supposed to be in my monitor? Is my monitor not working? Sweet jumping Jesus, this is going to be a train wreck!

I look around wildly. Trash Bag. Where is Trash Bag? I look offstage, scanning for someone. Where is the monitor operator? Where is Trash Bag? The locusts take flight.

Suddenly, a familiar face. Lark Dray. I beseech him with my eyes. "Read my mind, Lark. I've got a dead monitor at the Grammys, and I'm about to throw up on a $140,000 piano, not to mention myself."

Lark smiles that evil smile, then something odd. He gives me a thumbs-up.

Applause, and lots of it. I turn my head. Wendy Harper walks onto the stage. The funny lesbian scampers off.

"Thank you," says Wendy Harper, quite clearly through my monitor. She walks to center stage.

My head snaps back to Lark. He is still smiling at me, but now his hands are bouncing, palms down, softly, in front of him, and it is a genuine smile, not evil at all.

"Slow down," his hands say. "Breathe," his smile says.

The lights dim and a single follow spot hits Wendy in the middle of the stage. She looks terrific. This is a great seat. So much better than I had earlier. I am on stage. What am I doing here? Breathe, dammit!

Wendy's voice is in my monitor again. "This evening I am honored to be joined onstage by a wonderful musician and songwriter to whom I owe a great deal. He's nominated tonight for Song of the Year, for the piece we're going to play for you now. Ladies and gentlemen, Zack Fluett."

A spotlight blasts my face. I am utterly blinded. I smile reflexively. There is applause, perhaps even a bit more than polite. Time to go.

I settle myself, put a foot on the sustain pedal, still blind. Hopefully everyone in the band can see me. Hands fumble a bit shakily onto the keys. Hopefully no one can see me. What am I doing again?

D whole note in the bass, mezzo piano. Once again in the bass in octaves, add the D-minor tonic chord above high C in the right hand. Yes! There they are in the monitor, the cellos murmuring that same low D. I play the distinctive sixteenth note first-third-first in the treble, then into the down-beat grace note fourth-to-the-fifth as the cellos and my left hand move together to the B-flat in the bass. We're playing "I Turned Around."

Applause. I look up, and I can see everything. The conductor is locked on me, his eyes like lasers. Wendy has her back to the audience, her microphone clutched to her chest with both hands, eyes shining at me. God, she looks fantastic. I turn my head, and Huge is grinning at me, eyes wide, brush in hand, preparing to pull it across the ride cymbal right... now. I feather the A-minor with the repeating sixteenth note fourth-fifth pattern, and the violins kiss the high A. When we step down to the G-major, the electric bass joins us, along with the uprights in the orchestra, mezzo forte, and then quickly mezzo piano again as we flat the third, minoring the chord, reminding everyone that no matter how many times you hear it, this song does not have a happy ending.

Calmly and assuredly back to the D-minor, the B-flat minor, and the D-minor figure again, and Wendy turns to the audience and begins to sing. I close my eyes.

CHAPTER 41

Burton Fluett: 4/26/37-10/09/96
Burt Fluett, local rancher, died Sunday at the St.
Vincent Hospital in Billings after a long battle
with leukemia. He is survived by his wife, Cherie, daughter Mary, son Zack, and five grandchil-
dren. Burt was a local legend known to all. A
more full celebration of his life is planned for the
Sunday edition.

The Whitlash Promoter, October 12, 1996

I WASN'T THERE WHEN the Old Man died, of
course. He had been in remission for almost five
years, and we all had hopes that it would stick. I
checked in with Mom from time to time from the
road, and she told me that he was doing pretty well,
back on his horse roping calves and cussing out the
liberals on the television set. But when the blood
work came back bad once more, that was all she
wrote. He was gone in a matter of a couple of weeks.

I didn't figure he'd crater as fast as he did, and
I was taking a brief break from having Les Pauls
thrown at me by vacationing with an *Entertainment*

Tonight hostess in Belize, so I hadn't raced straight on home when I first got word he had fallen out of remission. When I got back to the States and Mom finally got through to me in L.A., I hopped on the first available bird, but the son of a bitch died while I was in the cab coming from the Billings airport to the hospital.

I'm pretty sure he knew I was coming and just didn't need to see me. Mom's look of disappointment at my appearance (not to mention my lateness) the moment I walked in was enough to make me understand why. There are times it's fun to dress and coif and smell like a rock star, but standing at your father's deathbed just isn't one of them.

The cancer had taken damn near all of him. At least he checked out having worn out all the machinery. My sister Mary stared balefully at me from the corner where she sat with her perfect little Christian family, praying and sobbing. I knelt down next to the bed where he lay, his eyes mercifully closed but his mouth agape. Gone. I lay my head on his unmoving chest and cried for the first time since I was a child. Cried rivers.

Eventually Mary kindly put a hand softly on my shoulder and helped me to my feet. She walked me over to Mom, who hugged me tightly and with forgiveness, and then Mary took me down the hall and down the stairs and out into the early fall air.

Mary and I had never gotten along very well. She was six years older than I, to begin with, and she was a Montanan through and through, and never understood what I hated about the place. She thought it was a good, safe place to grow up and ultimately to raise children, and, for the most part, she was right.

What she failed to understand was that I had no desire to grow up, and I certainly had no desire to raise children. We found a certain rapprochement during the first phase of the Old Man's illness, however. He first got sick during the waning days of August West, before I moved to L.A., and I did go up and spend a couple of weeks with the family after his first round of chemo.

Mary was pregnant at the time, but she still insisted on coming by and cooking all manner of meals and helping Mom with the laundry and generally fussing over the Old Man until he'd bark at her to give him some room, which made her happy because she could be certain then that she had done enough and was fully appreciated. I, on the other hand, hung around and smoked cigarettes and drank beer and watched ESPN and The Weather Channel with him and allowed him to carry out a slow-burn inquiry into what kind of life I was leading, and what the hell was I doing, and what sort of damn fool was I, and things of that nature. This also made Mary certain that she was fully appreciated. In this fashion, we got along pretty well.

We also got along just fine in later years when Claudia was around, because everyone liked her so much that some of it just naturally caromed over to me. Claudia and Mary got along very well, and the only reason that Mary hadn't come to our wedding was because she was close to due to give birth again.

I stood out in the blowing leaves of the Billings Hospital parking lot and lit a cigarette. "I didn't get to say goodbye," I mourned.

Mary's look of disapproval returned. The river of tears had only granted me a brief respite. The sight of her heavily tattooed, unkempt, unbathed, and most likely high brother angling for pity brought back the steel.

"Nope. You sure didn't. I wouldn't worry too much though. He wasn't asking after you or anything."

Cold. Cold and unnecessary, I thought, but probably fair.

I crushed out my cigarette. "No, I suppose he wasn't."

The Old Man and I pretty much had stopped talking. It wasn't like we had a fight or anything; he just got tired of being disappointed in me, and I got tired of him being disappointed in me. He was never really happy about the music side of things, although he did allow as to how I was obviously good at it and worked hard and all, once Cultural Wasteland started having real success. But he was never one to brag on me, either.

I think we got along the best during the time I was married to Claudia, because he figured I couldn't be all bad if I could get a girl that smart and funny and pretty to walk down the aisle. But when Claudia left and I took the first of many tumbles into the deep, dark places—where you don't answer your phone or even keep the same phone number, and you don't call your mother, and you don't ever come home—I figure it confirmed suspicions and concerns he'd had about me for years.

For my part, I didn't really have a problem with the Old Man. I honored him for who he was and what he did. Hell, as a kid I idolized the big sonofabitch because I knew he was the best rancher in the county. At the same time, I also knew I'd never be as big as he was or as hardworking, either. When I got older that idolatry turned to honest to goodness respect, but that didn't change that I wanted to live my life my way.

Unfortunately, looking at the Old Man became like looking at a mirror when you really didn't want to see your reflection. I didn't like what I saw in me when I was around him. Rather than try to change that, I just avoided the situation and hid out on the road with Cultural Wasteland. I did that with a lot of people, it turned out.

Mary and I reconciled, or something like it, during the time when I was taking care of Bobby. I would call her pretty frequently to ask her advice on how to handle some of his needs or just to unload, and she took to calling and checking in on me too. I grew to understand a phrase she and Mom used on those rare occasions when I had asked about the Old Man, and I could hear her smile on the other end of the phone when I reported that "We had a good day today." She sent me a beautiful hydrangea when Bobby died. I planted it in the backyard in Woody Creek, where it has thrived and is a constant reminder to me of the value of each day of life and of the people who share it with you as family.

CHAPTER 42

WE MAKE THE TRANSITION to the middle eight, the strings and woodwinds providing support as we crescendo slightly into the G-minor, then G-minor over E, then the F-major to A-major that gives the false sense of hope, before returning to the D-minor verse. Wendy sings the lyrics the audience knows by heart, but I hear the words as only I know them. I hear her sing about loss and disappointment, about regret and longing. I hear her sing about Claudia and Davy and the Old Man and Bobby. I crescendo, accompanying her as she sings about me too.

We are back to the G-minor, and I can feel the energy in the arena begin to build as the audience anticipates the soaring, powerful, satisfying climax as only Wendy Harper can sing it, the guitars ringing high, sustained notes and the orchestra preparing to swell. Wendy comes over to me, stands at my shoulder. The conductor locks onto me, his eyebrows questioning, alert, and ready. I nod and break back to the D-minor, the piano mournfully alone, as the strings hush. I feel Wendy's hand on my shoulder and sense a sharp intake of breath throughout the whole of the Staples Center, and Wendy drops her voice an octave, and she sings the right words, but now I feel as if everyone hears the same words that I do, the real words. "Too late. Too late. Too late."

I clutch the keys with talon hands and close my eyes and pray. Wendy's voice cracks low and dies softly with a cry as the cellos play the long, grief-stricken, final note. We all hold our breath as I tinkle the successive broken D-minors up the keyboard and off to heaven. The pain hangs in the air, dissipates into nothingness, and then is gone forever, leaving behind only fresh, clean silence.

Wendy squeezes my shoulder. I exhale, and with me the whole of the Staples Center exhales. A moment of dead silence, and then comes the applause. Thunderous. And cheering. I open my eyes and smile into Wendy's, and I am vaguely aware that we both have tears streaming down our faces on national television. She tugs at me. I stand and step away from the piano. We hold hands and together we bow, and the applause goes on even after the stage lights dim.

The houselights come up, and we are in the midst of the taping of a television show, but the audience still stands and applauds. Wendy and I walk to the front of the stage together and take one more bow, we acknowledge the band and the orchestra, and we wave to our peers in the front rows. Then we duck as the boom camera moves back to first position, and we hustle off the stage, stepping carefully over moving cables, the love of the room pursuing us.

CHAPTER 43

WILMA THEATER
131 S. Higgins Ave.
Friday 9:00 pm
ZACK FLUETT (Cultural Wasteland)
$5 cover/Ladies Free/$2 Jäger shots

Missoulian, August 24, 2003

I WAS BACKSTAGE AT the Wilma Theater in Missoula one evening before a show when there was a knock on the dressing room door, and the stage manager informed me that someone who knows me would like to come back and say hi. I had no interest in chatting with someone I had undoubtedly spent most of my adult life avoiding, so I suggested that the visitor cram it sideways.

"Is that any way to talk to your mother?" said my mother as she breezed in.

My mother was not on the list of people I had no interest in chatting with, though, in a sense, I had spent most of my adult life avoiding her.

"What're you doing here?" I asked, reasonably enough, I thought.

"We came by to see your show. The kids are getting a bite, but I thought I'd drop in for a little chat first. I hope you don't mind."

"Drop in? Mom, it's damn near four hundred miles. You just dropped in?"

"I love you darling, but not that much. We're here to get Tim settled."

Blank stare.

"Your nephew Tim. He's starting at the U this week. We're helping him get moved in, and you just happened to be doing a show, so we thought we'd come watch."

"Oh. Tim. Right. He's going to college? Isn't he a little young for that?"

"He's eighteen, dear. That's the standard age. Also, I brought you this."

She produced a small package from her purse and handed it to me. I unwrapped the butcher paper around it and extracted a weathered box I had seen many times before. The Old Man's harmonica. I opened the case, and there it was, the vintage Hohner Marine Band in the key of C. Made in Germany and everything. Granddad had brought it back from the war where it had helped him to keep occupied in the Meuse-Argonne when the Germans weren't shooting at him. Granddad had scratched his name on one end of the bronze comb where it extended beyond the cover plate, so he could identify it as his own. The story is that he was pretty good on it and used to play at local dances and the like back in the days before television kept folks at home.

In any event, he gave it to the Old Man at some

point before I was born. He scratched his name on the other end of the comb. Some of my earliest memories are of him tootling along on it after branding or shipping or some other event when the neighbors came around. He wasn't much good on it, but everyone got a kick out of this normally taciturn man playing along while Mom sang "Don't Fence Me In" or "The Ace in the Hole." It evoked warm memories.

"Turn it over," Mom said.

On the bottom side comb, opposite where Granddad's name was, the Old Man had scratched "Zack Fluett."

"I found it going through his desk. I'm sure he meant to give it to you, but you two just didn't get your schedules together at the right time."

I looked at my mother with a none-too-subtle combination of "Oh come on" and "Thank you for telling that thoughtful lie."

"There's room for one more name on there, you know," pointed out Mom.

"Maybe one of Mary's kids would like it. Any of them show any musical ability?"

"All of them, in fact. But I think you should keep it for a while, Zack. You never know what might happen. You might have a child of your own one day."

"Getting a little long in the tooth for that, Mom."

"Cary Grant was sixty-two when he had his first child."

"I, Mother, am no Cary Grant."

"Why Zack! That may be the first modest thing I've ever heard you say. I do believe there's hope for you yet."

I grinned. She was a funny thing.

"Have a nice show tonight, Zack. We're all excited to see you."

"Sure, Mom."

"And Zack? Please don't drink too much. You know how it bothers the kids."

I said nothing. She smiled tightly, gave me a little hug, and left. I turned the Hohner over in my hands and looked at the Old Man's name, and then I gave it an experimental toot. I reached into my bag and pulled out my neck brace, removed my blues harp from it, and inserted the Old Man's Marine Band in there instead. I thought about him in the moment that he had scratched my name on it, and I thought about the life I had chosen to lead and what he thought about that.

Then I got loaded. Again.

CHAPTER 44

THE ATMOSPHERE BACKSTAGE IS electric. Wendy doesn't let go of my hand. Huge thumps me on the back. Everyone is elated. Even Trash Bag gives me a thumbs-up. I assume that my imminent murder in the parking lot has been called off, at least for the time being.

We cruise into the Talent Lounge to warm applause. Everyone is smiling. The funny lesbian shakes my hand and hugs Wendy, then dashes off to continue the show. Huge blasts open a Dom Perignon magnum and pours. A glass appears in my hand. I toast Wendy and Huge and the rest of her band, and they toast me, and I slug back the cold fizz and hold my glass out for more. It magically refills.

Wendy pulls me over to a black leather couch, and we collapse onto it. I down my champagne, and Huge refills it once again.

"That was pretty awesome, Cowboy," Wendy says.

"You were fantastic," I reply.

"Did I miss something, or did you two just have sex?" rumbles Huge.

"*Better than sex,*" we both say.

"*What could possibly be better than sex?*"

Claudia plops down on the couch beside me and kisses my cheek.

"*Well, you've had him honey, so I guess I really couldn't say, but that was still a lot of fun,*" Wendy says.

"*I'll bet. That was probably the finest performance I've ever seen at the Grammys, Wendy.*"

"*It wouldn't have come off without Zack.*"

Huge refills my empty glass. I smile broadly. I am so pleased to be sitting here with these two women.

"*Now you just need to pick up the hardware,*" says Huge.

My stomach lurches. I had forgotten why I was here in the first place. It seemed like the night was over, but there's still the little matter of finding out who wins the miniature gold gramophone. A cold chill runs through me. Sweat breaks out on my forehead.

"*I honestly don't care anymore. I've accomplished what I came here to do,*" says Wendy, and I think she honestly means it.

"*Help me up, Huge,*" I mumble. "*I gotta go to the bathroom.*"

Huge yanks me to my feet, and I slug back the contents of my flute.

A PA appears. "*Mr. Fluett? Ms. Harper? Would you accompany me to the Media Room for a few pictures and a quote or two?*"

"*Certainly,*" says Wendy, hopping up. "*Come on with me, cowboy.*"

My heart is suddenly in my throat. "*I don't think so, Wendy. I'm guessing that they really just want to take pictures of you. Nobody knows who I am.*"

"*Sure they do, Zack,*" Wendy says, encouragingly.

"*If they didn't before, they have a better idea now,*" Claudia chips in.

"*Maybe on the next go round,*" I say. "*If I actually win. I'm a little wigged out right now, and I need to wash up again.*"

Wendy nods and turns away with the PA.

"*You really were great tonight, Zack,*" says Claudia. "*You should take your moment in the sun. You shouldn't run away from this.*"

"*Thank you,*" I reply. *I appreciate Claudia's kindness, but she's not the one who has to answer questions and who still doesn't know what the evening has yet to bring.* "*It's too bad that the awards have to ruin these awards ceremonies.*"

"*You do what you want, but I really think you should just come with me and see what it's all about. As I recall, the last time you were here you didn't get as far as the photographers. Your mother would probably like to see a picture of you on your big night.*"

Ah. She pulled out the heavy artillery. "*Come on, Huge,*" I say, "*And bring that bottle.*"

"*Media Room?*" he asks.

I nod. He grins at Claudia and helps her up off the couch, and she takes my hand and leads me out of the Talent Lounge.

We don't have to go far. The Media Room is pretty much next door, right off the first crash door outside the main stage. It is filled with photographers and reporters, and there is a small catwalk/stage with a gray curtain hanging behind it covered in Grammy logos and sponsors' trademarks. A knot of publicists stand ready to haul their artists up onto the catwalk to preen for the cameras and answer whatever questions these morons in the press pool can muster. It's been years, but I still hate this. I wonder if I can just talk about the gardens of the royal palace of Luxembourg. Probably not. They may be morons, but they speak English. Claudia squeezes my hand.

"I'll just sneak up there and get you on the walk with Wendy real quick." *She trots off. I look over the heads of the popping flashes to see who's up there now. It's Melanie, the GDT. I turn quickly and bump directly into Huge.*

"Let's go," *I say.*

"What?"

"I want to go. I don't want to see her."

Huge looks up and sees the source of my concern. He nods.

"Don't sweat it, Zack. She's almost finished and she'll go out that other door over there. You don't have to see her." *He points out the logical exit point for me.*

I look up and see he's right. "I still want to leave."

"Think of your mother."

"Hand me that bottle."

He does, and I take a few more big swigs of the champagne. I hand it back and he takes a swig too.

"That was fun tonight, Zack."

I can't help but smile. "Yes it was. Can't tell you how good it was to look across that stage and see your ugly mug behind the skins."

Huge smiles, and then nods his head toward the catwalk. "See there, she's gone."

I turn back to the little stage, and indeed, the GDT has left, and Wendy has taken her place. Warmth returns to my chest.

"Let's go," *says Huge, indicating a waving Claudia beckoning us from the front of the line. I hand the bottle back to Huge, and we make our way through the crowd. The photographers are snapping and Wendy is smiling* and posing for them. Claudia waves at her, catches her attention, and then points at me. Wendy sees me and smiles even more brightly. She beckons me up on the catwalk.

Claudia takes my arm as I reach the stairs and steadies me as I mount the stage. The champagne is starting to do its job. I feel pretty good, however, and I don't have far to walk. Wendy promptly links arms with me and we smile out at the photographers. Wendy reintroduces me to them, and indicates that her performance tonight would not have been possible without me. That's nice.

One of the reporters gives me a bored look and asks a rote question.

"What did it feel like to play out there tonight with Wendy Harper at the Grammys, Mr. Fluid?"

I grit my teeth in a smile. Out of the corner of my eye I can see Huge laughing into the ceiling, and although she looks serious and professional, I can detect a quiver of laughter in Claudia's lips as well.

"Great," I respond.

There is a silence for several seconds as a few more flashbulbs pop in desultory fashion. Then someone says, "Great. Could we get a few more shots with just Ms. Harper?"

"You bet," I think to myself. Wendy squeezes my hand and busses me on the cheek, and I return back the way I came. Someone by the stairs tries to point out the right direction in which I should make my exit, but I'm not going to comply. I head right back down the stairs, forcing one of the American Idols to move out of my way. Fortunately, Huge and Claudia are still at the bottom to greet me.

"Great," Huge says. "That was great!"

"Really great," giggles Claudia.

I give them both what I hope is a devastating look, but they know me too well. They can see the laughter in my eyes.

"I'll make sure to get a copy of the best shot from Wire Image for your mom," Claudia promises, "But now I've got to get back to my paying job."

"Go Greentricity," I smile back at her.

She heads off and I turn to Huge, who is trying very hard not to laugh in my face.

"I wasn't kidding before. I gotta take a piss. Come on you big ape, and bring that bottle with you."

"Your mother would be so proud, Mr. Fluid," he chortles, waving the half-full magnum in the air.

CHAPTER 45

CELEBRATE THE BICENTENNIAL!
There will be a special program celebrating the
nation's Bicentennial at the Middle School gym
on Thursday evening at 7:00 p.m. Join the students in a song and dance review of America's
history. Refreshments will be served.

The Whitlash Promoter, May 21, 1976

THE FIRST TIME I played the piano in public, that
is, in front of a group of people not strictly blood
related, was in the late spring of 1976, the Bicentennial year. It was the end of my first year of going to
school in town, at the Middle School, having spent
kindergarten through fifth grade at the country
school out near the ranch. The Middle School was
the old high school from the fifties, and as a result,
for a town of just over three thousand, it was pretty well outfitted, including as it did a proper Home
Ec room with kitchen, an industrial arts shop with
lathes and kilns and all manner of dangerous things,
and a decent gym with a stage for plays or musicals.

Like many schools around the country that year, ours determined to put on a grand revue and tribute to our nation, with band, chorus, drill team, and drama all coming together to perform a Middle School civics version of American history from Jamestown to the present. Well, almost the present. The powers that be agreed that leaving out Vietnam and Watergate and simply ending on a vague note of optimism for century three was the best way to go.

The Middle School music teacher and director of the Bicentennial salute was my Aunt Shirley, a blood relative the Old Man called Aunt Squirrelly. She decided that the segment on the Roaring Twenties should be set in a speakeasy with flappers and a jazz piano player along the lines of a white W.C. Handy. The chorus would sing of the excesses of the era, a continuing crescendo ultimately concluding in the hilarity of Black Tuesday and the ensuing Great Depression. The Great Depression was rendered by an audience sing-along of "This Land is Your Land," segueing without irony into a call to arms for the Second World War. But first we had to get through the Jazz Age. Of course, as a blood relative, I was just the perfect little piano player Aunt Squirrelly had in mind.

Why she thought it might be appropriate to put five scantily clad adolescent girls and one ridiculously attired pubescent boy into a setting representing a complete disregard for the law of the land at the time, I will never know. I do know that I howled mightily to my mother when I was drafted for the assignment. Up until then, the piano had been something I could keep secret from the other boys. It was a chore I was forced to perform, practicing thirty minutes per day with one hour long lesson a week. Mom and the Old Man didn't seem to care that I had no interest whatsoever in the piano and would have preferred to be on horseback or playing football or having a tooth pulled. They bought the piano for my older sister, Mary, and if we were going to have something that expensive in the house, then I was going to learn how to play it too.

My mother informed me that I would indeed bow to Aunt Squirrelly's wishes. She was, after all, my music teacher and could give me a bad grade, and also, she was still quite fragile after the loss of her fiancé in Saigon. This was really all she had left, so Mom thought it best for me just to go along and be a good boy.

This I did with bad humor, practicing the difficult (and, I must say, inane) salute to the early gangster years over and over at home, and then bearing the catcalls of my buddies when I plodded out of the risers over to the piano to accompany the chorus in rehearsals of the song. Worse yet was practicing with the girls who portrayed flappers, playing the same sections of the song over and over as they learned their faux Charleston steps.

It was all a nightmare until the evening of the dress rehearsal, when I donned my straw boater, sleeve garters, and bright red vest, and was then joined by the flappers and saw their costumes, or lack thereof, for the first time. Aunt Squirrelly, because she was, in retrospect, on lots of medication but none of it the right kind, decided to add in a few fun little twists, such as putting one flapper on top of my piano where I could see up her skirt. She also had all of them gather around me at the end of the number, kissing me up, tossing my hat, and playing with my hair, as I pulled a fake flask from under the piano bench and toasted the audience with a wink.

Of course, we all pretended that this was just horrifying, all this kissing and groping and leering and the like, but none of us actually objected to a bit of it. Deep down I was secretly excited suddenly to be surrounded by touchy-feely-not-completely-dressed girls, even though I wasn't entirely certain about why this was working so well for me. Also, the verbal abuse from the other boys came to a screeching halt, almost certainly because they sensed the same thing. I suppose the opportunity to show off some of their nascent sexuality did the same thing for the girls, but all I know is that when the show finally went down, we were the hit of the whole thing. I played like there was no tomorrow, the flappers flapped, I saw Rhonda Smedsrud's underwear, and I watched as my mother and the Old Man, along with half the town, clapped and cheered while the girls hugged and kissed me as I toasted the onset of the Depression. Rock Star.

CHAPTER 46

I REPLACE THE FLASK in the Old Man's boot and wash my hands. A quick jolt or two of the Esperanto during my bathroom break has me feeling pretty damn good again. Champagne has never been my best medicine. I like distillates better than fermentations.

I've recovered from the embarrassment of the Media Room and actually found the humor in it, but now I'm actually starting to get downright nervous about my category. I have to admit that I really would like to win. I know that Wendy is right. I know that we gave a once-in-a-lifetime performance that will be remembered (or at least she'll be remembered for it). I feel good about that. On the other hand, Wendy probably will win Album of the Year, and even if she doesn't, she'll undoubtedly win in any number of categories in the future.

This is pretty much it for me, though. Unless I pull a Bobby Craft (and he wasn't alive to collect the hardware), I am unlikely to get nominated in any category other than for a songwriter award, and I'm not at all sure that I didn't blow my wad with "I Turned Around."

I know I shouldn't care. I know it's just a Grammy. I know it's not going to change my life (you need an Oscar to do that). A week ago I wasn't even going to come and two hours ago I was ready to leave. Yet what an experience I just had! So deep down I obviously wanted to come and was meant to be here.

Now I want to stand up there and give a speech. I want to say something about the artists who are still out on the road playing small venues and scratching by, giving it all they have, even though the industry has left them behind. I want to look up on my mantle and watch that shiny thing justify twenty years of refusing to play by the rules. I want Mom and Mary and the kids to have that experience too. I want, whenever I see my name in print (as rarely as that might be), to have "Grammy Award-winning artist" appended to it. Sort of like Esq. or Ph.D.

"You working on your speech?" asks Huge, who has suddenly appeared in the mirror behind me.

"Beg pardon?"

"You looked like you were thinking, so I figured maybe you're working on your speech."

"Nah. No. Not expecting to win anyway. Don't really care. Wendy's got it right. Might as well just go home now."

"You know, Zack, for someone who lies as much as you do, you're sure lousy at it."

Huge hands me a proper drink glass with ice and brown liquid in it.

"I figured we'd had enough of that champagne, so I brought you a real drink."

"Jack and Coke?"

"Figured you could use the caffeine. It's pretty light

on the Jack. Bartender got a little parsimonious with me after it turned out that was some guy named T-Pain's Dom I grabbed."

"Rock & Roll rules," I shrug.

"Yeah, but I think there's some rap rules too that we're probably not fully aware of, and I don't really want to learn the hard way, so let's stay away from the Talent Lounge for a while."

"Roger."

We exit the men's room and amble away from the artists and media and back toward the dressing rooms down one of those broad cinderblock corridors in the backstage greenish light. I take a drink. Tastes good, but I need to be a little careful. I'm out of practice, and mixing champagne, tequila, and Jack is probably unwise. Jesus, I miss cocaine, but I'm just not prepared to go down that road ever again.

I stop under one of the ubiquitous No Smoking signs and pull out a cigarette. I offer the pack to Huge knowing he will decline, and I light up. I'm glad to be with Huge. I feel more relaxed. What was it that he reminded me of a minute ago? Something fleeting that I should remember to do. What was it again?

Speech. Yes, that was it. He asked if I was preparing my speech. I have not prepared my speech. I will probably not need it anyway, but just a minute ago I was hoping that I would win and wanting to give a speech, so I should start thinking about it in case I do win. Of course, if I don't prepare something, then I'll probably win. That's the way the universe works. So it's prepare something meaningful and memorable that doesn't get used and hangs around in your head, or else just get up there and do what everyone does, thank God and the first five people who come to mind, and then let *the orchestra drown you out. I ought to be able to do a little better than that.*

Hey, there's Lark Dray. Now what was it that I was thinking about him?

"Looks like the big man's getting ready to play. Let's watch," says Huge.

Lark carries his old Les Paul. I recognize it as the one he threw to me when we played "This Is Gonna Get Expensive" on the Grammys over a decade ago. There's no Cultural Wasteland tonight, though. Just Lark Dray. I crush out my Marlboro and we follow his entourage back toward the stage, where the lights change from green to blue.

A security guy steps up to check our laminates and then steps aside graciously. Huge and I sneak forward and stand in the wings. Huge smiles as Lark plugs in his Les Paul and steps up to the microphone. The lights come up and the funny lesbian does her thing.

I am usually annoyed when I see or think about Lark Dray, but not right now. Is it the booze? I am starting to feel a little floaty. No, I remember. He was encouraging to me when I got panicked on stage just a little while ago. Jesus, that seems like a lifetime. This Jack & Coke is empty. But that isn't what I was trying to think of. Maybe I'll just pour a little Esperanto into this ice. Just pull it out of this boot here. What was I thinking again?

Lark starts to sing, his voice gravelly and tough, lyrics still poetic and smart. I actually enjoy listening to him. I pour the tequila and take a drink. Ah. Thank heavens for that nice little gay PA Alain who filled up my flask.

There it is. That's what I was trying to think about. Lark Dray is gay?

CHAPTER 47

KNICKERBOCKERS
Wednesday 9:00 pm
BOBBY CRAFT
Cultural Wasteland
Tickets $20

Lincoln Journal Star, March 4, 1993

WE WERE IN OMAHA on tour with Bobby Craft the night we wrote most of "Graveyard Shift." We were staying in some dive place on the edge of town, having played earlier in Lincoln. Huge had taken Winston, Bobby's long-suffering driver and roadie, out to get a little break from Bobby, and the Ramos brothers were cruising the campus for coeds. Lark and I were hanging around in the room doing pretty much nothing. I had made my phone call to Claudia and made lovey-dovey sounds until Lark pretended to vomit in the background, so Claudia told me to tell him that she loved him too and signed off.

About then, Bobby showed up at our door. He

was out of sorts because Winston was not keeping to their ordinary schedule. We invited him in and listened to him bitch about life on the road for a while. Then I chimed in and pointed out that at least he had an RV with a bed in it, while we were usually trying to sleep on a stinky bus. I also pointed out that he seemed to have a female fan in about every other town who would take him to bed in an actual home of some description with sheets that most likely hadn't been slept in by three hundred different people in the last year. I groused about not seeing my girlfriend in well over a month and spending all of my time with smelly guys, rarely seeing the sun.

"So what's your fucking point?" snapped Bobby.

"I'm getting sick of the graveyard shift, that's all."

"So become an accountant."

"Yeah, Zack. What you got against workin' nights? I love it," said Lark.

"I just get a little tired of it all the time."

"I hear they've got a good accounting school here in Kansas," Bobby injected.

"We're in Nebraska," I pointed out.

"Not knowing what state I'm in is the state I'm in," barked Bobby.

"Oh, that's great. Can I use that?" enthused Lark, picking up his guitar.

He started messing around on the guitar and started singing the line with a syncopated rhythm, stressing the word "is." When he came around to the obvious chorus, I sang out, "I'm workin' that Graveyard Shift." Bobby grinned and started drumming his palms on his knees in the style of "Marrakesh Express," a locomotive beat that Huge would later bring to life.

Lark started jotting down lyric ideas about being a midnight worker. He used our recent late night experiences in the studio with Leon, our time out on the road with Bobby, and he threw in what we saw on the road or after the show: the overnight truckers, the cops, the emergency workers. Bobby and I added lines here and there, but Lark stayed with a formula of seeing the night as a nocturnal sharing between men—teams and partners and crews—spending the nighttime hours with someone you trusted, who had your back and you his as you ventured out to come face to face with the things that go bump while everyone else is sleeping. He made it sound sexy and dangerous and cool. I started missing Claudia less and less the more he sang.

Lark and I were a good writing team because we had complementary talents and also an ability to communicate clearly on a musical level. Lark was far more of a poet than I, and I was the more accomplished music theorist.

Not that Lark wasn't a good musician. Lark was good for a three-chord verse with a two-chord chorus and a walk-down bridge. Sometimes this is just what a song needs, no question. But other times, especially, it seemed to me, when Lark was trying to convey something a bit more complex or metaphorical, having something a little meatier in terms of structure was not a bad thing. Also, despite frequent screams of "Manilow" from the Ramos brothers, changing keys was also not necessarily a bad thing in conveying new meaning to an already-heard chorus. For those things, you came to me.

On the other hand, sometimes Lark got a little too metaphorical for his own good, and it was up to me to make things a bit more straightforward. Hence the line in "Old Girlfriend" that always got the big cheer when it was live and we inserted the verb: "I miss [fucking] my new girlfriend; good thing you're here." Lark would never have thought to say something like that, but once it was out there, he knew it was all there was to say.

After he went solo, Lark started working with a wide array of other songwriters and producers, and some very good tracks came of it, but few were as popular as the big hits that came out of Cultural Wasteland. I would eventually start working alone, and while I think I improved lyrically over time, I would certainly not have anything big until "I Turned Around."

CHAPTER 48

LARK IS SNARLING ABOUT the Republicans, the best I can tell. I think this is an anti-war song, but I haven't been listening to the radio, so it's new to me. It's still pretty good. The structure is typical Lark, and his voice is even more powerful and emotional than it was a decade ago. I do feel the hurt and betrayal there. The band is slick, but Lark still manages to sound raw, and his guitar playing is very percussive and strong, probably because he has two additional lead guitar players both imitating Peter Ramos behind him.

I take another swig of tequila. Huge grabs me by the collar and stands me up straight. Ooops. Must have been swaying. Subpar. Subpar indeed.

"Coffee," Huge and I say at the same time.

"Indeed. Fine plan," I say.

Huge takes the glass from my hand and tosses it into a trashcan as we amble back toward the Talent Lounge. It shatters and we get stares.

"My bad," Huge growls.

"It's just a glass. They'll have more."

"No, my bad for giving you too much champers. You lost your hollow leg."

"Nonsense. I'm just out of practice. I'll get better."

"I really don't think so, Zack, but that's your business."

We arrive at the Talent Lounge and Huge gets me a cup of black coffee. It tastes terrible. Has probably been brewing there the whole show. Who drinks coffee at the Grammys?

"This is terrible."

"Think of it as medicine."

"What's all this about Lark being gay?"

"Drink your medicine."

"No really, Huge. It's hard to believe. When did it happen?"

We find a black leather couch and sit down.

"Well, I assume that what you're really asking with that question is when did I find out."

"Well, that too, but not exactly. I mean, the Lark Dray I knew was straight."

"Funny how you can know a fellow and not really know him at all, isn't it?"

"Are you telling me that Lark was gay back in the day?"

"Look, Zack, I don't know that I'm the most expert person to answer your questions. I can tell you this—after you left the band…"

"I got kicked out of the band."

"All right, after you self-immolated, Lark became more and more separate from the rest of us, and he had this series of 'assistants' that were all kind of the same faggy type who traveled with us on the road and were always around him. He always had his own bus to himself by then too. They carried his cell phones and stuff, but we all started to suspect that there was more going on there. It was nobody's business, of course. Lark can do what he *wants. And then after a little while he announces that he's doing a solo record, and that's all she wrote."*

"So you don't really know for sure."

"Well, a while back I ran into Anastasia. You remember her?"

Name rings a bell, but I can't quite place it. I focus. This is important stuff.

"Vegan chick? Caught the lunker at the ranch?"

Huge nods. *"I ran into her at an organic market in Nashville a while back and she asked after Lark, and I tell her I haven't talked to him, and then I ask whatever happened to them, you know, small talk like you do."*

"I don't."

"Yeah, but you're rude. Anyway, Anastasia says that she met her soul mate, Irene, and decided it was time to stop being a beard."

I ponder this revelation. *"No shit."*

"No shit. She tells me that at first she was just friends with Lark, then he started giving her money for that t-shirt line she was running back then, and they got to spending a lot of time together, and she told him she didn't really like men, and he told her that he really did, but that nobody could know because of his rock-star image, and so she just started playing beard. They didn't really discuss it or anything, supposedly. She just did it, and he treated her like a girlfriend, investing in her hippy-dippy businesses and letting her travel around with us and shit."

"She told you this?"

"Yep, and she was pretty surprised I didn't know. Then she told me that old Carol from San Francisco was one of his beards too. Remember her?"

"Rain in her eyes?"

"That's the one. He made all that shit up about cheating on her with another girl. He was with some guy in

the Castro. They had a fight about something else. I don't know what, but he wanted her out of the picture so none of us would talk to her."

"I recall that she was a college volleyball player."

"Nuff said."

"What about that actress? The one on the Internet?"

"I thought about that, and I think he was more worried about getting outed than anything else. I looked at some of the old corporate records at the end of Cultural Wasteland, and I noticed that she was on the payroll back then. I wondered about it a little at the time, but I didn't really put it together until I got to thinking about what Anastasia told me. And you've heard all about Melanie already."

"Fuckin' A." I am stunned on the one hand, but deep down in the very far back of my mind a small voice whispers that it always knew and why couldn't the rest of the brain stop talking about me for a minute and listen to it.

"I don't care if he thinks it isn't rock-star and wants to hide it from the world, but why the fuck didn't he tell us? We wouldn't have cared."

"I don't know that that's true, and I sure don't know that Lark could have felt for sure that it was true. You never know how somebody's going to react to the news that you like cock, especially a couple of Latin Catholic Lotharios, a former dockworker, and a cowboy."

I had forgotten that Huge had worked on the docks in the days of Danger Zone.

"I think he wasn't just hiding being gay or being in denial about it, he was hiding how he felt about you especially," he continues.

"Don't lay this on me, man. What makes you think he was in love with me?"

"Where the fuck is my gawdamn motherfuckin' Dom

Perignon?" yells a voice from across the Talent Lounge. I am betting it is T-Pain.

Huge hops up and scampers away, leaving me with my thoughts. I don't think Huge is right, exactly. Maybe Lark was in love with me, but back in the day, I was in love with him too. I just happen to be straight. And Lark knew that, so even if he was in love with me, he never acted on it in a way that could possibly make me feel uncomfortable.

It would explain why he got so pissed at me over cheating on Claudia when the other guys really didn't, even though they all loved her. The three of us were thick as thieves, and cheating on her probably made him feel like I was cheating on him too. I don't know. This stuff could drive you crazy. All I do know is a lot of what I have thought and felt about Lark Dray for a long time is turning out to be wrong. I don't feel so good right now.

"You look pensive. Don't worry, it'll all be over in a few minutes."

Claudia is back. I smile at her sadly. I pat the seat next to me on the couch.

"No time, Zack. We have to get you into your seat. They're announcing Song of the Year in the next segment."

I look at the monitor and can see that we're in commercial.

"Help me up, please. I'm a little worse for wine."

Claudia lends me a hand, frowning at me. I feel terrible.

"I'm sorry."

"Just keep your speech short, Zack. You tend to get a little loud and longwinded when you've had too much."

We head out of the Talent Lounge. Claudia takes my hand and gives it a squeeze. I suddenly feel truly awful, like I'm going to cry.

"I'm really sorry for everything."

"I know you are, Zack."

"I'm sad that Lark felt he had to hide his, well, you know, hide from me."

"Well, that's his deal, not yours."

"I should have let him play on Bobby's album."

"Probably." Claudia waves at a clutch of PAs, indicating that she has found me and for them to take me back into the auditorium.

Claudia kisses me on the cheek and turns loose my hand. "I wouldn't worry about the past too much, Zack. We've all done things we're sorry for, and you've come a long way. Now, remember, short speech."

She turns and disappears as Alain the PA comes to collect me. The line of seat fillers is waiting to fill out the seats just emptied by the last set of losers. I take a deep, cleansing breath. I feel strangely calm now about the award. I know I am not going to win, and I don't really want to hang around afterward and hear consolations. Even if I were to win, I don't think it's going to make me feel any better, now or at any time in the future. Almost all of my life I have been a shit to the people I loved, and no gold gramophone can justify twenty years of that. Funny what a difference five minutes can make.

"I need to go to the bathroom," I tell Alain.

"We need to get you to your seat as quickly as possible, Mr. Fluett. Your award is in the next segment."

"I don't care. I have to go."

I turn down the hallway toward the dressing rooms and quickly slip into the men's room again. I've spent too much time in here tonight, but that's what addicts do. I'm finished with this party. Time to get out of here. Head for the hills, as the Old Man used to say. I pull the flask from his boot and finish the tequila. Not much left, *but enough of a warm boost to get me out the back door and into a limo—anyone's limo—or even a cab if I can find one. I quickly wash my face and hands and head out the door, prepared to give Alain some line of shit and then scamper for the emergency exit and safety.*

There is no sign of Alain, but Lark Dray is standing outside the Talent Lounge, leaning up against the wall. He looks a little tired. I wish I hadn't just finished all the tequila; I could offer him a drink. It's been a long time since we raised a glass together. Suddenly I realize that I need to reach out to him. He was there for me earlier, and I need to go apologize to him. Maybe it's the booze talking, but it was the booze talking when I picked this fight in the first place, and it's time to end this feud.

I walk right up to him, and he ventures a smile at me.

"Nice performance, man," I say.

"Thanks, but it wasn't in your league."

I decide just to leap right in. "Jesus Christ, Lark. All this wasted time. Why the hell didn't you tell me you were gay? I wouldn't have minded."

Lark's eyes go wide. I suddenly get a bad feeling. Lark looks over his shoulder, and I realize that we're not alone. Alain pops out from behind Lark and titters, "Hell-o!" He's holding a wireless mic set-up in his hands that he has clearly just removed from Lark's back. I didn't see him there! He's like a fucking remora on a shark!

Alain looks at Lark with what appears to be amazement, and probably just a little joy. Lark opens his mouth to say something, his head shaking. I realize I need to backtrack, and fast. Suddenly I see something out the corner of my eye and turn my head. I briefly glimpse the GDT with a look of pure venom on her face, and I realize for a microsecond that she is throwing a punch at me.

Then my nose explodes.

CHAPTER 49

Bobby Craft: 11/8/51-4/1/06
Just over a year after being diagnosed with terminal lung cancer, singer/songwriter Bobby Craft,
age 54, died in his sleep in Woody Creek, Colorado, according to his long-time friend and col-
laborator Zack Fluett. "That he should choose
April Fool's Day to check out pretty much sums
up the man," said Fluett, who produced Craft's
universally acclaimed final album, *The Death of
Fun*, released just months before Craft's death.

Rolling Stone, April 14, 2006

CLAUDIA HELD MY HAND at Bobby's funeral,
which took place at the Hillside Cemetery in Cul-
ver City. He was buried under his real name, Ira
Liebowitz, but the marker also read "Bobby Craft"
underneath it in smaller letters. There was a nice
turnout, and I said a few words.

Afterwards, Claudia and I met Bobby's sister. I
didn't know he had a sister, but he did. Like in my
situation, she was older than he, and they hadn't spo-

ken for a long time. Unlike me, he hadn't reconciled things with her. He had just left instructions with his lawyers on how to contact her upon his death.

She let me know that she appreciated my comments about Bobby but that I had left out mentioning that he was a miserable sonofabitch. She explained that he had left his affairs in utter disarray and died without leaving a will, so she had to clean up the mess. She recognized my name as the fellow who had produced Bobby's last album and asked if I thought there would be any money coming in from it in the future. I explained that she would have to take that up with the record label but that in my experience, it was less than likely that she would see much cash, as we were likely to stay in recoupment hell for quite some time. I told her to be sure to get with Bobby's music publishers, because any money to be found would most likely come from them.

I remember being struck at the time by how you could think you knew someone pretty well and then find out that you didn't really know much of anything at all. Here I had spent almost a year watching Bobby get ready to die, eating most meals with him, working with him, and trading stories in the evening, and I didn't even know that he was Jewish, that his real name was Ira, and that he had a sister named Selma. I commented on this to Claudia over coffee at a little place in the shadow of the Sony water tower, and she pointed out that I didn't tend to ask a lot of questions, but rather told stories or held forth on my own opinions without overly concerning myself with the details of everyone else's existence.

I thought this was a little harsh, and I said so. Claudia then asked me to tell her the names of her

two older sisters, both of whom had been in our wedding. Of course, I drew a blank.

Claudia bummed a cigarette and lit it. "It doesn't
really matter, Zack. It's not like you spent a lot of
time around them before or during the wedding, and
we didn't stay married long enough for you to get to
know them at family reunions or things like that."

"You have family reunions?"

"Never. That's sort of the point. We used to summer in Sagaponick together, but I stopped going
when I met you. I didn't care that much about you
becoming part of my family, because I was happy to
become one of yours, but then I realized that the only
real family you seemed to care about at that point in
your life was Cultural Wasteland. I realized too late
that there was no way I could marry into that family."

"I really did feel awful about what happened, you
know."

"Oh, I'm sure you did, Zack, in your own narcis-
sistic way."

"That's not a very nice thing to say."

"Look, Zack. You're an amazingly warm and
friendly person, when you want to be. You're very
funny, and you're nice and kind, for the most part.
You're talented beyond belief, and you have the ability to light up a room, but you also have a very pro-
tected place deep inside you that you won't let people
into, and it prevents you from caring about trying
to find the deep private places in other people who
might want you to find them, to know them, and to
care about them too."

I looked at her in some amazement. Lots of this
was ringing true, but I certainly didn't want to hear
it!

"I'm sure you don't want to hear this," Claudia continued, accurately. "But it's really not that hard to let someone in or to go ahead and take the responsibility for accepting someone else's invitation to come into their private place, if you just let yourself do it. And if you do, you're going to find that it's safer there than you thought, or even if it's not, it's still worth it for the sense of connection. It's a connection you obviously have and want to communicate in the abstract. It's what you do with music, with your songwriting, especially these last few years. When you find out how to do that with another person, you're going to be much more complete, and I think you'll find that you like yourself a lot better too."

"Me? I'm crazy about me."

"Don't bullshit a publicist, Zack. I'm a professional. I'll grant that you're better than you used to be. You're a lot better off the booze. But you've still got some shit to work on, and you can't count on dying rock stars to teach you all the lessons. Some of them you're going to have to figure out yourself."

"And how exactly do I do that?"

"I don't know. Just keep telling the truth all the time and listening for the truth all the time. If you let a little self-forgiveness in there, it'll allow you to take it easier on everyone else at the same time. I'm trying to take my own advice these days too, just so you know. I know I can be hard."

Claudia stubbed out her cigarette, kissed me on the cheek, and walked away again. I went back to Woody Creek and thought about it.

CHAPTER 50

BLOOD IS EVERYWHERE. MY *nose is lighting up like I'm the guy on the table in a game of Operation. My eyes are watering—let's face it cowboy, you're crying—and I'm seeing everything through a fog. The best I can tell, I'm sitting on my ass backstage at the Staples Center. I reach up and wipe my nose. Searing pain. Don't do that again. I look at my hands. They are covered in blood. I realize that blood is still gushing out of my nose. My new tux is getting bloody, and my nice white pleated shirt looks like T-Pain decided I was the one who stole his champagne and busted several caps in me.*

"*Zack? Are you all right? Can you hear me?*"

Claudia swims into view; she reaches out and touches my face. Searing pain again! I wave my arms wildly. She jumps back.

"*I love you honey, but pleathe don't touch be ride dow,*" *I mumble.*

I shake my head a little and my eyes begin to clear. I see Lark and Alain the PA looking down at me with concern. The GDT has adopted a stance that indicates if

*I get up, she's going to put me back down. She's in bet-
ter shape than I am. I consider this fight officially over.
Melanie Locke by knockout.*

"You fucking bitch!" *screams Claudia. Claudia is in
better shape than I am too and appears to be ready to go
to the mat with Melanie. It occurs to me that I really do
not want to see which one of my ex-wives is the better
ultimate fighter. Lark steps in front of Melanie, who has
her dukes up and is ready to go.*

"Sthop, Claudia!" *I call out through the pain.* "It
wasth by fault. All by fault. I detherved that."

*Everyone stops and looks at me. With the exception
of Melanie, no one seems to believe that it was my fault
or I deserved it, so I must look pretty bad. There is a lot
of blood, and I'm quite certain that my nose is broken. I
can't breathe through it, and my voice sounds far away
and muffled to me. The old cymbal player in my head has
brought in a buddy on cannon, and they are rehearsing
the finale of the* "1812 Overture."

"I toad an ode Party Poopersth Incorporated joke.
Called da Jet Jock here a butt pirate. Melanie didn't
know it wasth a joke between uth."

*Alain does not look convinced with this version of
events. Lark shuffles his feet uncertainly. Melanie remains ready to go. Claudia tosses her hair back and takes
a deep breath.*

"That shit wasn't funny in the nineties, Zack. I always hated it when you boys did that. I guess your time
in Woody Creek didn't make you any more politically
correct."

Suddenly Lark grins a big, evil grin. "Yeah, you little
cum dumpster. You need to get more politically correct."

*Alain sniffs in disdain at Lark and looks at me as if
I deserve to be bleeding out of my ears too. I don't blame*

him. I'm sorry to have been rude, but better this than a full-scale cage match between the exes.

I look pleadingly at Alain. "Towel? Ithe?"

"Get it yourself," he snaps, turning on one heel. "I have seat fillers to get organized. You're in no condition to be seated at the Grammys." He swishes off.

The four of us look at each other for a moment, and then heave a collective sigh. Melanie lowers her fists. Lark looks at me, grinning, then starts chuckling. Claudia grabs a wide-eyed passing PA and makes a terse and powerful demand for towels, ice, and the backstage medical personnel immediately.

I look up at Lark, and so help me, despite the awful pain, a little chortle comes out of my nose and mouth.

"I thing it'th broken," I manage.

"Hurts, doesn't it?" he snorts, between hiccups.

"Way worthe than by finger did."

"You really are a menace to the Grammys, man."

"I keep telling you. The Grammyth are to blame. They know bedder than to inbite be."

"I really don't think there's much concern about that happening again," says Claudia, kneeling next to me once again and surveying the damage.

I look up at Melanie and make my best approximation of an apologetic smile. "How'th your hand?"

She inspects it and adjusts the sparkling diamond that is no doubt responsible for some of the blood on my tuxedo. "Fine," she says.

"That figuresth," I say, and then I start laughing again. Lark joins me. Claudia grins. Melanie does not look amused. I get it together a little; the throbbing in my nose and head is bad enough that I really don't enjoy laughing right now, even though there is a spot in my chest where it feels really good.

"I really owe you an apology, Melanie. I'm bery thsorry."

This appears to catch Melanie a bit off guard. She stands up straighter and gives a sniff, then makes an effort to regain her dignity and the upper hand. She makes to say something, but just then the cavalry arrives in the form of the medic and a couple of PAs. Claudia steps aside, and the medic takes a quick look at me.

"What happened here?"

"Walgged into a door," I hear myself saying. Lark starts to get the giggles something awful in the background. Some weirdo on a highly amplified Theremin joins the cymbal player and cannon guy. It's still kind of funny, but it really hurts a lot too. Claudia holds my hand, and I feel a weight lift. Whatever happens next, it's going to be OK. I'm going to survive this.

"Fluett! Where is Fluett! I'm going to kill him!"

Trash Bag is pissed again.

The medic says, "You've got a broken nose and a laceration here. I'm going to set it and get the bleeding stopped, and then we'll get you to the emergency room."

"Justht hide be from Trash Bag. He'th almostht ath mean ath Melanie."

Lark puts his hands on his knees and starts to whoop in earnest. I can't help but grin too. Melanie pivots and walks determinedly away.

The medic grabs my throbbing nose with both hands and inflicts grievous bodily harm on me. The Grammy laser show has migrated backstage and is going off in all directions. I see nothing but lights and stars. It feels as if Dr. Pricey is ramming a Stryker drill into the front of my skull. I hear a grisly crunch followed by the distant sound of a coyote yelping, which I realize, moments later, is my own voice.

Then air comes in through my left nostril and the pain returns to a more manageable throb, as if I am merely repeatedly hitting myself in the nose with a tennis racket. I can see again, and the first thing I see is Lark Dray on his hands and knees, eyes tearing, still laughing, but looking at me with genuine concern at the same time.

"Fag!" I splutter, because I can think of nothing else to say. Lark starts laughing hysterically again.

"Hit him again, doc," says Trash Bag, now standing behind the medic. "Hit him for me. I want more blood!"

Lark rolls over on his back like a dying cockroach and gasps for air. The medic shoves something up my right nostril. It hurts a little, and I realize that I am squeezing Claudia's hand pretty hard. I loosen my grip, but she squeezes hard back. The medic applies a butterfly bandage to a diamond-induced gash under my right eye, and then wipes up my face and gives me a towel. I wipe my hands on it, and then he hands me an ice pack. I apply it to my forehead, just above the bridge of my throbbing nose. The cymbal player blessedly returns to solo mode.

"It's a good thing you're already bleeding, asshole. I hate to get that shit on my hands while I'm working." Trash Bag is really torqued.

"I'm fine. Honest. Never better," I say. Lark appears to be having an asthma attack.

"Upsy daisy," says Huge. I didn't see him show up. He puts his hands under my armpits and effortlessly raises me to my feet. I can see all right now, and I keep the ice applied to my face.

"Really, Trash Bag. Don't worry. I'll be fine in a minute."

"We don't have a minute, dipshit. Your category is being announced right now."

CHAPTER 51

Burt, Cherie, Hugh, Lark, Zack, Claudia,
Gloria, Molly, Cynthia, Preston

Head Table, Rankin/Fluett Wedding, July 26, 1994

LARK MADE A VERY eloquent speech at the rehearsal dinner for my wedding to Claudia. Best Man speeches are rife with opportunity for embarrassment and general fuckups, but Lark didn't fall victim to any of the typical mines in the minefield. He didn't talk about any ex-girlfriends. He didn't mention anything about the bachelor-party fuckup that landed all five of us in jail for stealing range balls at my old college, not to mention the four sheets of (thankfully fake) blotter acid (turns out it's not illegal to purchase fake LSD, but for six hours in the Oakland jail, we thought we were all going to the pen for a long time). He didn't talk about groupies on the road, and he didn't talk about the contents of my medicine cabinet.

All he did was make a series of comments about how Claudia was flatly too good for me. This was done with quite a lot of good humor, self-accompanied on guitar, something like a latter-day Henny Youngman. Everyone enjoyed it, especially Mom and the Old Man.

"Claudia grew up in a country club. Zack grew up in the country. Well, check that, Zack never grew up and the country in which he was raised sent him away."

"And we don't want him back!" shouted the Old Man, bourbon flask in hand. Everyone laughed.

"Claudia rode for the Wellesley Equestrian Team. Zack cartwheeled through the alfalfa for our amusement."

"Oh, be nice, Lark," called out Huge. "That horse was fast as the wind!" The Old Man really appreciated that one.

"Claudia graduated at the top of her class. Zack dropped out."

That one didn't seem to sit as well with either the Old Man or Mom.

"Claudia is beautiful. Nuff said."

I grinned at that. Claudia did look stunning that evening, as she would the next day, and most every day of her life thereafter, save for a few brief moments at the Hotel du Cap in Antibes. Even then she was still at least exciting to watch.

Lark went on in this fashion for an appropriate and funny length of time, but then said that despite all of these problems, he was there that day to point out the good news: "I'm honored by both Claudia and Zack to be here today. I am grateful to Zack for his friendship and for asking me to stand up for him.

I love this man dearly, and I want nothing but the best for him for all of his life. That's why I'm so very happy he found Claudia. Because when he fucks up, and he will fuck up, he'll always have this incredibly talented and terrific woman to fall back on!"

I led the applause.

CHAPTER 52

8:09 p.m. PST

HUGE HAS ME HALF off the ground, hands still under my armpits, as he propels me toward the wings. I look like one of the Team America *puppets walking along, feet dancing lightly off the floor, albeit, a puppet that has been shot in the face. I can't really see where I'm going. I have my head back, balancing the ice bag gingerly on my nose. Claudia is still holding my hand, and I can hear Lark giving directions to people to get out of the way and get us to nominee mark stage left. Trash Bag is muttering directions, presumably into the walkie-talkie that is permanently fused to his left hand.*

"OK. Right here. No, get out of our way, honey. Right here. Stand him up," I hear Lark say.

"Here?" says Huge.

"Yeah."

"Tell them that I've got him at nominee left. He's not in his seat!" growls Trash Bag.

I am standing on my own two feet now, Huge just balancing me a bit. I take the ice bag off and open my eyes. Lark and Claudia huddle in front of me, looking concerned. Lark's no longer laughing; however, his eyes are smiling. Claudia isn't smiling, but at least she doesn't look angry or frosty. She doesn't even look sad. I give them a grin.

"You look terrible," says Lark.

"Awful," agrees Claudia.

"I feel fantastic," I say, not kidding.

"I'm very happy to be here this evening and honored to present this award," says a Cockney accent nearby. I look around and find the source of the sound to be a video monitor above my head. Look at that. The Grammy Awards are on!

"Last year it was an honor to be nominated. This year it's even nicer to be able to attend!" continues the girl from the monitor. This gets a nice laugh and applause from the audience. I recall her as the artist who won a lot of awards for a song about being in rehab, but she missed the show because she actually was in rehab. Irony of all ironies that she is to introduce my award tonight. Perhaps I would be better off if I were in rehab right this instant.

"Song of the Year is a songwriter's award given to a song that was first released or reached prominence during the eligibility year. And the nominees are. . ."

"No! I said he's with me! Nominee left. He's not in his seat," Trash Bag hisses.

"'I Turned Around.' Songwriter, Zack Fluett. Performed by Wendy Harper."

The orchestra strikes up the main theme to our song. The onscreen image cuts to the audience where Wendy Harper sits next to a nice-looking young Asian man. He is clapping enthusiastically. Wendy applauds politely but looks a bit strained, her eyes flicking back and forth from the seat filler to the camera. I detect a swell of applause *that drops off quickly, as the audience grows confused. I turn to Claudia to comment, and suddenly, backstage gets very bright. I return my attention to the monitor and see a tuxedo clad form with his back to the camera and Lark Dray in the background, grinning evilly and giving the old thumbs up. I smile.*

Rehab girl appears on the screen. "Another Whole New World (Gilligan's Theme).' Songwriters Alan Menken, Tim Rice, and Sherwood Schwartz; Original Artists, Michael Bolton and Natalie Cole." Two geezers wearing white scarves with their tuxes appear on-screen to the orchestral accompaniment of an overwrought derivative of the theme from Gilligan's Island. *I look at Lark, and then I have to look away or I know I will go into a completely spastic laughing fit that will really cause my head to hurt.*

I wipe at my nose absentmindedly. It hurts, and my hand comes away with blood on it again. I turn to Claudia for a towel.

"How bad is it really?" I ask her.

"Repeat after me: 'Yo, Adrian!'" she responds. Very clever girl. Adore her.

"I'm telling you, it's not my fault. The guy's been a pain in my ass for ten years. He got in a fight backstage and didn't get back to his seat!" Trash Bag hates explaining himself, and he hates it when anything goes the least bit wrong on his watch. He is going to kill me later.

"'The Streets of Orlando,'" continues the presenter, whose name I now remember is something like "wino." "Bruce Springsteen, songwriter and artist."

The Boss is in his proper seat, smiling self-deprecatingly at the camera. His lovely wife/bass player sits next to him holding three gold gramophones. Underneath the orchestral strains of "The Streets of Orlando," a subtle male announcer's voice points out: "Bruce Springsteen is nominated in six categories tonight and has already won for Best Rock Vocal Performance, Best Rock Album, and Best Song Written Specifically for Motion Picture or Television."

"You'd better beat him, Zack. I don't think I can," *says Lark. I am reminded that Lark's big competition for Record of the Year is "The Streets of Orlando."*

"I don't stand a chance," *I say.*

"'I Turned Around' is the best song of the year, hands down, dude. You're gonna win." *Lark looks at me dead seriously, and suddenly he looks just exactly like the man I spent so many endless hours with in tiny rehearsal spaces so many years ago.*

I am so happy to be speaking to Lark Dray again. Why didn't I know I would feel this way? I could have done this years ago. I look at Claudia, and her eyes are shining. I can tell she shares this feeling with me, this feeling of reconnection.

"'I Love You Because I'm Lonely,'" *intones the rehabbed wino.* "Songwriters Diane Warren, Richard Marx, Max Martin, and Andreas Carlsson; performed by TJ Corey." *As the strings saw away, heroically attempting to repeat the main theme from TJ's hip-hop power ballad, the screen divides into four squares showing each of the songwriters, none of whom appears to be sitting in the same auditorium or paying a huge amount of attention.*

"I'm not kidding, the fuckhead got in a fight. He looks like he's been mugged. He's got blood all over him. It's not my fault!"

I am beginning to guess that the director of the Grammy Awards telecast is displeased with Trash Bag and that I am the cause of that displeasure.

"'*Insanity Salad.*' *Songwriter and Artist, Lena Rifka.*"

I look back up at the screen and see the young, pretty, soulful guitar player from earlier in the rehearsal room. She is sitting cross-legged in her seat out front, smiling shyly, hands on her knees palms up—meditation style. The male announcer's voice intrudes on the very pretty melody the oboes are playing over the cellos: "*Lena Rifka is nominated for six Grammy Awards tonight. She has already won for Best Pop Vocal Album, Best Pop Female Vocal Performance, and Best New Artist.*"

It occurs to me that she is also nominated for Record of the Year and Album of the Year. That was a terrific song she wrote. I loved that song. What a darling girl.

"*She's going to win,*" *I murmur.* "*She's going to run the table.*"

"*Nobody's done that since Christopher Cross,*" *says Claudia. Woman knows her stuff. Love her.*

"*The chick on stage almost did and probably would have if she hadn't really been in rehab when the voting took place,*" *comments Huge.*

"*That didn't hurt her too much. She still won five,*" *replies Lark.*

"*We're all in big trouble,*" *I say, not really caring.*

"*How can we be in trouble?*" *says Huge.* "*I thought we didn't care.*"

"*Fluett. You're in big trouble,*" *says Trash Bag.* "*You can't go onstage and collect the award. You'll cause a riot looking like that.*"

"*Don't worry, TB. I'm not going to win,*" *I say.* "*The kid's going to run the table.*"

Trash Bag looks at me strangely. "*Just don't go out there,*" *he repeats, and turns away.*

Huge, Claudia, and Lark all turn slowly and look at

me, smiles beginning to play on their faces. A thrill of adrenaline runs through me. We all look up at the monitor as an evening gown clad model hands the envelope to Rehab Girl. She opens it.

"And the Grammy goes to…"

CHAPTER 53

Then and Now

DESPITE HAVING SPENT OVER two decades on stage, I have never been particularly comfortable with public speaking. Singing or playing an instrument or even talking between songs on stage is one thing. It's a performance of something rehearsed and allows the adoption of a particular role. Now, you can argue that public speaking is just that as well, but if you're really trying to be honest and share something of yourself, it requires an openness that is not my forte.

I had to give the valedictory address to my high school. I would have liked to have said something of value, but I didn't have anything of value to say. I would have liked to have told them all that they were a bunch of idiot jerkoffs who were going to spend the rest of their lives struggling to get by and keep food on the table for the numerous moronic children they would doubtless soon have (some of them were already well on their way), but I didn't feel like getting beat up on my own graduation day. In the end I found a book of famous speeches in the library and cut pieces of a few together into something that resembled a valedictory, using segments of Churchill, Douglas MacArthur, and Martin Luther King, Jr., as I recall. The speech didn't really make any sense, but everyone applauded politely. Mom looked mildly confused, but the Old Man seemed satisfied that I hadn't said something to embarrass him.

The one time I do recall speaking in public openly and honestly required only that I say two words. All I had to do was to look out on the gathering of our dearly beloved and then look Claudia in the eye and firmly say, "I do." It was the most important public statement I ever made on the most important day of my life. On that day, both Mom and the Old Man looked genuinely proud.

My subsequent stupid and rotten behavior would reverse all the good intentions and hopes and dreams I had when I said those words. It would provide me with a path to follow of self-abuse and self-loathing. It took years to traverse that road, and I had to learn the way not once, but many, many times. The lesson I think I have learned is that it is a damned long road, and even though it's full of bumps and potholes, there are also, from time to time, turns.

CHAPTER 54

"'I TURNED AROUND,' ZACK Fluett, songwriter."

Claudia grabs me and kisses me, ignoring my bloody face and damaged nose. The pain is excruciating, but it is the best sensation I have ever felt.

Lark and Huge jump up and down, slapping each other on the back and otherwise acting exactly like they're hearing "Cry for Me (This Sucks)" on the radio in a smelly old bus between Tucson and Flagstaff.

On the monitor, Wendy Harper is kissing the nice-looking Asian seat filler. He shakes his fist in delight, as if he's actually done something other than rent a tuxedo. I am very happy for Wendy and him. Jackson Harper enters the picture and gently separates his wife from the perfect stranger and gives her a squeeze. He has a huge grin on his face.

Ms. Wino reappears on the screen. An evening gown clad model hands her the Grammy Award. My Grammy Award. She looks around expectantly. The orchestra plays the same strains of "I Turned Around" it did just a moment before. The on-screen image cuts briefly to Bruce

Springsteen, who is applauding with what appears to be genuine enthusiasm, then briefly to Wendy Harper again, who is looking around, undoubtedly for me, then to the orchestra conductor, then back to the model and the beehive at the podium. There appears to be some confusion.

"Come on, dude. Get out there. Go collect your hardware," says Huge.

"Trash Bag told me not to go out there," I point out.

"Fuck that," says Claudia, somehow managing to make it sound ladylike. I am so in love with her.

"Zack Fluett couldn't be here this evening..." says the male announcer's voice. Presenter Wino looks around confused, certain that she was supposed to hand the statue to someone.

"Bullshit!" screams Huge. "He's right here!" It's not loud enough to be heard on TV, but everyone on stage hears it, as do any number of staff and orchestra members. Everyone looks confused. It occurs to me that this should come as no surprise to anyone paying any attention. I was on stage less than an hour ago.

Trash Bag is studiously twiddling knobs on his walkie-talkie and shaking it, as if he is suddenly having technical difficulties. He looks at me out of the corner of his eye with the tiniest of grins, then turns his back on me and shakes his walkie-talkie again, walking slowly away.

"So the Recording Academy is happy to accept this award on his behalf."

"Bullshit!" yells Huge again. "He's right here. He's coming!"

Lark grabs my right arm and gives me his best-ever evil grin.

"Come on, Cowboy. Let's poop this party."

Claudia kisses me on the cheek and lets go of my hand. Huge grabs my left arm, and he and Lark march me out of the wings, toward the stage. There are a couple of yellow-jacketed security guards standing there, looking confused, but they don't seem to want to get involved with almost thirteen feet of rock stars accompanying a blood-covered Grammy Award winner.

The funny lesbian reaches the stage before us, heading for the podium, looking to give some guidance to the confused wino and get the ceremonies back on track. The evening gown-clad model slinks into the far wings.

Lark and Huge walk me several steps onto the stage. I can see the audience now and hear confused chatter. I look down into the orchestra pit just as the conductor looks up and sees the three of us. He drops his hands, his eyes staring at me in disbelief. The orchestra dies.

Lark and Huge give me a little shove and I am making my way across the stage, a bit unsteadily, but determined. I lock my eyes on Ms. Rehab, who is holding my Grammy Award. She notices me over the shoulder of the funny lesbian. Her eyes go wide, and she lets out a shriek and drops my Grammy!

Everything slows down. I am cognizant of the look of horror on my presenter's face, and I recall at that moment Claudia's description of me. I am aware of the blackening around my eyes, of the red wreck that is my nose, of the fresh blood weeping from the butterfly bandage on my cheekbone, and mostly of the vast crimson stain down the front of my white pleated shirt, a color I'm sure will show up very well on camera. I feel bad about surprising the wino in this way. This was a bad idea. I shall have to discuss this with the other principals in Party Poopers, Incorporated. This is going too far, even for us.

The funny lesbian makes a dive for my Grammy

Award. I'm certain Jackson Harper will be impressed. An audible intake of breath by all present fills the Staples Center. The funny lesbian makes a spectacular catch, grabbing the miniature gramophone's horn just inches from the stage. She rolls on her side and holds up my Grammy Award. The wino wrings her hands and races off stage. The silence is complete and eerie.

The funny lesbian seems disappointed that her spectacular catch has gone without the level of appreciation it should have received. She looks around and finally notices me. I grin at her and give her the old thumbs-up.

"Nice catch," I mouth.

She looks at me, troubled but forever the professional, then gives a shrug of surrender and raises her eyebrows as if to say, "Well, are you just going to stand there, or are you going to help me up?"

I help her up and she smiles as she hands me the gold gramophone. It occurs to me that she knows good television when she sees it. The room is still silent. I step over to the podium and approach the microphone. I look out on the sea of people, all there for "Music's Biggest Night." I look into the front rows and see Wendy Harper looking terribly concerned. I smile comfortingly at her and then at everyone there, most of whom are looking at me with varying levels of shock or distaste.

Then I catch sight of Bruce Springsteen, and he is smiling at me and shaking his head in what appears to be amusement. His gleaming eyes meet mine, and he gives me a wink.

I take a long look at the statue in my hand. I am happy to have it, but I know it doesn't change anything. I know it doesn't change anything because before I even touched it, everything changed anyway. This has been my biggest night. My biggest performance, my biggest heroes, my best song, and my best friends all back with me, and all at once. I am no longer alone. I am truly blessed. I only hope my mother is watching. I'm going to call her as soon as I get off this stage, which, it occurs to me, I should do with alacrity.

But I have to make a speech first. Claudia's advice on public speaking rings in my ears. I just want to get off this stage and into her arms. I'm hoping she's my karma.

I hold my Grammy Award high over my head, lean into the microphone, and enunciate as carefully and clearly as I can through my stopped-up, shattered nose.

"Thang God!"

And then I turn my back on "Music's Biggest Night" and look around for my friends.

THE END

ACKNOWLEDGMENTS

I AM MOST GRATEFUL to Suzanne Ciani for her trust, faith, and love and for giving me my start in the entertainment industry, among many other things. My very dear friend Wendy Thorlakson Svehlak made it possible for me to continue my life in entertainment and opened many doors for me. Much that I learned about storytelling came through her. Phillip Rosen is a wonderful friend and the best law partner anyone could ask for, always encouraging my interests outside our practice.

I am very grateful to my former producing partner Lance Bass for providing me access to his utterly insane but wonderful world at the height of *NSYNC's fame. I also must thank my friends Chris Carmack (for chucking guitars at my skull), Dr. Mark Price (for teaching me all about boxers' fractures and reflex sympathetic dystrophy), and Tom McCann, Brian Scanlon, Will Walgren, and my niece Alexa Fey Schnee for much-appreciated comments on early drafts of this book. Although their expertise and guidance is greatly appreciated, all responsibility for the accuracy of anything in this novel is mine alone.

I could not have completed this project without the generous support, encouragement, and housing provided by my wonderful roomies Daniel and Nana Howell, and I'm grateful to the whole gang at Maya Restaurant in Sonoma for always making me feel that my stories were funny and worth listening to and for introducing me to really good tequila.

I am especially grateful to my family the "Ander-Schnees" for all their love and support throughout this crazy life of mine.

Finally, most profound thanks and love to Willow for everything else and that is yet to come.

ABOUT THE AUTHOR

Joe Anderson is an entertainment and digital media attorney, record and film producer, musician, and writer. In the 1990s, he was the keyboard player in a San Francisco rock band and ran a small record label that earned three Grammy nominations. In 2001, he moved to Los Angeles and got into the movie business, producing the Miramax film *On the Line* and the Weinstein company film *Lovewrecked*. Joe's experiences in the music and film industries and growing up in Montana inform the writing of his first novel, *Face the Music*.